Every Pretty Thing

Chris Mooney is the internationally bestselling author of the Darby McCormick thrillers. His third novel, *Remembering Sarah*, was nominated for an Edgar for Best Novel by the Mystery Writers of America. His books have been translated into more than twenty languages. He teaches writing courses at Harvard and the Harvard Extension School, and lives in Boston, Massachusetts, with his wife and son.

By the same author

The Missing
The Secret Friend
The Dead Room
The Killing House
The Soul Collectors
Fear the Dark
Every Three Hours

Every Pretty Thing

CHRIS MOONEY

PENGUIN BOOKS

PENGUIN BOOKS

UK | USA | Canada | Ireland | Australia
India | New Zealand | South Africa

Penguin Books is part of the Penguin Random House group of companies
whose addresses can be found at global.penguinrandomhouse.com.

First published 2017
001

Copyright © Chris Mooney, 2017

The moral right of the author has been asserted

Set in 12.5/14.75 pt Garamond MT Std
Typeset by Jouve (UK), Milton Keynes
Printed in Great Britain by Clays Ltd, St Ives plc

A CIP catalogue record for this book is available from the British Library

ISBN: 978–1–405–92245–6

www.greenpenguin.co.uk

For Jen and Jack
Not enough time for all my love

New Year's Day

I

Whenever Karen woke up – night or day, violently or peacefully, or simply kicked awake by her constant nemesis, insomnia – she reached under her pillow for the handgun she had affectionately nicknamed Baby G: a subcompact 9-millimetre Glock 43 sold to her by a smug, twenty-something gun-store owner in Ohio who had called it 'the perfect little sidearm for ladies in your age group'. She'd been fifty at the time – not exactly old, as far as she was concerned, but not exactly young either.

The punk kid had been correct in calling the G43 the perfect little sidearm. It *was* little, just over six inches long, and surprisingly light and easy to shoot. Grabbing the handgun whenever she woke up was as much a habit as it was a ritual: she needed to hold it long enough to calm herself down, to remind herself that she was safe, that the man who had killed her family and tried to kill her hadn't found her.

Only that wasn't strictly true any more. *She* had finally found *him*.

Karen sat up, the nightmare she'd just had already on its way to a fast exit. A dull square of moonlight splashed against the end of her patchwork quilt, and she saw the neon-blue numbers glowing from her alarm clock: 1.32 a.m. She was alone in the bedroom because she lived here alone and, most importantly, her bedroom door was

3

shut and locked, the deadbolt she'd installed the day she moved in firmly in place. The windows were cracked open to let in the cold air; she loved sleeping with the windows open, even during the winter – especially when, like tonight, she felt hot, like she was coming down with a fever. Had she caught that virus that was going around? Or had the stress from the past few days taken its toll, screwing up the hormone levels in her body and placing her in what her doctors called adrenal fatigue?

Get up, her mind screamed. *Grab your keys and leave.*

But there wasn't any reason to leave – not now. Not yet. The house was locked up, secured. She was safe, and she was armed.

She eased herself into a sitting position and her heart rate, which was already spiked, seemed to crank itself up to an alarming level, leaving her feeling lightheaded. There was a brief moment where she thought she was going to pass out. That had been happening a lot these past three days, her heart jackhammering so hard against her breastbone that it reminded her of the old *Bugs Bunny* and *Tom and Jerry* cartoons she had watched in hospitals and psychiatric wards. She pictured her heart exploding out of her chest, grabbing the car keys and getting in her truck and driving off, leaving her here.

Running away was the smart thing to do – the *right* thing to do. But the governing principle these last seven or so years had had nothing to do with what was right or smart but rather what was *needed*. And she needed to stay here in this oddball town in northern Montana, because now, after thirty-eight years of searching and praying, she had found him. The man who had killed her family and

4

had almost killed her was living right here in Fort Jefferson. The Red Ryder.

Karen ran a forearm across her eyes, feeling the damp and greasy slickness of her skin. She grabbed the bottle of water she kept on the nightstand and polished it off.

Going back to sleep was off the table; she felt wired from head to toe. She was afraid, yes (okay, *terrified*), but there was some excitement too. The culmination of her life's work – her life's purpose, mission, whatever you wanted to call it – wasn't coming to an end, but she was finally going to get some closure. Finally, she would be accepted back into mainstream society. Finally, she would no longer need to hide or sleep with a gun under her pillow and a deadbolt installed on her bedroom door – that is, *if* she played her cards right. *If* she could remain vigilant and patient.

Holding Baby G was delivering the jolt of comfort she needed. Karen pulled back the warm but damp flannel sheets and got to her feet, groaning. The surgeon had removed all the slugs except for the one still lodged near her spine, the man afraid of paralysing her if he removed it. And, despite the multiple surgeries to repair her muscles, all the years of physical rehabilitation, she still walked with a slight limp. During the winter and before a thunderstorm, she experienced a dull but debilitating pain throughout her body, as though it were trapped inside a vice and slowly being squeezed.

When she reached the other side of the bed, Karen lifted up the mattress and removed a Colt .45 that had belonged to her father. She carried it back with her to bed, where she gathered up the pillows and propped them against the headboard. Then she got comfortable and, tucked back under the warm covers, held the Colt against her stomach. Its reassuring weight, the feel of the cold steel seeping past her T-shirt and touching her skin, always did the trick on nights like this.

She closed her eyes.

Thought, *I want to be thirteen again.*

Thirteen had been a magical year for her. Not Disney fairytale magical with unicorns that crapped rainbows, but something close to it. The year she turned thirteen she became a straight-A student for the first time. She ran for class president – and won. She became one of the top five long-distance runners in New England and, at the school's winter social the week before Christmas, she kissed the cutest boy in her class, Duncan Monroe, a tall, comic-book-loving nerd from Australia all the girls called Duncan the Delicious and then simply Mr Delicious, a nickname that was fully justified later in high school, when that great purveyor of youth culture and taste, Abercrombie & Fitch, selected him as a model the summer before his senior year, his perfectly chiselled chest and ripped stomach not only featuring on a big black-and-white poster at the local store but also on all the A & F shopping bags.

The best part about the year she turned thirteen, though, was her father, who had returned home – again, miraculously, in one piece – from yet another overseas secret mission he couldn't discuss. This time, he came back with some great news: he had officially retired from the Navy. His new job? Full-time dad. That year, he shuttled her back and forth to school, to her field hockey and soccer games, and at least once a week the two of them went to Bluey's Diner for lunch or an early dinner, where she talked to him about the music, movies, books and TV shows she liked – they even talked about Delicious Duncan and 'the kiss'. The year she turned thirteen she learned she could talk to her father about anything, no subject off limits.

She wished she could talk to him now.

In a weird way, she still could. After he died, the calm but extremely cautious voice within her, the one reminding her to look both ways before crossing the street, to be a good and kind person who said 'please' and 'thank you' – the voice she assumed was her conscience – that inner voice had taken on the blunt, no-BS tone of Lieutenant-Commander Samuel Decker, a SEAL Team Six sniper awarded two Purple Hearts. That voice spoke to her now:

Pick up the phone and make the call.

She couldn't. She had a solid and well-documented history as the girl who'd cried wolf. The FBI wouldn't take her seriously unless she had concrete proof – which she believed she finally did, now that she was sober. She wouldn't know for sure until the Bureau's lab geeks tested the evidence she'd mailed out yesterday.

Now came the hard part: waiting. The Federal lab was backlogged, always. Even with her connections, she was looking at at least a couple of weeks. No more than a month. She didn't want to wait that long – no one in their right mind would – but she could because she had been careful. The Red Ryder didn't know she was here.

If the Red Ryder really is here, Karen, he may come after you.

7

Prudent advice. *Sage* advice. She might have said those exact same words to her own child if the roles had been reversed. But she didn't have any kids, thank God, because she'd had her tubes tied. She had never married or gotten anywhere close to it, because she had never been in a serious relationship. She was alone by choice but not lonely – an important distinction.

The Red Ryder had no idea who she was. She wasn't using her real name, and she looked nothing like the thirteen-year-old he'd seen that night or anything like the photos of her as a teenager posted all over the Internet, on the Red Ryder fan sites and, at last count, in the eighteen crime books published on America's favourite unknown psycho. Leaving Fort Jefferson was not an option. Do that now and everything she had worked and suffered for – had literally *bled* for – could and would vanish. At fifty-one, she didn't have another thirty-eight years to devote to her cause. She didn't have –

The bedroom exploded with light.

2

Shit, Karen thought, slamming her eyes shut against the sudden light. She had forgotten to draw the light-blocking shades before turning in, and now her bedroom glowed like a searchlight, courtesy of the insanely bright halogen bulbs the rangers from Montana Fish, Wildlife and Parks had installed in the backyard's motion-sensor lights to help scare off the black bears and grizzlies. Animals had started making their way down here, to a lower elevation, looking for food. It was a big problem this time of year, she'd been told, from mid-September all the way to December, thanks to global warming; and yet locals like Gina Miller, the Bible-thumping old bird who lived up at the top of the road, kept feeding bears from her back porch despite several warnings from the rangers. The only saving grace was that Miss Miller hadn't had any children to carry on her stupidity.

Karen was way too comfortable and way too warm and cosy to get up and draw the bedroom shades – and she should, because if some animal were moving around out there, the backyard lights would continue to shine on, preventing her from getting a good night's sleep. She thought about getting up as she stared out the window, at the trees lining her little stretch of backyard and beyond them, the seemingly never-ending stretch of forest packed with massive pines and other trees (the names of which she did not know, having lived in cities most of her life) that blocked out the sun on even the brightest of days, casting the hiking and, in the winter, snowmobile trails in perpetual gloom.

Her father said, *You're in danger.*

No, Karen told her father. I played it nice and cool yesterday. He didn't notice a thing. No one noticed a thing.

You don't know that.

I do. I'm in the clear.

Then explain to me why you're sitting in bed with not one but two loaded handguns.

You're forgetting about the Mossberg in my bedroom closet and the other shotgun stored inside the closet by the front door. I've got handguns hidden in just about every room inside this house, Pops. I've been living this way for years.

Because you're scared.

After what happened to us that night? You're goddamn right I'm scared.

Then, as if to prove her point, her mind replayed the nightmare that had just woken her up – only it wasn't a nightmare but a home movie, and it always began with her, at thirteen, sitting in the back seat of the family station wagon, with its plastic blue seats and fake panelling along the sides. They were parked in a dirt lot in Vallejo, California – the site of a campground. Her father, an avid outdoorsman, had decided to take them hiking and camping along the California coast. They were eating burgers and drinking milkshakes and sharing thick steak fries from a white bag splotched with grease when a car driving fast across the dark and quiet road suddenly pulled into the dirt lot and came to a sharp stop behind them – an unmarked cop car, she guessed, like the one she'd seen on her favourite TV show, *ChiPs*, because a searchlight exploded through the station wagon's rear window. The piercingly bright, white light began to move and come closer, and she thought it was the portable kind the police used to check vehicles for alcohol and drugs, just like on TV. Her suspicion was confirmed moments later, when her father told everyone to relax, that it was just a cop checking to make sure they weren't riffraff up to no good. It was the start of the long Fourth of July weekend.

Karen *did* relax, because she'd seen the driver's licence and registration pinched between her father's fingers. She turned to her two-year-old brother, Paul, with his gap-toothed grin, and was about to feed him a French fry when the shooting started.

The first shot hit her father – it was like a cherry pie had exploded inside the car – and, by the time the man who would later become known to the world as the Red Ryder turned his silenced 9-millimetre Luger on her mother, she had already draped her body over her brother's, her shaking and red-slicked hand covered with her parents' blood reaching for the car door.

Now she was sitting in a bed in another state thirty-eight years later. Was she scared? No. She was *terrified*. But on the subject of terror, what people generally forgot about was how it could sharpen the mind. How it cleared away the bullshit and focused your attention so you could zero in on the heart of the matter, which was this: no matter how scared she felt, no matter how much she wanted to leave (and there was certainly a part of her that did), she had to stay here and keep an eye on him *until* the evidence came back. Once it did, then she could decide what to do, and only then.

The outside lights clicked off, plunging the bedroom back into its gloom, and she thought she heard the snap of dry branches from the backyard – an animal moving through the woods, searching for food, maybe. It alarmed her for a reason she couldn't explain, and for a moment she felt as though someone – or something – was sitting on her chest.

Make the call, her father said. *At least do that.*

No. Not until I have some more information. Besides, talking isn't going to change anything, and you know it.

Do you want to end up like the others?

That wasn't going to happen. She'd been living here for four months as Melissa French. Before coming to Fort Jefferson, Montana, she was Cindy Otto, living in Cheyenne, Wyoming. Before Cindy she was Sandra Jane Healey, and before Sandra she had been someone else – the list of names went on and on, every one of them with bland back stories. And, while all roads led back to Karen Lee Decker, that life – her first life, as she called it – had been successfully erased. Karen Lee Decker was, for all intents and purposes, dead and buried. She had hired trained professionals – erasers, as they were called in the businesses – who could turn you into a ghost as long as you followed the rules, the first of which was you were never to contact anyone from your former life, for any reason. No problem there. She had followed the rules, so no one, not even the FBI, could find her. She had made certain of it.

You can never be certain of anything, Karen. That's why you —

I'm not asking for your advice, she told her father. But, since we're on the subject of putting one's life in danger, let's not forget that you willingly signed over *your* life, not once but *several* times – *and* left your family, not once but *several* times – all to help the good ole US of A. I love you, but you don't get a say in this one. Sorry.

It was then Karen noticed she had traded the comfort of her dad's handgun for the comfort of the second and last item from her first life: the St Christopher medal that hung from a gold chain as thin as a piece of thread. The oval, gold-plated medal, not the chain, had belonged to her father, a gift from his parents for his first Communion. Lieutenant-Commander Samuel Decker, he of great religious faith, had carried it with him during his secret missions, believing it would protect him. And it had.

The backyard floodlights came to life again. This time she whipped back the covers, thinking about how no one could be protected forever, no matter how many saints or angels were on your side. Good ole Saint Chris was the perfect example. After carrying little baby Jesus on his back across a swollen river (and almost drowning in the process), Chris went off to spread the good word, and how was he rewarded for his devotion? Decapitation.

Karen had her fingers pinched on the shade, listening to the snap, crackle and pop of dry twigs and small branches, when she was struck with a new thought: *Whatever animal is coming this way, please don't let it be a baby cub.* When a cub appeared, the mother wasn't too far behind, and momma bears were extremely vicious and –

A girl stumbled out of the woods.

Karen slammed her eyes shut, sure she was hallucinating. *Yes, that's it*, she told herself. It had happened before, a handful of times – one of the not-so-common but very real side effects of extreme exhaustion brought on by adrenal fatigue. Another common symptom was an elevated heart rate. She had that too; her heart was jackhammering furiously inside her chest.

But when she opened her eyes she saw the girl running across the backyard – and not just any girl but someone she recognized *and* knew well: Miriam, the daughter of her next-door neighbour. Karen had babysat for Miriam and the older daughter, Tricia, a number of times, and now the eight-year-old was in her backyard – in the middle of the night – wearing her knee-high green boots and lavender winter jacket with a Dora-the-Explorer patch on her breast pocket.

'*Let me in*,' Miriam screamed. She banged on the back door with her fists, her long, stringy blonde hair blowing in the wind and scattering across her pale, chubby face. '*Let me in right now!*'

Karen was turning away from the window, frightened, a greasy sweat breaking out across her skin, when she saw the deadbolt on her bedroom door slowly turn then stop with a soft *click*. Again she had a moment where she wondered if she was hallucinating, but that thought quickly vanished when she saw the doorknob turning.

Her father's Colt .45 was still gripped in her hand. She brought it up as the door swung open and there he was, the Red Ryder, dressed in the exact same clothing she'd seen him in over thirty years ago: the dark-red hoodie covering his head, the chino slacks and dark military boots.

He didn't come into the bedroom, just stood in the dark hallway, his head bent slightly forward and his face covered in the gloom. Miriam was still kicking the back door and screaming to be let in when Karen pulled the trigger and heard a dry *click*.

Valentine's Day

3

As Darby hustled through Logan Airport's bright and noisy corridors – shit, she was late, so late – she found herself thinking about how this seemed to be the only way they saw each other these days – airport layovers or by driving to some randomly picked chain restaurant or bar that was a halfway point between them. They were either in the air or on the road for their jobs, and, while talking on the phone, texts and emails were great for keeping in touch, no technology – not even a video-conferencing program like Skype – could ever replace or even come close to replicating the feeling you got sitting next to someone, talking and sharing beers. Which was why, when Coop told her about his layover at Logan, she told him she'd meet him there.

It wasn't a long drive from Hartford, Connecticut – a little over an hour and a half, according to Google Maps. She was meeting him at night – shortly before ten – so she wasn't expecting to hit any significant traffic. Still, she gave herself an extra forty-five minutes, because she didn't want to risk being late. She had a lot of things she wanted to discuss with him during his hour-plus layover. Personal things.

By the time she reached Logan, she figured she had fifteen, maybe twenty minutes before Coop had to catch his flight.

One of their favourite meeting spots inside the airport was a retro-lounge called Lucky's. It had stucco walls, dark mahogany furniture and cherry-red leather chairs and stools and lots of mood lighting – the sort of place you'd see Frank Sinatra and the Rat Pack hanging out back in the fifties. Coop was sitting at the bar, his back to her. His arms were crossed and resting on the bar top, and the fabric of his thin grey sweatshirt was stretched over his massive back, shoulders and biceps.

The tall man standing beside him, in tight jeans and an even tighter white T-shirt, had to be one of the most perfect-looking men she had ever seen: Mediterranean skin, thick black hair, all chiselled features and perfectly sculpted. The type of guy you'd see in an ad for cologne or underwear. Men and women paused to look at him, but right now the guy only had eyes for Coop.

The guy tucked a business card under Coop's glass, smiling. He picked up his ski jacket, and by the time she reached Coop the man had already walked away.

'I'm sorry I'm late,' she said, slipping out of her jacket. 'There was a major accident on Route 26, and the main garage next to this terminal is closed for repairs.'

'It happens.' Although she thought he looked sad when he said it. 'I ordered you a drink,' he said, sliding the glass to her. 'Knob Creek, double neat.'

Darby pulled out the chair next to him and picked up a black down jacket resting on the seat.

'Patagonia,' she said, and whistled. 'Aren't we moving up in the world?' She was about to hand it to him, but stopped when she saw the inside collar. 'Why is there a black X on the label?'

'To let the world know you bought it at a heavy discount at an outlet. You're a girl, you're supposed to know these things.' He took the coat from her and then, before she could sit, stood and hugged her.

She loved the way he smelled. Like home.

'Way, way too long,' he said, and, when he kissed her cheek, the personal feelings she kept buried (mostly) came to the surface. It didn't take much effort to push them away; she'd had a lot of practice over the course of their fifteen-year friendship.

'I saw that you made a new friend tonight,' Darby said, and removed the business card from underneath the glass. She waved it playfully.

'I most certainly did.' His eyes were shiny with alcohol. Mischievous. 'His name is Andy and he owns a yoga studio.'

'That explains the body. You mind if I keep this?'

'Sure. But I'm pretty sure he's more interested in my equipment than yours.'

'How sure?'

'Well, he told me he lives in the South End.'

'Gay clue number one. What else?'

'He also told me, "I'd really like to see how you look when I'm naked."'

'Confident. I like that in a man.'

'The final clue came when he told me I had a great ass. Asked me what time it opened.'

Darby laughed, realizing just how much she'd missed him – how deep her feelings for him ran.

Tell him.

'Then he slipped me his card, you know, just in case I

changed my mind,' Coop said. 'But, seriously, keep it. I'm sure he'd make an exception for someone as beautiful as you.'

Darby felt warm under her clothes. 'Why, thank you, Mr Cooper.'

'I like the hair, by the way. That shade of brown looks good on you. When'd you do it?'

'Last month.'

'Why?'

She shrugged. 'Wanted a change.'

'Well, you look stunning. As always.'

'Okay, what's going on?'

'What's going on with what?'

'All the compliments.'

'Just stating the obvious.' Coop glanced at his watch, frowned.

'How much time have we got?' she asked.

'About five minutes.'

'*Five?*' Her heart sank a bit.

'They bumped up my departure time,' he said. 'I was going to call and tell you to turn around and go back, when you texted me that you had just parked. But I'm glad you're here, even if I only get to see you for a few minutes. It's been, what, four months?'

'Almost six.'

'Math was never my strong suit.' Coop sighed and pinched the bridge of his nose and massaged the skin there – Darby was amazed, as always, at how slowly he seemed to age compared with other men. Maybe the crow's feet around his eyes were a bit more pronounced, and there was no question he looked tired, but his hair was still that same shade of brown and blond, not a single grey, and he looked as fit and trim as a guy in his thirties.

She pointed to the two empty glasses on the bar and said, 'Bad week?'

He shook his head. 'Just felt like tying one on before my flight,' he said. 'Helps me sleep.'

'Where you heading?'

'Big Sky, Montana.'

'Ski country.'

'So they say.'

'Only you don't ski.'

'I do not.'

'Vacation?'

'That's what the Bureau is officially calling it.'

'And unofficially?'

'That consulting gig you're doing in Hartford, for their Special Victims Unit,' he said, staring into his glass. 'Could you get away for a few days?'

'For you? Sure.'

'Don't you have to check with people?'

'Just tell me when you need me.'

'Well,' he said, smiling and turning his attention to her, 'I'll *always* need you, Darb.'

His smile felt forced, his normally playful words empty. She glanced at the empty highball glasses, then leaned closer to him and said, 'How about you tell me what's going on?'

Coop sighed. 'Look,' he said, 'it may be nothing. In fact, it probably is.'

'I'll be the judge. Let's hear it.'

She saw something inside him relax. Then it vanished

and turned to anger when he heard his flight called. Boarding had started.

Coop got to his feet. 'I need to get moving,' he said, taking out his wallet. 'I've still got to go through airport security.'

'I'll walk with you.'

She did, wondering if she should bring up what she needed to tell him. *No*, she thought. There wasn't enough time, for one, and she needed his full attention – his full *sober* attention. She had never seen Coop drink so much before a flight.

'Just answer me one question,' she said.

'Yes, it's true.'

'What's true?'

'What they say about the size of a man's foot being a good measure for penis length. I wear a size fourteen shoe, which means that I'm exactly –'

'Is there a problem?'

'With my penis size? No. Girth? I'd say I'm a little above average in that department.'

'Coop, I'm being serious.'

'So am I.'

They reached the back of the security line, which was surprisingly long, given the hour. She leaned in close to him, smelling the bourbon on his breath as she said, 'Are you in trouble? Danger? What?'

'No, no, and no.'

She said nothing, stared at him.

'Honest,' he said. 'If I was, I'd tell you.'

Darby saw that this was true.

'Reason I asked if you'd be willing to come to Montana

is . . .' He looked up at the ceiling for a moment and then his gaze scattered around the sea of faces coming and going, before settling back on her. He sighed. Looked embarrassed.

'This is going to sound stupid,' he said, 'but the truth is I would simply feel better having you around. We've always worked well together, and you're maybe one of three people in my life I trust to have my back.'

'So let me go book a ticket and I'll come with you.'

'Flight's full.'

'Then I'll take the next one out.'

They had reached the first security checkpoint. Since Darby didn't have a boarding pass, she had to step out of line, and did.

'Give me a couple of days and I'll call you,' Coop said. 'Just don't call me, okay? My employers will be watching every single phone call, text and email I make on both my business and personal cell phones.'

He handed his licence and boarding pass to the bored and slightly pissed-off-looking TSA agent sitting behind the raised desk. Then he turned to her, Darby expecting him to say goodbye, when he hugged her again, fiercely, his body tensing against hers.

He kissed her fiercely on the cheek. 'Thanks for coming,' he said.

'Whatever you need, I've got your back.'

'I know.' He sounded so sad when he said it.

Coop walked away, into the security line feeding into the adjoining room, with its X-ray machines and body scanners. Something told her to call out to him, to tell him to come back so they could talk here or back at the bar or at a hotel room, any place he wanted. He could take a later flight, or, if there wasn't one available, he could take the first one out tomorrow morning, the afternoon or evening, whenever. The important thing is that they should talk. He needed to tell her what was bothering him, because something clearly was; and she needed to share some long overdue things with him.

No more waiting, a voice told her. *Do it now.*

But the moment had passed. Coop had already moved through the security checkpoint and stepped into the adjoining terminal. He stood there with his back to her, looking at the signs for the gate numbers and the flat screens announcing the arrival and departure times for hundreds of flights, and when he finally turned and walked away she saw his face and thought he looked like a man who had willingly entered a familiar building and yet had no idea where he was.

4

Coop contacted her three days later, by text, while she was taking a much-needed long lunch with a couple of the Hartford officers from the Special Victims Unit: NEED TO TALK. YOU AROUND?

Darby texted back: GIVE ME HALF AN HOUR.

OKAY. BATTERY ALMOST DEAD. WILL CALL FROM PAYPHONE.

Darby insisted on walking back to the station, despite the cold. She needed the fresh air.

She had spent a good part of the morning trapped inside an interview room with a female social worker and a ten-year-old girl who had been repeatedly raped by her uncle. The girl pulled her sweater over her head – it was the only way she would answer their questions.

Her desk in the squad room was too busy and loud, so Darby fixed herself a paper cup of coffee and carried it with her through the back of the station and into the small parking lot. She was watching a pair of pigeons fighting over the picked-over remains of a half-eaten candy bar when her phone rang. 'Fort Jefferson, Montana' flashed across her Caller ID.

'Your offer to come to Montana,' Coop said. His voice sounded casual to her; she detected no undercurrent of urgency or concern. 'Does it still stand?'

'Tell me when and where.'

'You'll want to fly into Bozeman. There's a motel in town called the Rose Courtyard. Place looks like a dump from the outside, but it's neat and clean and cheap. I'll meet you there.'

'When do you want me to fly out?'

'Tonight or tomorrow, latest. Don't worry about the cost. I'm picking up the tab.'

'I'll check flights and call you back.'

'Don't call me on my business phone. Bureau keeps track of everything.'

'What about your personal phone?'

'I'd rather keep the lines clear, just in case.'

'Just in case of what?'

'I'd rather not let the Bureau know I'm bringing you into this. You two still don't play well together.'

That was true, but that wasn't the issue. The issue was she had embarrassed the Bureau too many times, especially in the media, which was a mortal sin. The FBI would never forgive her for it, and Coop had to tread carefully in order to protect his career.

'Contact me through the email account we set up back when we worked together in Boston,' he said. 'You know the one I'm talking about?'

'The Gmail account.'

'You remember the password?'

'The unfortunate name of your high-school chemistry teacher, a Mr Richard Fingerhut.'

'Or, as we called him, Dick Finger.' Coop snickered like a twelve-year-old boy.

'I'll see if I can get a flight out tonight.'

'Book everything on your credit card and I'll reimburse you.'

'Done. You need anything else?'

'No,' Coop said. 'Just you.'

Darby wanted to fly out that night. Problem was, every single flight out of Hartford, New York, Boston or Rhode Island had at least two layovers, and every flight was ridiculously expensive. She wanted a direct flight, and there wasn't a single one to be found until early the following week.

She didn't want to wait that long, so she booked a flight leaving that night out of Hartford, at eight. It had two stops. If everything went according to plan, she would touch down in Bozeman early tomorrow morning. Thursday.

You didn't have to go to Alcoholics Anonymous to practise their best-known motto, which was to live one day at a time. And you didn't have to be Jewish to appreciate the Yiddish expression 'Man plans and God laughs.' These two philosophies had not only kept her sane and her anger in check during the tough spots in her professional and personal lives, but they had also proved especially useful when dealing with what she considered was the single most disorganized and frustrating bureaucracy on the planet: the Federal Aviation Administration.

When she reached her first layover in Atlanta, Georgia, she was told that the second leg of her flight had been accidentally overbooked; she didn't have a seat on the plane. Darby told the woman she had urgent business in Montana and flashed her 'special investigator' badge, which was essentially meaningless. Fortunately the woman working the counter didn't know that, and with a few keystrokes a seat suddenly became available.

But, in the end, Mother Nature made the final call. A major thunderstorm that had been waffling through the day decided to move into Atlanta with a vengeance, shutting down the airport. All flights were cancelled.

Darby flew out to Seattle the following morning, Thursday, after a fitful sleep at a nearby airport hotel; but her next flight had been cancelled because of mechanical problems. By the time she touched down at Bozeman on Saturday, fifty-nine hours had passed since she'd left Hartford. Using her iPhone, she logged on to the private Gmail account she and Coop shared and sent him a message saying she had arrived.

Darby rented a Jeep Grand Cherokee. It took her a few minutes to familiarize herself with the SUV's on-board navigation system, and then she was on her way, the land flat and covered by snow.

The Rose Courtyard was a squat, brick building that had a decrepit sign planted high on a pole by the side of the road, the floodlights pointed at the writing advertising FREE HBO AND WI-FI!!! Darby was given a room out back, the only one that didn't face the street. It had beige walls and smelled of carpet cleaner, and sitting on top of a cathode-ray TV set was a tented placard advertising free HBO, just in case she'd failed to notice the sign out front.

Darby dumped her suitcase and then went outside, to the Jeep, and drove to the downtown area. Everything was closed except for a handful of restaurants and bars. She parked and then started walking around the area, ducking down side streets and through alleyways, before entering a pub called the White Tail. She picked a spot at the bar where she could see the front door and a good part of the dining area.

She was halfway through her burger and drinking a beer when she took out her smartphone and, for what seemed like the hundredth time that day, checked the Gmail account. Still no word from Coop.

5

She was great to look at, even on the computer monitor. The wireless camera he'd set up on a tree branch across the street from the Rose Courtyard offered HD-quality video and night vision. Fortunately, there was still enough light in the afternoon sky for him to take in her striking features.

What he didn't understand was why she had on the exact same clothes he'd seen her in since Saturday: tight-fitting jeans, leather harness boots and a white collared shirt worn underneath the kind of stylish black motorcycle jacket the late, great actor Steve McQueen had favoured. After she zipped up her jacket almost to the top of her neck, she put on her sunglasses, a pair of Ray-Ban Caravans with dark-green lenses and gold frames, completing her badass vibe.

Only she was the real deal, if the stories posted on the Internet were true. Not only did she have a Ph.D. in deviant criminal behaviour from Harvard, she had killed fourteen people, the majority of them men, who, like a rabid dog, needed to be put down, the sooner, the better. The other strange thing about her? She loved to fight. This good-looking and slightly muscular woman who had the body of an Olympic volleyball player, all cut muscles and chiselled features, had no problem getting into fistfights with guys.

And winning.

Repeatedly.

She shut the door to her room and then tested the knob to make sure it was locked. She walked down the steps and got into her rental car, a Jeep Cherokee, and, as she drove out of the parking lot, the stars already visible in the late-afternoon sky, he switched his attention to the second monitor, the screen showing a satellite map of the area. Her first night in Bozeman, he'd placed a GPS tracker on the engine block of her SUV, and the device was still broadcasting perfectly.

The man yawned, shivering beneath his winter jacket. He had killed the van's engine, so there wasn't any heat – which was good. He wouldn't be tempted to fall asleep. He'd been at this for three straight days, catching catnaps whenever he could.

He threaded his fingers behind his head and, leaning back in his chair, watched the GPS screen while thinking about where he should take his next vacation. He knew he should try someplace new, like Italy or France, take in a few museums and shit. But that wasn't him, and he always wanted to spend his vacation – his retirement, God-willing – in Mykonos, a Greek island where every day felt like a summer party, the beaches made of golden sand and the water crystal clear.

Twelve minutes later, he watched the Jeep slide into one of the parking lots in front of the Happy Cup diner. Except for her first night in town, she'd eaten all her meals there. It was a great place, with a big menu, but why not go a little crazy and explore some of the other restaurants? His father had been like that, a creature of routine, and it

33

always mystified him why his old man insisted on going to the same places and ordering the same food over and over again.

The man got up and made his way to the driver's seat. The van was parked on a quiet road less than a mile away from the Rose Courtyard. As he drove, he answered a couple of phone calls.

Her room was Number Eleven, along the east corner of the building, practically around the back. You couldn't see it from the motel's front office, which would make what he had to do much easier.

The winter sky had grown even darker by the time he pulled into the parking lot. He scanned the area to see if anyone was outside, maybe grabbing a smoke, or on their way out for an exciting night on the town in cow country. The only sign of life came from a truck for the local power company, Western Grid. He drove past it and didn't see anyone sitting inside, but the driver had left the headlights on and the engine running.

The man parked in the back of the hotel. He killed the lights and engine and stepped out with his toolbox. He pulled the Western Grid cap he was wearing a bit lower across his forehead out of habit, just in case someone on the road drove by and saw him. He didn't have to worry about security cameras. The motel didn't have any, inside or out.

He heard music, some hillbilly country shit, coming from inside the room, the music growing louder with each step.

Why had she left the radio on?

It was a simple lock. Eighteen seconds and he was

34

in – and that music, Jesus, it was awful. All the shades were drawn, so he turned on a light.

The room was rustic and surprisingly homey: queen bed with thick quilts and pillow, a fireplace that had been recently used, the room smelling pleasantly of ash and pine. The music wasn't coming from a radio but from the MacBook Air sitting on an oak desk, the screen on, tuned to one of those online music services like Pandora.

He left the music on even though the guy singing sounded like he had recorded the song while receiving a prostate exam. His work required what was called 'minimum disruption', which was a fancy way of saying touch only the things that absolutely needed to be touched, because you never wanted the target to have even the slightest inkling that someone had been inside his or her room or home. And before you moved anything, you took multiple pictures first, so everything was back in the exact same spot it had been originally.

He decided to work on the computer first, while he waited for his partner, Billy, to join him. Not only was it the most important item but also the easiest to tackle. He slid the disk key into a USB slot and the sleeper software on it came to life and began to install itself on the Mac. The software would allow him to read her emails and view her browser history, and also to see whatever she typed in the search boxes from here on out, because the software provided him with root access. As a side bonus, the software also turned the MacBook's camera into a surveillance device – full video and audio, all of it streamed to the equipment inside his van.

Next and final stop: listening devices.

He placed one underneath the bedframe – a 'quick-and-stick' bug the size of a pencil eraser equipped with a battery that would last seventy-two hours. A second bug, this one with a battery-operated 'peeper' camera, went inside the bathroom vent. He cleaned up the dust that had fallen to the floor, and after he flushed it down the toilet he left the bathroom and came back with a can of spray dust to replace clumps that had fallen from the vent, because you never knew when or if someone would notice such a small thing – and the McCormick woman had been trained to notice the smallest things.

The quick-and-stick bugs often failed, so he had to leave behind a hardwired listening device. The best locations for those were electrical outlets. He decided on the one beyond the front door, as it offered the best acoustical coverage. He got the battery-operated screwdriver with the silent motor from the toolbox and went to work.

Kevin had removed the faceplate, his gloved fingers moving deftly to hardwire the bug into the motel's electric system, when the front door swung open. Darby McCormick wasn't wearing her sunglasses any more, but she was still wearing leather gloves and already swinging her arm. Kevin registered her smile and the look of delight on her face, like a kid who had stumbled upon a hidden Christmas gift, just as the police baton gripped in her hand exploded against his temple.

6

Deputy Chief Stan Davies stood in his office doorway, kneading a piece of Nicorette gum between his front teeth and studying the two men who had just stepped inside the lobby of the Bozeman police station. Both were tall and broad-shouldered, and both wore dark wool over-coats over their suits. *Got to be from the marshals' office in Great Falls*, he thought. All the US Marshals he'd ever met were built the same way – and, like these two, itching to show you just how tough they were. Time for another big swinging-dick contest.

Davies sighed, flicking a glance to the wall clock. Quarter to six. Whatever bullshit had just arrived on his doorstep had to be wrapped up and tied with a pretty little bow in the next half-hour, come hell or high water, or he'd be in the doghouse again with the missus – and his daughter. Dealing with one pain in the ass was enough.

The guy with the neatly combed brown hair stepped into the bullpen first. He was taller than his partner but not as wide through the shoulders; he looked more like a middle-aged guy into swimming or long-distance run-ning. He had the big, sorrowful eyes of a dog you had just caught chewing on your favourite shoe. *He's the one in charge*, Davies thought, crossing his arms across his chest. *He's gonna do all the talking.*

The man's partner was the one who really stood out. First, he was butt-ugly. Looked like the Mr Potato Head toy: a big, shaved head; big ears jutting out a bit; and a thick black paintbrush moustache. Not a good look. Second, and far more interesting, was how the guy was carrying himself: tense and watchful, like at any moment he'd be asked to take a bullet for Mr Brown Eyes.

Davies noticed something else: they were both dressed a little too slick for cattle country.

Not marshals, he thought. *Federal agents.*

Mr Potato Head spoke first. 'Chief Porter?'

'He's not here. Stomach flu. I'm Deputy Chief Davies. How can I help you boys?'

'Phil Bradley. Assistant special agent in charge here in Bozeman. I don't think we've met before. This is Noel Covington.'

Mr Brown Eyes – Covington – extended his hand and gave his top-wattage smile – the kind, Davies was sure, that not only melted the panties off plenty a lady but also charmed his way through plenty of tough situations. The man's palm was smooth, no doubt from daily moisturizing, and he barely had a wrinkle on his face, no doubt from some skincare regime using products he picked up from reading one of his homo magazines. Davies disliked him immediately.

Mindful of the nearby ears, Mr Potato Head – Bradley – moved in closer and spoke in a low, hushed voice. 'I understand you have her in custody.'

Davies nodded. 'We do,' he said, tired and bored. He sure as hell wasn't going to miss this, being the little errand bitch for Fart, Barf and Itch, when he retired.

'Have you spoken to her?' Bradley asked. His forehead was shiny with sweat.

Davies nodded, smiled a bit. 'We have. Several times.'

'What'd she tell you?'

'Oh, lots of real interesting things – *especially* about your man Kevin Fields and the other, the taller gentleman with black hair, Billy something or other.'

Neither Covington nor Bradley provided the man's last name.

Davies snapped his fingers. 'Vieira,' he said, taking real pleasure at the pissed-on-my-parade expressions these two government yoyos were wearing. 'Billy Vieira. He was wearing the same Western Grid uniform as your man Fields.'

Covington stared down at the tops of his fancy shoes. Bradley didn't look away – seemed, if anything, ready to take charge of the situation.

'She called 911,' Davies said, enjoying this. 'When my boys arrived, they found Fields and Vieira on the floor, unconscious and hog-tied. She told them a third man was involved, but she didn't know his name. Said he was following her and gave us a physical description. I take it he's also one of yours, the third man from your Tactical –'

'Sir,' Bradley began.

'*Sir*. Wow. You two must be really deep in the muck. How are they doing, by the way? Fields and Vieira? Last time I heard, they were, ah, still incapacitated.'

'They're recovering, thank you for asking,' Bradley said. 'Have you spoken with your attorney general?'

'Sure did. Got off the phone with Miss Banks about forty minutes ago, when she called me at home and told me I had to come in on my day off to attend to some urgent business. She informed me some people would be coming but didn't give me any names, said she couldn't explain what the fuss was all about. So, how about it, fellas?'

'You have the cell phones?'

'Confiscated them, just like Attorney General Banks asked.'

'The computer?'

'Got that too.'

'You view the contents?'

'Nope, and neither did my men.' *Although I certainly tried*, Davies added privately. He had wanted to see what might be on 'em, figure out what had gotten the AG's panties all in a bunch, but the phones and the laptop were password protected.

'What about your men?' Bradley asked. 'They take any pictures?'

That got Davies's dander up. 'I'm gonna pretend I didn't hear that,' he said. All his men knew taking pictures of a crime scene with their phones was against regulations. Still, he had checked 'em to be sure, and they hadn't.

'Today is my grandson's birthday,' Davies said. 'It was arranged for my day off so I could be there. He's at my house now, waiting on me, and I've been standing here for a good hour waiting on you, so my patience is about worn thin. You've got ten minutes to clean this shit up.'

Covington spoke for the first time. 'I only need five,' he said, and invited himself into Davies's office.

7

Noel Covington entered the interrogation room alone.

It was cleaner and neater than the ones he had visited over the course of his career, although this one, with its white-panelled walls and yellowed overhead fluorescents, was a bit smaller than the normal 8 × 10 construction, giving the room a boxy and slightly claustrophobic feel. He found the three standard folding chairs, but he needed only two. Bradley wouldn't be joining him. No one would.

Noel had conducted a number of successful interrogations – conversations, as he liked to think of them. He moved the chair out from behind the table and slid it to the corner, so he could be seated next to the subject, which eliminated the psychological belief that the table was a shield or a barrier, which encouraged lying. You always wanted to have full view of the subject's upper *and* lower body movements, both of which were critical for interpreting non-verbal behaviour.

Noel, wanting to feel comfortable and to appear confident, turned his chair so it was facing the door. He had another reason for doing this: he didn't want Bradley to see the letter Karen Decker had written to him.

It was written in blue ink, on white college-ruled paper torn from a spiral loose-leaf notebook, and stored inside a clear plastic protector. The fingerprints the lab had pulled from the paper all belonged to Karen Decker. She was going by the name of Melissa French now, and she was living in Fort Jefferson, Montana. The name and return address were written on a legal-size envelope, which was stored inside its own clear plastic protector in the file.

Noel had read the letter countless times during the past month. He read it again now to punish himself.

Noel,

AA has taught me the importance of taking a personal inventory and accepting responsibility for my actions. Jesus Christ, my personal Lord and Saviour and guide these last seven years, has taught me the importance of forgiveness, especially when it comes to forgiving myself.

I know you've heard me say the AA speech before, too many times, so if the words sound hollow I don't blame you (or Vivian, let's not forget her) for feeling that way. I know the two of you will always see me as the pain-in-the-ass girl who kept crying wolf. Not only is that a fair description, it's a hundred per cent true.

Before you continue reading, know this: I've been clean and sober coming up on seven years. I take my meds every single day, and I haven't gotten into a lick of trouble since we last saw each other. Please keep that in mind when you hear what I'm about to say. That's all I'm asking. Please keep an open mind and heart this one last time, okay?

Ready?

I've found the Red Ryder.

DO NOT put the letter down.

And please don't throw the letter away.

PLEASE.

42

Just stay with me for a moment and hear me out, PLEASE, I'm BEGGING you.

Have I said these words before about the Red Ryder? Yes. Too many times. I've lost count, as I'm sure you have. All I ask is that you examine the evidence I've included and you'll see I'm right this time — you'll <u>know</u> I'm right.

I'm not giving you my phone number because I want to share this great moment in person with you and <u>only you</u>. No Vivian. Please respect my wishes on this. It's not because of what she said the last time the three of us were together (although I still consider what she said to be unusually cruel, even for her). It's because you're the only person I trust, and because I want to share this moment with you.

You'll find my house key taped inside the gas grille on my back porch.

And Noel?

I'm finally free.

God Bless,
Karen

The evidence Karen included was tucked inside a clear sandwich bag: a 5 × 6 piece of white scrap paper stained by coffee, cooking grease and ketchup. It had been previously crumbled into a ball before Karen (at least he assumed it was Karen) had retrieved and cleaned it up and smoothed the paper flat.

Fortunately, she hadn't touched the scrap paper with her bare hands: not a single one of her prints was found anywhere on it. Unfortunately, she had most likely used a paper towel, tissue or towel to blot away the ketchup and coffee. That, and smoothing out the paper, had turned the partial latent fingerprints and palm print to dreck – or, as the co-head of the Bureau's Latent Prints Lab, Jackson Cooper, had told him, the prints were possibly dreck right from the start.

Cooper had decided not to use ninhydrin, the standard chemical for lifting latent prints from paper, but rather a new method recently developed by Israeli scientists: the use of gold particles that strictly adhered to paper instead of the amino acids left by sweat. When the silver-treated developer was applied, the paper turned black and the fingerprints stood out in relief as a high-contrast white.

The latent fingerprints on Karen's piece of scrap paper, six in total, were of good to very good quality. But not a single one came back with a likely match inside the Federal database. Disappointing, absolutely, but not totally unexpected as the Red Ryder hadn't left any fingerprints at any of the crime scenes or on any of the thirteen Halloween cards and pieces of clothing he had mailed to the *San Francisco Chronicle* over a five-year period in the late seventies.

The only piece of evidence the killer *had* left behind was a palm print on the receiver of a payphone in Vallejo, California, 2.6 miles away from where he had shot Karen Decker and her family in the summer of 1978. The Red Ryder had used the payphone to call 911 to report the shooting. The detective who had pulled the wet palm print from the receiver was wanted at another job that night and had to work quickly, using a hot light and blow-drying to accelerate the process. The palm print, fortunately, was solid.

The palm print left on the crumpled piece of paper was, for all intents and purposes, useless. Cooper had found two possible points of identification that matched it to the Red Ryder's palm print. There was no way a judge would ever sign off on a search warrant because the comparison would never hold up in court.

Noel had better luck with the lab's 'Questioned Documents' section.

The scrap paper contained a handwritten list in black ballpoint of grocery items: kale, apples, raspberries, eggs, Nutella, doughnuts. Two other items were written and circled at the bottom: Preparation H haemorrhoid cream and Just For Men hair colouring. After comparing the Halloween cards with the list, 'Questioned Documents' confirmed that they had all been written by the same person, in all likelihood the Red Ryder.

'Questioned Documents' also confirmed Karen Decker had written the letter to Noel. He had asked the unit to examine the handwriting because he hadn't heard from Karen for almost seven years. No one had. He thought she was dead – had finally killed herself and done it someplace where her body would never be found. To punish Vivian.

And me, Noel thought. *I played a part in this too.*

8

The curvature of some of Karen's letters suggested she was under the influence of alcohol, cocaine or a psycho-tropic medication – or all three. If Karen was to be believed, she had been clean and sober for seven years – and taking her medication to treat her major depressive disorder: lithium, a psychotropic. She had been diagnosed with major depressive disorder following her second sui-cide attempt, at twenty-three.

Karen was living in Omaha, Nebraska, at the time. Her roommate had left to celebrate her parents' twenty-fifth wedding anniversary, only to turn around forty-minutes into her planned two-hour drive when she realized she'd left the gift in her bedroom closet. When the roommate returned, she found Karen slumped in a beach chair in the backyard, an empty bottle of vodka next to her and a series of cuts along her wrist. She had passed out before the razor blade had hit a vein.

Alcohol had been involved in all of her suicide attempts (four), her arrests (nine), and just about every other single incident listed in the classified file locked inside his brief-case. The cocaine came two years later, followed by a brief dance with heroin that, mercifully, didn't take hold.

It was the time that had elapsed since she mailed the letter that consumed him.

The letter had arrived at his office after he'd left on the

3rd of January, the beginning of a spur of the moment ten-day trip. His colleagues – Vivian included – thought he was going to Key West on vacation, and were pleased. Great, they told him. Wonderful. You've been working too hard, they said. Sit on the beach and get some sun. Turn off your phone. Better yet, leave it at home.

Florida was his destination, but Noel had lied about Key West. He was heading to the Daytona Beach area – more specifically, the Murphy & Stein funeral home. He had served with Billy Diaz over in Kirkuk and trained with him in Florida, at the Naval School EOD unit – bomb disposal – located at the Eglin Air Force Base in Fort Walton Beach. Billy had died when a roadside bomb hidden in a garbage heap on the road exploded outside the crowded Al-Hawija district of Kirkuk. The funeral was a closed-casket affair, as the IED had removed Billy's head and limbs.

Four days of hard drinking and swapping stories well into the night, and then Noel hopped back on the plane and flew out to New Mexico to the funeral of another EOD brother, Barry 'Bee-Bee' Buckley, who had completed four tours and returned home, in one piece, to his family. On a summer afternoon Bee-Bee had complained to his wife about a severe headache after playing in the backyard with his three boys and went inside his house to take a nap. He died of a brain aneurysm. That funeral was, depending on your point of view, a blessing, because the family had an open casket.

Noel had used much of his vacation time over the past few years to attend funerals. His colleagues and the few friends he'd made nodded in understanding, but he could tell they thought what he was doing was morbid.

47

Vivian, his boss, put it more succinctly: 'No more funerals. Send a card and flowers like everyone else. Your next vacation, you're to go somewhere sunny and get drunk and laid. If you don't, don't come back to work.'

Noel returned home late on a Saturday night and stopped by a liquor store and stocked up on a case of beer and several bottles of good Scotch. When he woke up Monday morning with an Olympic-grade hangover and his liver begging for mercy, he took the day off. Come Tuesday morning, he'd hit the ground running completely sober, beginning with his voicemails and emails because he had, in fact, left his phone at home. He didn't want anyone tracking his movements.

Friday afternoon, when he came up for air, he didn't sort through his mail and the printed copies of department memos, meeting agendas and other meaningless shit his secretary had piled in his in-basket. He changed into his running clothes, got into his car, and met his buddy and fellow EOD brother Chad for a five-mile run.

The postmark on Karen's letter said it had been mailed on Monday, the 4th of January. When he opened the letter, it was the 29th of January, the last Friday of the month. Twenty-six days later.

Seven years with no contact and now he was holding a letter in which Karen was claiming – again – that she was clean and sober (the Jesus thing, though, was new). She had included evidence (again) that she had found the Red Ryder (again). And what did he do? Tossed the letter aside, of course. He had been sucked down Karen's rabbit hole too many times. No one knew who the Ryder was – there had never even been a viable suspect – or why the monster had decided to stop killing. He had mailed out his last Halloween card to the *San Francisco Chronicle* with one written word inside it: Goodbye.

Maybe the son of a bitch had quit or gotten the Big C and died. Maybe he had started up again somewhere else and decided not to play the pen-pal game with the local newspaper. Whatever the reason, the monster – or at least the version in California – had vanished.

Twenty-five days had passed – almost a month – and what did he do? He waited another week before taking action. In all fairness, it took that long for the stew of anger and loss and guilt and every other goddamn thing he felt to cool down and settle. And, in the spirit of full disclosure, he took action not because he believed Karen (he didn't; he had been burned too many times) but because he wanted a clear conscience.

Noel heard the approaching *clink-clink-clink* of prison chains coming from somewhere down the hall and closed the folder, thinking of that last time with Karen seven years ago, inside a police station in the town of Weiser, Idaho, home of the National Oldtime Fiddlers Contest and Festival. Karen had been arrested for smashing a beer bottle against the head of a 69-year-old retired postal worker because she was convinced he was the Red Ryder. She had been shitfaced, of course, and coked-up, of course, and after she was arrested the police entered her name into the system. Vivian was alerted, and fourteen hours later Noel found himself sitting with her and Karen inside an interrogation room. Again.

It was summer. Karen wore shorts and a white 'Hello Kitty' tank top that looked like it had been retrieved from the bottom of a dumpster. Her bare feet were cut up pretty badly – she had lost her flip-flops while running from the police – and she was shivering and sweating from the coke withdrawal and hangover, the air-conditioned room reeking of BO and urine and a whole host of other nasty odours Noel had become accustomed to every time he saw her. But he had never gotten used to seeing her scars: they ran up her back and across her shoulders and arms and legs, a Frankenstein mess of raised red lines, some an inch wide. It was like a map that charted her story, one that had begun in the summer of 1978 when she was thirteen and ended years later, after multiple surgeries that freed her of her colostomy bag and allowed her eventually to walk without a cane.

Vivian was reading her the riot act (again!), threatening her (again!), the three of them playing the same tired roles in the same tired scene they knew by rote. Karen, looking pale and wan, hugging herself and rocking back and forth, was supposed to sit there and cry and apologize and make hollow promises.

Instead, she broke character. She stopped rocking and dropped her arms. Her eyes were bloodshot and her lips were cracked, and one side of her face was cut and swollen from a drunken fall on the street.

'Just go. Go and let me die,' she said in a soft, almost listless voice – the voice of someone who had finally arrived at the sad acceptance of who she was and what she had done – someone who had finally summoned the courage to unburden all her sins inside the privacy of a confessional and was now waiting for absolution. 'Please.'

'Then *die*,' Vivian hissed. 'Die and be done with it.'

Noel opened his mouth, about to tell Vivian she was out of line (again!) and come to Karen's defence (again!), but the words tumbled back down his throat because a part of him – a small part but a part nonetheless – had secretly agreed with Vivian. *Yes*, that part of him had nearly screamed, drowning out all his other thoughts. *Yes, Karen, do it. Kill yourself before you kill me – before you kill all of us. I can't do this any more – I refuse to do this again. I care for you, Karen – have gone to hell and back – we all have – but I've got nothing left. Nothing. Either clean up your act and get your shit together or kill yourself and be done with it, because, as of this moment, I'm done.*

Karen recoiled – not from Vivian's words but from *him*. Karen had seen the look in his eyes and knew he felt the same way as Vivian. Noel had spoken to Karen alone afterwards, apologizing, saying he was tired from the long flight and suffering from a hangover himself. All lies. Karen had seen right through them.

A pair of burly guys in neatly pressed blue uniform appeared in the doorway. They had taken extraordinary precautions with their prisoner: handcuffs connected to a special heat-treated belly chain with padlock rings designed for maximum security; leg shackles that restricted walking. Noel turned his chair so it faced the table and silently watched the men escort Dr Darby McCormick into the interrogation room.

9

Darby McCormick came in wearing dark, form-fitting jeans and a tailored, white-collared shirt that showed off a slightly muscular figure. Dried blood was splattered against the front of her shirt, and the sleeve cuff on her right hand – her fighting hand, he guessed – was smeared with it. With the exception of her knuckles, which were scraped and cut and slightly swollen, she didn't have a scratch on her.

It didn't take long to figure out how the op went to shit. The tracker, Danny Timmons, whose job was to have eyes on the target at all times, had watched McCormick enter the Happy Cup diner. There was no need to follow her inside; the store's front windows allowed him a clear view of where she was sitting.

After ordering, she played around with her phone, no doubt checking her email for messages from Cooper. She shoved the phone in her pocket as she stood, Danny figuring she was going to use the john because she had walked down the hall leading to the bathrooms and because she had left her sunglasses and keys on the table.

What Danny didn't know was that McCormick had ducked through the diner's back door, which didn't have an alarm, and hopped in a Honda Civic parked in the rear of the diner, out of Danny's line of sight. No one on the team had any idea McCormick had made previous arrangements with the motel owner, Ted Duffy, to borrow his Honda. McCormick told the man her rental car was acting up and, per the rental company's instructions, she needed to bring it to a mechanic downtown. McCormick was feeling stressed about not having a car, and said she had to meet a friend at the Happy Cup about a job. Since Bozeman didn't have a taxi service, Ted Duffy, being the gracious and accommodating gentleman that he was, offered her the use of his son's Honda for a few dollars, Duffy even going so far as to park the car, at McCormick's request, in the small lot the diner shared with the Rite Aid pharmacy, so she could have access to it after she met her friend. She had deliberately left the music on, Noel figured, so she could mask her approach to her motel-room door.

As the two Montana boys eased their prisoner into the chair, Noel looked to the door and saw Bradley hovering a few feet beyond it. Bradley pointed to the two-way glass – the signal that he was going back to the alcove to ensure no one listened in on the interview.

'Would you like something to drink?' Noel asked her.

'Bourbon, please,' she replied, her voice a bit hoarse and raspy. 'Knob Creek, if you have it. Or Woodford Reserve, I'm not picky.'

'I was thinking more along the lines of water or a Coke.'

'I'm fine, thank you.'

Noel turned to the patrolmen. 'Thanks, I'll take it from here.'

The cowboys left, but not without a pair of parting glares to let him know they were *really* unhappy about his presence here – completely understandable, given today's circumstances. The FBI had been caught playing in their sandbox without their permission, and now they were being asked to be a prisoner-delivery service, fulfilling drink orders for the inmates.

The door shut, and he was alone with her, finally.

Today, in between the rush of phone calls and meetings, Noel had scraped together a plan on how to best approach questioning her. She was smart enough to have an idea about *why* she was here, but getting the information he needed out of her was another matter entirely. She knew he had the upper hand here. Given everything he'd read in her file, Noel knew she wouldn't care.

'My name is Noel Covington.' He waited to see if his name meant anything to her; if it did, she didn't show it. 'Darby – may I call you Darby, or do you prefer Dr McCormick?'

'Seventy bucks.'

'Excuse me?'

'You ruined my favourite shirt. Got blood all over it. You owe me seventy bucks.'

Noel smiled politely. 'You put on quite a performance today,' he said. 'They teach you how to fight like that at Harvard?'

'Yes. It's a part of their Ph.D. programme.'

Noel couldn't help it; he chuckled softly. Karen would have taken an instant liking to her, he thought. 'When did you know you were being watched?'

'I'd like to speak to my lawyer please.' She sounded listless. Bored.

Noel wasn't buying it. Underneath that beautiful exterior there must have been a storm of anxiety about why

54

her best and only friend, Jackson Cooper, still hadn't called her back.

'This is strictly an informal conversation,' he said.

'Really? Then what am I doing in these?' She held up her bound hands.

'Given what happened today,' he said, 'I feel safer with you in restraints.'

A thick lock of auburn hair fell between her piercing green eyes. Sitting this close to her, he could see the faint hairline scar on her left cheek. Bleached white, it was nearly invisible against her slightly tanned skin.

An axe had done that. A decade ago, she had been protecting a young woman – a teenager – inside a dungeon of horrors when an axe blade split through a closed door. The surgeons had to replace her shattered cheekbone with an implant. She was damn lucky she hadn't lost an eye.

'You're currently consulting for the police department in New Haven, Connecticut. Their Special Victims Unit,' Noel said. 'You're contracted to work with them until the end of the month. Now suddenly you're here in Bozeman, Montana.'

She said nothing.

'You told your employer you had a personal matter you needed to attend to.'

'Have you worked with victims of sexual abuse, Agent Covington?'

Noel shook his head. Fortunately, he had steered clear of that particular world.

'Then you wouldn't understand the need to get away,' she said. 'Get some distance and some fresh air.'

'Why Montana?'

Darby looked to the two-way. 'Are you recording our conversation?' she asked. 'If you are, you're legally obligated to tell me.'

'No. No recording, audio or video.'

'What about the people behind the two-way?'

'Only one person there, and I assure you he's not recording us.'

'Agent Bradley?'

'Yes. Before we get into why you're here, I need you to help me clear up some housekeeping matters.' Noel opened the folder resting on his lap. 'Tell me when you knew you were being watched.'

Dr McCormick said nothing. Noel wondered if she was going to play nice or clam up. He was sure Cooper had given her critical information about Karen Decker – otherwise, why else would she be here in Montana?

'Saturday,' she said. 'That's when I spotted Penis Nose.'

'Who?'

'The short, reedy guy with the grey hair. He's got a thick and bulbous nose that looks like a penis.'

She had just described Kevin Fields, the man who had broken inside her motel room to install the listening devices.

'I saw him twice that day,' she said. 'The first time at the airport, the second time after I'd checked in and gone to a bar downtown. His name is Kevin Fields.'

Noel kept his face blank. *That doesn't mean anything*, he reminded himself.

She said, 'The next time I saw him he was inside my motel room, wearing a uniform for Western Grid. I met the other one, Billy Vieira, about ten minutes later. He tried to contact Kevin Fields, and when Kevin didn't answer Billy decided to let himself into my room.'

Noel pretended to write something in his folder.

'I told all this to the police, by the way, when they arrived. I called them the moment I subdued the two *intruders*. I'm sure it's in their report.'

There is no report, Noel added privately. He and Bradley had confiscated the paper file and shredded it – had removed everything from Bozeman PD's computer system.

'Agent Covington?'

'Noel will do.'

'Okay, Noel.' She smiled, like they knew each other and were sharing the same secret. 'How about we skip the whole getting-to-know-you business and get to the part where you tell me why three Federal agents were following me?'

Three, Noel thought, feeling his stomach sink. *She spotted the entire goddamn team.*

'Those two men you assaulted weren't carrying any government identification.'

'The agents who work for TacOps usually don't.'

Noel managed to keep the surprise from reaching his face.

'Tactical Operations,' she said. 'The section of the FBI that deals with –'

'You attacked two men. One is getting his jaw rewired, and the other suffered a massive concussion and a broken arm.'

'I didn't figure out the TacOps part until I saw what was packed inside his toolbox,' she said. 'Pinhole cameras, listening devices and a bunch of the usual clean-up tools – portable vacuum and cans of spray dust, to make sure everything was just the way I left it.'

She smiled at him with her eyes. She seemed unflappable. In total control, everything tucked behind the heavily fortified castle she'd built for herself, he suspected, after the murder of her father, when she was thirteen.

He took no pleasure in what he was about to say next, but it was time to knock her down.

'Jackson Cooper is missing,' he said.

IO

Missing.

The word exploded through her head and ripped through her organs.

It took her a moment to find her voice. 'How long?'

'Three days,' he said. 'Today is day four.'

Darby felt her entire midsection disappear.

Missing, she thought.

Four days.

Coop.

A missing Federal agent would be front-page news, and there hadn't been a single mention of such a thing in the Montana papers, TV news or on the Internet. She had checked.

Covington forged ahead, using a gentle tone. 'Needless to say, we're very concerned.'

Which was complete and utter bullshit. If Covington was concerned about Coop's welfare, he would have come right out and asked her about Coop at the *beginning* of the interview. If the man really cared, he would have gone straight to the hotel and asked her in person. He knew why she was there. He could have picked up the phone at any point and called her, or dropped by for a face to face.

But Covington hadn't done any of these things, because his job was about one thing and one thing only: protecting the Bureau's image and its own self-interests. The public thought the FBI was all about protecting and defending the US against terrorism and foreign intelligence threats, and providing services to Federal, state and local law-enforcement agencies, but its main business was brand management, and the brand had to be protected at all costs. The Bureau had been caught with its pants down here in Montana, and Covington needed to fix that – by any means necessary. His job wasn't finding Coop; it was collecting information. And, once he got it, he'd pack up and leave. She had seen it happen time and time again.

'We've combed through Cooper's phone records – all the calls, texts and emails he made on his Bureau phone and his personal phone,' Noel said. 'The last person he spoke to, it seems, was you.'

Darby felt something cold and hard move through her chest.

'Cooper sent two texts to your phone last Wednesday. The first one was at 1.54 p.m., Mountain Standard Time. It said, "You around?" You replied yes. Then, at 2.08 p.m., he sent you a second text, which read, "Battery almost dead. Will call from payphone." Did he call you?'

'You know he did,' Darby said. 'You already checked my phone records.'

'Why did he ask you to come to Montana?'

'Why didn't you pick up the phone and call me?'

'Because several people – Cooper, included – told me you have an inherent bias against the FBI.'

Not true, Darby thought. She said nothing.

'You also have severe anger-management issues. You get results – your record proves that. Your success rate is, without a doubt, stunning.' His voice was tinged with what sounded like sympathy, maybe even understanding. 'But, at the end of the day, the only thing you care about is serving your own personal agenda, which is why you were ultimately fired from the Boston Police Department. Why is that?'

'I have a problem with assholes – and liars,' Darby said. 'Especially liars.'

'Why did Cooper ask you to come to Montana?'

The truth was, she didn't know; Coop hadn't gone into specifics.

She said, 'Show it to me.'

'Show you what?'

'The court order.'

'I'm not following.'

'Tactical Operations need one to break into someone's home.'

Agent Covington glared at her from across the table.

'Show me the court order,' Darby said, 'and I'll answer all your questions.'

'I don't think you're fully grasping the reality of your situation.'

'I understand the reality of my situation just fine. The question is, do you understand the reality of yours? Both you and your friend behind the glass know you can't allow me to go in front of a judge because you'd have to inform him – or her – of the particulars of my arrest, which would open your covert division to all sorts of questioning, and we know the Bureau isn't going to allow that to happen.'

'You knew you were being watched. Instead of calling the police, you lured them into a trap where you assaulted two men –'

'I worked this cult case with the Bureau about five, maybe six years ago,' Darby said. 'I don't know the cult's name – I don't think it has one – and I don't know the names of the people involved, but I can tell you they're very secretive, and that they're still after me. I'm sure all the details are in that big, fat file on me you've got there. I'm sure the judge would love to know the details.'

'You don't want to go down that road.'

'The court order. Show it to me.'

'Don't need to. I have what's called a "self-written search warrant". It allows me all sorts of special powers.' Covington's tone was unquestioningly polite, but it also carried a clear warning. 'It means I can break into anyone's home – or motel room – and not only search it but take possession of any single goddamn thing I want. Your computer or phone, your chequebook and wallet, even your dog.'

'My ovaries are tingling. Tell me more.'

'I also have what's called an "emergency letter". That means any phone company, Internet service provider, financial institution or credit card company has to hand over any single piece of information I want – again, without court approval. And the best part? It's all perfectly legal, thanks to the Patriot Act.'

'I want to find Jackson Cooper. What do you want, *Noel*?'

'For you to tell me why Cooper asked you to come to Montana.'

'If I cooperate, will you drop the charges?'

'I'll seriously consider it.'

No, you won't, she thought. *I'm willing to bet my life savings you'll tuck me away in some secret Federal detention facility until you solve this thing, whatever it is, and clean it up. You're afraid Coop told me the reason why the Bureau sent him here. That's why you put the Bureau's best undercover agents on me, to try to bug my computer and motel phone.*

Darby looked down at the table. Every second wasted increased the probability of not finding Coop – and the chances of finding him alive were already slim because he'd been gone for three full days. She knew the statistics.

'Ball's in your court, Doctor.'

Every cell screamed at her to cut through the bullshit and cooperate with Covington – to answer every question and do everything he wanted as long as he brought her into the fold so she could help to find Coop.

Covington took out his pen, a fancy Montblanc. Uncapped it.

'Not one piece of evidence seized under the Patriot Act has, to date, been introduced in a Federal court,' Darby said. 'Why? Because the Federal government can't risk a judge ruling that the Patriot Act is, in fact, unconstitutional. You're not going to bring charges because you can't. You don't have a leg to stand on in court.'

Covington slid the cap back on his pen.

'Obstruction of justice,' he said. 'We'll start there and work our way down the list to assault.'

Darby said nothing.

Covington stuffed her file back into his briefcase. When he stood, she said, 'If it's after eight in Boston, then you're too late.'

Covington took the bait. 'Too late for what?'

'For you to speak to my lawyer. Rosemary Shapiro. I

spoke to her right after I called 911 and explained what had happened at the motel room. How the three men following me weren't members of this dangerous cult but actual Tactical Operations agents.'

'Goodbye, Doctor.'

'She'll have seen the video by now, I'm sure,' Darby said. 'I'm talking about the one I took of your man Kevin Fields breaking into my room.'

Covington stood as if rooted to the floor.

'I set my MacBook to record when I left my room,' Darby said. 'The camera streamed video directly to my lawyer's office in case something happened to me. I also sent her the pictures I took of Kevin Fields, his ID, his toolbox, everything.'

Covington's eyes were bright with anger.

'She's probably already getting everything ready for the press conference, so it'll make the eleven o'clock news cycle,' Darby said. 'I'm sure it will be all over the Internet by morning.'

Covington turned to the two-way mirror.

'It's 6921,' she said. 'That's the code to unlock my phone and MacBook. Go ahead and take a look.'

11

Instead of going to the alcove to join Bradley, who was no doubt already typing the password into Darby McCormick's phone and laptop to see if her story added up, Noel decided to take a moment to use the john at the end of the hall. *Let her stew in it,* he thought.

Only he knew she wasn't going to change her mind.

The cheaply framed sign above the crapper and the one hanging to the right of the small mirror held the same message: DON'T BE A PIG. WASH YOUR DAMN HANDS. Noel took a long time washing his hands, thinking about Darby, how calm she had acted back there, how she'd refused to be intimidated – which was about what he had expected. Everything that he had expected to happen with her had, in fact, happened.

He had been warned she was smart and cunning and exceedingly stubborn. She didn't back down from a fight. Cooper had put it to him more succinctly: *Nothing seems to scare her. She never backs down.* Then, almost as an after-thought: *I've never met anyone who loves fighting as much as she does. I think she gets off on putting men in the hospital.*

What was really bothering him was the feeling he'd had after leaving the room – the feeling that she hadn't been looking *at* him but *inside* him. Like she was rooting around the locked rooms inside his head, searching for things that were none of her goddamn business. *You're imagining things*, a voice cautioned. Maybe. But that had been his experience with shrinks – and women. Especially women. They were always looking for you to tell them your secrets, and when you didn't they would push you, wanting you to get angry and spill everything. They did that far too much and far too often, in his humble opinion.

As a kid and then a teenager, he'd been forced by the state of Connecticut to meet with social workers and state-appointed therapists, most of them young women with newly minted degrees in psychology, to discuss his impulse control and anger-management issues. They all wore bad clothes and smelled of fast food and cigarettes, which they'd chain-smoked during his therapy sessions. They all seemed to carry the same air of desperation, as if they had suddenly realized that everything they had sacrificed, worked so hard for and believed in was a monumental waste of their time and energy.

Later, after completing two successful tours in Iraq, he had been ordered to attend twice-a-week mandated sessions with a military therapist. The sum of those visits resulted in something he'd already known about himself: he could turn his emotions on and off with the simplicity and ease of flicking a light switch, a trait that had come in especially handy when he had to make the initial approach to an IED some shit-stinking, turban-wearing kook had planted inside the ground or left inside a junked car parked alongside a road.

Cooper was the sort of man who knew how to keep a secret – which was why Noel (and Vivian, she had played a major part in this decision) had selected him to come to Montana and look into Karen Decker. Yes, Cooper had called Darby, but that didn't mean he had shared details with her, no matter how close they were. Cooper was a professional. Noel had vetted him thoroughly. Trusted him.

So why had Cooper called and asked her to come to Bozeman?

Noel splashed cold water on his face, then dried his hands meticulously with rough paper towels. He used them to turn the doorknob, to prevent any viruses from attaching themselves to his clean hands. The last thing he needed right now was to catch the flu. It would knock him flat on his ass.

Actually, that wasn't true, he thought. The good doctor had already knocked him flat on his ass, if what she'd said about the video and pictures were true.

If so, game over.

He couldn't wait to tell Vivian. Noel smiled at the thought.

When he returned to the alcove behind the two-way, he found Phil Bradley leaning far back in a padded leather desk chair and staring through the glass while rubbing a Dentastix, the fancy brand name for what was nothing more than a glorified toothpick, in between his bottom teeth. Noel had known the guy for a little more than forty-eight hours and thought Bradley had some sort of OCD thing when it came to oral hygiene. If Bradley wasn't picking at his teeth, he was excusing himself to brush them or use mouthwash. He was always chewing mint gum.

'I found the thermostat for the interrogation room and cranked up the heat,' Bradley said.

Dumb move, Noel thought. The textbook interrogation trick screamed amateur hour. 'Good,' he said, wanting to keep Bradley feeling satisfied, like he had some skin in the game.

Noel shut the door. McCormick's password protected iPhone and MacBook sat on the small table in front of him.

'The video and the pictures?'

'It's all true,' Bradley replied. 'McCormick sent everything to Rosemary Shapiro, a Boston-based lawyer.'

'Let me see it.'

'Can't show you the video. She had her MacBook set up to stream directly to the lawyer's office computer *and* cell phone. The pictures are on her iPhone.'

There were four: two of Kevin Fields, unconscious and bleeding and tied up; one a close-up of his fake credentials; and the last a picture of his opened toolkit, its contents exposed.

Christ, Noel thought. 'Phone calls?'

'Two,' Bradley replied. 'First one was this morning at around 10.30 our time. They spoke for roughly fourteen minutes. If I had to guess, I'd say McCormick was guiding Shapiro through the technical aspects of having video streamed and downloaded on to the company computer – firewall issues and all that.

'The second time they spoke was this evening, about two minutes after McCormick called 911. That call lasted less than a minute. After McCormick hung up, she emailed the pictures she took of Kevin Fields to the lawyer's phone and company email.'

Bradley rolled his head to him, moving the Dentastix

back and forth between his teeth. 'Your girl really screwed the pooch,' he said.

Sparks of anger flew through Noel's bloodstream. It wasn't targeted solely on McCormick. In fact, the majority of it was directed at Vivian, who had insisted on using the TacOps agents.

'What's the status of the search?' Noel asked.

'Helicopters just packed it in. Still no sign of Cooper's rental,' Bradley said, turning his attention back to the two-way. 'The last time you spoke with Cooper was, what, Wednesday?'

'Wednesday night.'

'Northern part of the state got about eighteen inches of fresh powder since Thursday. If his Ford Explorer veered off the road and got stuck somewhere or if he was in an accident, then the SUV is buried, which means we're not going to find it.'

'Before you go . . . You gonna tell me what Cooper was really doing here?'

'Vacation.'

'Right.' Bradley shot him a look that practically screamed *bullshit*.

Noel opened the door. 'Keep an eye on her,' he said.

'No problem there.'

12

Noel needed fresh air. He put on his overcoat, scarf and gloves and went outside.

The sun was long gone, and it was bitterly cold out now, and windy. The main street facing him was busy with traffic, but the parking lot in the back of the police station looked quiet, and it was well lit. He made his way there, dialling the number.

Two rings and the line on the other end picked up; he heard the familiar prim voice that never betrayed any emotion. 'You spoke with her?' Vivian asked.

'We had a conversation. It wasn't a fruitful one.'

'She refused to tell you why Cooper asked her to join him.'

'That about sums it up.'

'Melissa French or Karen Decker?'

'She didn't mention either name.'

'I told you she was stubborn.'

'Which is why I advised a direct approach right from the start,' Noel said. 'We should have made contact with Darby the moment she arrived in Bozeman.'

'*Darby?* I didn't realize you two were on a first-name basis.'

'If I had spoken to her directly, told her Cooper was missing, she would have played ball with us. Instead, you wasted time –'

'No, you're *assuming* she would have cooperated. You

don't know her, and I can tell you it wouldn't have made a lick of difference. The Irish are as stubborn as a grease stain, as my dearly departed mother liked to say.

'If she's not going to talk, we'll sideline her,' Vivian said. 'Treat her to an all-expenses paid vacation to Rancho de la Relaxo.'

It was the nickname for the private Federal detention facilities used to give certain guests an opportunity to unwind and come to their senses. If that didn't happen, which was almost always the case when it came to dealing with terrorist suspects, other methods could be employed to help a guest get his or her priorities in order.

'There's one less than an hour away from Bozeman,' Vivian said. 'I'll call and book a room.'

Noel told her about McCormick's lawyer, the pictures and the live-streaming video.

'Jesus Christ,' was all she had to say when he finished.

'I haven't talked to the lawyer yet,' Noel said. 'I wanted to call you first.'

'We can't have videos and pictures of Tactical Operations agents out in the public domain. The Bureau will crucify me. This is a major problem, Noel.'

'I agree. What do you want me to do about it?'

'You think she knows about Karen and the Red Ryder?'

'My guess is no.'

'Too bad we're not in the guessing business.'

'If she knew specifics, she would have taunted me with them, and she didn't,' Noel said. 'If she knew anything at all, she would have hinted at it, and she didn't.'

'Or she could be playing this close to the vest. That's what she does. She's very cunning, that one.'

'She wants to help us find Cooper.'

'Naturally. They're in love, the two of them. They're not fooling anyone. Why else would Cooper keep her so close all these years?'

'Because she gets results. Darby knows Cooper better than –'

'You can't be serious. Noel, the woman is a killing machine – has the highest body count of any law enforcement officer in the country. The only reason she isn't in jail is because she's a woman, and because she has a Ph.D. from Harvard. I don't want any part of her.'

'I can control her.'

Vivian barked out a laugh. 'That's like saying you can control a tornado.'

'Any additional evidence we uncover, she won't know.'

'If there was any additional evidence, Cooper would have found it on his first day. Time to pack it in and come home. Bradley can take care of things from here on out.'

'Not until I find Cooper.'

'He's been missing for three days. Today is day four. You can't honestly think he's still alive.'

'I gave Cooper my word.'

'He's dead. Your word doesn't mean anything to him any more.'

His left eye started to twitch – nothing major, not yet, just a few spasms – and he found himself thinking back to a hot and sunny afternoon in Fort Walton Beach, Florida, a day when he had felt not only proud but, for the first time in his life, whole and complete, all doubt about who he was and what he was capable of finally erased: graduation day from the Navy's Explosive Ordinance Disposal school at the Eglin Air Force Base. It had been a brutal affair; only a few people graduated.

The EOD badge was called the Crab, and the moment it was pinned to his chest he had been accepted into a family where you never, under any circumstances, left behind your brother or sister. You lived for them and they lived for you. The words still lived and burned inside his blood now, and they would mean absolutely nothing to Vivian, who operated in a world where words and promises held little value – unless they could advance your career or agenda.

'When you speak to McCormick's lawyer,' Vivian said, 'tell him or her that the Doctor is to leave Montana. Make that a condition of having the charges dropped. I'll see you tomorrow.'

'Not until I find out what happened to Cooper and Karen.'

Vivian didn't answer. She had already hung up.

13

Darby sat alone in the interrogation room, facing the two-way mirror. There was no other place to look. She couldn't turn her chair around – couldn't turn her body either, thanks to the wrist and ankle chains that had her conveniently tied down to the bolted chair.

She had no idea how long she'd been sitting here because the room didn't have a clock. She had no way of knowing if Noel Covington was behind the glass, watching her, along with the other one, the big Fed with the lumpy face named Bradley. She had met him after the two Montana men had escorted her out of her cell. Bradley popped two sticks of Dentyne in his mouth and insisted on checking her restraints himself. He approached her without trepidation and, smiling, began a leisurely exam of her wrist and ankle cuffs. She felt his bicep and then his forearm brush up against her breast, and she was sure she heard his breath catch in his throat when he tightened her handcuffs. She had almost headbutted him right then and there but stopped herself. Better to hurt him later so she could really savour the moment.

Having witnessed and performed dozens of interrogations over the course of her career, Darby had a strong idea about how this whole thing would play out. Covington was going to let her sit here all chained up and feeling uncomfortable, which was the reason why Bradley had given her cuffs an extra, special snap; why they had shackled her in wrist chains and leg cuffs; why they had turned up the heat inside the room to an uncomfortable level. Changing the temperature to hot or cold was an old interrogation trick – and generally an effective one when used against someone who wasn't accustomed to being locked inside 'the box'.

The charges, she knew, wouldn't stick. It was a bullshit threat meant to frighten her into submission. *Good luck with that*, she thought, and almost grinned. She had played her trump card: Rosemary Shapiro and the incriminating video and photos of the TacOps agent calling himself Kevin Fields. Rosemary was a well-known pain-in-the-ass in both state and Federal circles, and the powers that be knew she would delight in sharing her client's story and incriminating evidence with the media. The FBI and the other alphabet agencies despised publicity that wasn't overwhelmingly positive in their favour *and* something they could fully control and spin for their benefit. When the Bureau was unwillingly kicked into the spotlight or, worse, their investigative methods were exposed, careers were flushed. Arrest her and Covington knew he'd have a major PR shitstorm on his hands – one that would tank his career.

Covington and his partner were the least of her concerns. What had happened to Coop? He had come to Montana on 'unofficial' FBI business, and because he was missing the Bureau had, twenty-four hours later, put not just run-of-the-mill agents on her but highly coveted trained surveillance agents from Tactical Operations. Why? Because Coop was here on some highly sensitive or classified matter, and the Bureau wanted to watch her and monitor her phone conversations and emails in case she knew something about what had happened to him. Because they knew she wouldn't share any information with them if asked.

And the Bureau was right. She didn't trust them; never had, never would. The FBI played by its own set of rules. She had learned that lesson the hard way and had the physical and mental scars to prove it.

Why did they send you here, Coop? What the hell did you get yourself involved in?

The door swung open. Covington came in alone. No briefcase this time, but he was wearing his jacket, gloves and a scarf.

He didn't sit. Just stood on the other side of the table and looked at her with this odd, tumultuous mix of sympathy and fear – and anger, yes, she definitely saw some of that too.

'We found Cooper's rental car,' he said. 'We also found a body.'

14

Two weeks shy of her thirteenth birthday, Darby had been at home reading *A Separate Peace* for her English class when her mother entered the living room and in a calm, clear voice, as though she were just popping in to tell her dinner was ready or just to say hello, announced that her father had been shot and rushed to Boston for emergency surgery.

Then, almost as an afterthought, her mother added, 'Before we leave, I should go next door and feed Mr Birmingham's cat.' Sheila McCormick, still oddly calm, turned and walked away without any urgency.

Her mother's parting words and mannerisms were obviously crazy given the circumstances. It wasn't until much later that Darby realized the root cause: her mother was in shock. In that moment, though, Darby wasn't thinking at all about her mother because she too had gone into shock. All the light had been sucked out of the room, and her body felt like it had been packed in dry ice. Coldness spread through her, like a spill. She couldn't speak or move.

But her mind, strangely, was alive and in overdrive, sprinting like a medic through a warzone to reach the wounded soldier screaming to her from across the battle-field. *There has to be a mistake no there's not Big Red is dead no he's not my father will get through this no he won't yes he will he's strong and tough and he was a Marine but what if he doesn't make it?*

Now she was sitting in another room, this one boxy and overheated, with a Federal agent who, with his perfect hair and smile and chocolate puppy-dog bedroom eyes, looked like some pretty-boy actor from a soap opera. Those eyes were full of mourning, but not for Coop. The man was mourning the failure of whatever had brought him here to Montana.

Covington put his hands on the back of the chair and, gripping it, bent slightly forward. He spoke in a low voice. 'Car accident. Happens a lot on this particular stretch of road, I'm told, especially in the winter. They're waiting on the crane.'

'Crane,' she repeated flatly.

'The SUV is at the bottom of a ravine. They need a crane to pull it up.'

'But it's Coop's SUV. The one he rented.' Why did she say that? Of course the SUV belonged to him; why else would he have told her?

'Yes. They ran the plates.'

'And the body?'

'Buckled in the driver's seat. White male. That's all I know at the moment.'

That doesn't mean it's Coop, she told herself.

Another voice said: *It doesn't look good*.

She blinked and kept blinking, Covington coming back into focus and standing next to her now, working on her restraints. Three quick turns of the handcuff key and she was free.

'Four days,' Darby said. 'Four days and you're telling me no one saw him.'

'It's an isolated area, and there's been a lot of snowfall.

78

The SUV got buried. Only reason it was found was because snowmobilers were out late this afternoon and saw it on their way home and called it in.'

'I'll do it,' she said.

'Do what?'

'Identify the body.'

'We don't know if it is, in fact, Cooper yet.'

'But if it is, you'll need someone to identify him – the sooner, the better.'

Noel sighed. 'I'm not sure that's a good idea,' he said.

'His mother and his sisters live in Boston. I don't want to put them through that – and I'm already here.'

Again, Covington took in a deep breath. This was the part where he would put up a fight – a gentle fight, given the circumstances, but a fight nonetheless. Yes, he wanted someone to identify the body as soon as possible in order to get things moving, but he wouldn't want her anywhere near the crime scene even if it were nothing more than a simple car accident, because if she got even the slightest whiff of what was going on here in Montana, the case Coop couldn't tell her about, Covington knew she wouldn't let up. The smart play was for him to do everything in his power to keep her as far removed as possible.

So she was surprised when he said, 'Are you sure?'

No. 'Yes,' she said, and felt her throat close up.

'Okay,' he said softly. 'First thing tomorrow, I'll drive you –'

'No. Tonight.'

Noel thought about it for a moment. Nodded.

'What about the charges?' she asked.

'Dropped – provided you call your lawyer and tell her

to hold off on releasing the video and pictures. We also want the originals.' Covington reached into a jacket pocket and came back with her iPhone.

Rosemary had tried to call her several times over the past few hours. Darby's hands were steady as she dialled Rosemary's private number.

He's not dead, she told herself, listening to the phone ring on the other end of the line. *Not until I see the body.*

Rosemary answered on the first ring. 'Darby, thank *God*. I've been calling you for hours.'

'I'm with Noel Covington from the Bureau.'

'I spoke to him and the other one, Bradley.' Darby could hear the smile in Rosemary's voice. The woman's whole day – her life's mission – was structured on finding ways to become a boil on the collective ass of law enforcement. The more powerful the players involved, the more excited she got.

'Hold off releasing the stuff I gave you.'

'Did they threaten you? If they did, tell me right –'

'Coop's been missing for four days. They just found his SUV. Some sort of car accident. That's all I know.' Darby swallowed. Cleared her throat. 'I'll call you tomorrow.'

'No, you'll call me *tonight*,' Rosemary said, her voice strangling on tears. 'You want me to come out there, I will.'

'I'll call you.'

'You sure?'

No, Darby thought. *I'm not sure of anything. Not any more.*

15

The site of the accident, Noel Covington told her, wasn't in Bozeman. It was further north, in a town called Fort Jefferson. Coop had called her from a payphone there. She didn't tell this to Noel. He probably already knew it, anyway.

'Fort Jefferson is about 300 miles north of Bozeman,' Noel said. 'We're going to drive for about half an hour and then take a copter. When we land, we'll take a Sno-Cat to the site, on a road that's slightly east of the major highway, 86. Taking the Sno-Cat will be quicker and safer than driving, because a good majority of the roads leading into Fort Jefferson either haven't been properly ploughed or are too risky to drive on, with all the ice.'

'What was Coop doing up there?' Darby asked.

'I honestly don't know.'

And I honestly know you're lying to me. I know the Bureau sent him here.

As she followed him out of the station into the winter evening, the sky black, the wind cold and mean, she fought the urge to grab Noel, as he kept insisting she call him, by the jacket collar, spin him around and beat the truth out of him. Doing so would satisfy a lot of urges but it wouldn't help Coop – at least not yet. She had to wait.

Noel Covington had invited her to the crash site. If she could manage to put her anger aside and stop herself from indulging in her grief, she might be able to think clearly. Logically. If she gave in to any of her emotions, she might miss some clue or crucial piece of evidence, if there was anything to find.

You only have one shot at this, Darby told herself. *Indulge your anger or your grief and it's over, and you'll never know what happened to Coop.*

Noel, ever the gentleman, held open the back door of the Chevy Suburban parked at the kerb on the main road. Darby slid into the warm back seat, with its ample room and tabletop desks so agents could juggle their papers. A privacy screen separated the back from the front, and she saw Bradley seated behind the wheel – and, to his right, a console-mounted laptop, the glowing screen containing a GPS map of the route to Fort Jefferson.

Noel shut her door, plunging the SUV into gloom, but he didn't open the door to the passenger's seat. Darby looked through the tinted window, squinting, and saw him take out his phone and dial a number.

'Hey, Bradley.'

He rolled his shaved, potato-shaped head to the rear-view mirror.

'What's your first name?' Darby asked, watching Noel pacing near the driveway leading into the Bozeman station.

'Phil,' he said.

'Has anyone ever told you that you have the charm of a date rapist?'

Bradley chuckled.

Darby turned her attention to him. 'The way you groped me when I came out of lockup,' she said. 'Do that again, Phil, and you'll be picking your teeth out of your shit for the next month.'

Bradley smiled brightly. 'You're a real class act, McCormick.'

'You've been warned.'

Noel opened the door. As he slid into his seat, Bradley put the car into gear.

Bradley pulled away from the kerb. Noel turned around in his seat and, looking through the opened partition, said, 'There are a couple of fast-food places along the way to the copter. If you're hungry, we can –'

'I'm fine, thank you.'

'That box next to you has a bunch of bottled water. I suggest drinking up, to prevent altitude sickness. Your jacket, how warm is it?'

Darby glanced out her side window. Underneath the streetlights she saw long stretches of empty and flat land, most of it covered in a pristine white.

'Your jacket,' Noel said. 'How warm is it?'

'Warm enough.'

'I took the liberty of having one of the agents pack up your stuff. Everything's in the trunk.' A beat as he tried to take her measure, and then he said, 'I need to make some phone calls. Do you mind if I put this partition up?'

'Do whatever you need to do.'

'You need anything, just knock.'

As the motorized privacy screen slid up to the ceiling, Darby stared at the back of the man's head. *If I find out that you or Agent Bradley or anyone else was responsible for what happened to Coop, or in any way negligent, I will make it my life's mission to punish you. To make you suffer. And if none of that works, I won't hesitate to put a bullet through your head.*

The thought comforted her. Not much, but some.

What Noel had told her was essentially true: he did have calls to make, the first of which was to Vivian, who had to be told about the car accident, and Cooper. The sooner she found out, the better, so she could use the details to fill in any potential holes in their story. They would need to keep away any politicos or career climbers who might start sniffing around to see if they could uncover anything in Fort Jefferson, Montana – and there was a lot to uncover, starting with Karen. He had no idea how strong her 'Melissa French' identity was, whether it would hold up under intense scrutiny.

He decided not to call Vivian until he'd gathered more details. The best thing he could do right now was to use the time to think, so he did.

When they reached the helicopter pad on the outskirts of Bozeman, he had a solid idea of what he wanted to do.

Noel insisted Darby sit up front, next to the pilot. She did, without complaint, and when she turned her back Bradley shot him a look of mock disappointment. It was meant as one of those playful high school boys' locker room 'thanks for denying me the chance to sit next to the hot chick on the bus' sort of things, but Noel had caught a distinct undercurrent of contempt and anger behind the expression – the same one he'd seen back at the police station, when Bradley went back to ogle her privately through the two-way, as though she were responsible for having stolen something precious and important to him.

Guys like Bradley, though . . . Noel had the misfortune of meeting men like him over the years. When it came to anything they either outwardly or secretly desired, they all acted the same way: like little princes in waiting who had suddenly and inexplicably been denied the throne that was theirs by birthright. Some managed quietly to nurse and stoke their anger, waiting for the right time to strike. Others did a piss-poor job of hiding it. You couldn't count on them saving you a seat in the mess hall, let alone saving you on the battlefield, and they never had your back because they were terminally insecure and always looking out for themselves and their own self-interest. No matter how many times you spoke to them, no matter how many examples you gave them, they would always fail to comprehend that mental and physical toughness and virtues like bravery and courage were genderless. They could never be trusted, under any circumstances.

Noel continued to dwell on Bradley in an attempt to stave off his twin terrors: his intense fear of heights coupled with a disorienting and stomach-churning claustrophobia. They introduced themselves to him during his second month in Iraq, after he had travelled a dozen or so times by military helicopter, every single one of which was designed not for comfort but for transporting cargo – and you were cargo. The best ride was the hurricane seat on a Black Hawk, but he never got to experience it, damned to always travel, it seemed, inside the dreaded Chinook – what everyone called 'Shithook'.

The countless blast waves he had endured in Iraq had turned his brain to Swiss cheese, nearly wiping out memories from his early childhood; but, as the helicopter took off in Montana, he could still remember every single ride inside the Shithook, each one exactly the same: sitting shoulder to shoulder with forty or so other sweating men crammed into the outside jump seats, the centre loaded with two or three pallets; everyone dehydrated within a few moments of takeoff and breaking in the same hot, toxic stew of main engine exhaust, dust, soot and grime trapped inside a windowless oven that, when it wasn't vibrating, was spinning or shaking. If he didn't throw up from the heat, he threw up from the motion – and he always puked on himself because he couldn't turn or move.

Noel had a window, plenty of windows, and plenty of room to move, and clean, fresh air. As the copter gained altitude (it felt like a flying coffin, an image he couldn't get out of his head), a slick and greasy sweat broke out across his body. He stared down at the tops of his shoes – a trick he had learned from Kimberly Jackson, a Marine staff sergeant from the Marine Corps Forces Special Operations Command – the first female allowed into MARSOC and one of the bravest people he had ever met. He suspected Darby McCormick possessed the same type of courage.

Maybe Cooper had died in a car accident. Or maybe it was something else entirely. He would soon see. And if his gut instincts were right – if he allowed Darby McCormick to take a look at the accident site and if she could manage to think past her grief – then maybe she would see something of value, provide him with a new direction in which to explore. Maybe, just maybe, she could provide him with much-needed hope.

16

The Sno-Cat – a bright neon-yellow Ford F350 truck refitted to include an enclosed rear cabin with benches and satellite-equipped GPS maps displayed on not one but three custom-built monitors, all four tyres replaced by caterpillar treads – was called 'Winston Fur-chill'. The name was painted in big black block letters on both doors, to let everyone in on the joke.

Noel had insisted she sit in the front, which was fine by her – the more distance between her and Bradley, the better. Noel and Bradley sat in the rear, studying their phones, hoping to get a signal in someplace this out of the way. The Sno-Cat's gas-guzzling engine rumbled underneath their seats and drummed steadily against their ears, the entire cabin shaking, bouncing and vibrating as it chugged and clawed its way across yet another wide, groomed path she assumed the locals used for snowmobiling. The engine was loud enough to discourage talking, but that didn't prevent their bearded and baseball-hat-wearing 26-year-old driver, Jonas Cutler, from speaking, the man taking great delight in telling them about wildlife in this part of the state – especially the bears.

'Worked in Yellowstone for five years,' Cutler said, his callused hands gripping the wheel fiercely at two and four o'clock, fighting like hell to keep the Sno-Cat steady as it chugged across the snow. 'Back in the fifties, they drew up these promotional brochures – colour drawing of a smiling pretty little girl in pigtails sitting on her daddy's lap inside the family station wagon and holding a jelly sandwich out the window to feed this big, friendly Yogi Bear-type bear. Big hit, those brochures. Massive. Tourism at Yellowstone skyrocketed. Then it all came to a crashing halt when the bears decided to eat a few fingers, sometimes an entire hand, along with the jelly sandwich.'

Either Jonas Cutler hadn't been told about the nature of their trip or he was simply trying to fill the awkward silence. Bradley and Noel weren't speaking – at least not loudly enough for her to hear. Every now and then she saw, over her left shoulder, Bradley lean in and say something to Noel. Whatever Cutler's reason, Darby was grateful for the distraction. It helped keep a part of her mind tethered in the real world and prevented her from drowning in her thoughts about Coop, his mangled body.

Darby sucked air deeply into her lungs and held it as Cutler said, 'Momma bears, both the blacks and the grizzlies, they hibernate during the winter, as everyone knows. The same isn't true for their cubs.'

Outside the front window and in the distance she spotted a bright, white cone of light shooting up over the snow-covered treetops and into the night sky – a grouping of portable searchlights, was Darby's guess.

'When the cubs aren't sleepin' or feedin',' Cutler said, 'they're playing inside the den, having themselves a grand ole time. They even do their bathroom business right there in the den, all while momma snores away.' He rolled his head to her and, smiling widely under his handlebar moustache, added, 'You ever wonder how momma bears do numbers one and two during the winter?'

'Can't say I have,' Darby said absently. The Sno-Cat had moved on to a flat patch of land, and through the gaps between the trees she saw flashing blue-and-white police lights. The driver didn't notice her discomfort, or her hands resting on the seat cushion, grabbing the edges and squeezing.

'Momma bears don't got to worry about doing a number two because right before hibernation, they treat themselves to a final meal of pinecones, bark and their own fur,' he said. 'It creates their very own special, one-of-a-kind butt plug.'

Someone chuckled from the back seat – or had she imagined it? She turned her head slightly and glanced over her shoulder and saw Bradley staring impassively at whatever was displayed on his phone's screen. Noel, though, had been watching her and listening, and said, 'Mr Cutler, how about we –'

'Accident site's up ahead; we're almost there,' Cutler said. Then, to Darby: 'You're looking a little green. Riding in one of these, with all the shaking, can give you motion sickness. You want me to pull over?'

'No, thank you. How much farther?'

'A mile or two. Roll down your window and get some air in here, you'll feel better.'

As the outside lights grew larger and brighter, her imagination provided a gruesome image of Coop's badly beaten and mangled body restrained by the seatbelt of the SUV, its frame dented and crushed from the fall. Her mind kept providing more images, as though they would somehow inoculate her from her grief.

You need to prepare yourself, an inner voice whispered.

The Sno-Cat came to a full stop.

No matter what happens, she thought, opening the door, *keep your shit together.*

Darby got out and trudged her way across the groomed path, making her way to the bright lights as tides of dread flooded her heart.

17

The human nervous system reacts in the same primal way to grief as it does to any physical threat or danger: the adrenal glands kick in, heightening your senses, putting them – and you – on high alert. The first thing Darby noticed was the cold. She had grown up in New England, where winters were harsh and grim, so she was used to snow and biting subzero temperatures but this coldness felt different. It pressed at her exposed skin like needles and seemed to be seeping past her jeans and the thick black leather of her jacket – the kind of cold that killed quickly if you weren't careful.

The second thing she was aware of was something she couldn't see but could definitely hear: a steady and persistent roar of running water. Not quite the thundering or deafening drum of a waterfall but a sound close to it, and it was growing louder with each step. It didn't belong out here in the woods, where everything was pristine white, the branches sagging with fresh snow.

When she stepped on to the main road, which had been badly ploughed, the pavement covered in ice, the rushing sound of water vanished, replaced by the rumbling chug of a diesel engine coming to life further up the road – the crane Noel had told her about back at the station. The crane was a truck-mounted model designed for highway travel, so it could be easily transported. Equipped with outriggers, it sat on a level section of road. Three portable floodlights, the kind used in road construction, had been set up, and she could see everything clearly now: the sheriff's trucks and the flatbed used to transport the crane; the wind-burned faces of the six men huddled near the guardrail, plumes of breath exploding around their faces and scattering in the wind. They all wore identical clothing: forest-green trousers, black winter boots and thick black parkas. Some wore earmuffs. Five wore black baseball caps with the words SHERIFF DEPT. embossed in white on the brim. The sixth, the shortest of the group, wore a Stetson.

Probably the sheriff, Darby thought, switching her attention to the portable floodlight on the edge of a precipitously steep decline. As she drew closer, she saw, in the bright LEDs, the wide and jagged path carved through the snow by the tumbling Explorer. On its way down, Coop's rental had taken out some skinny trees and saplings before crash-landing in the river, where it now rested, overturned and partially submerged. The running water she had heard earlier now had an explanation: this section of the river contained rapids. She could see the water pounding against the SUV.

The crane's hydraulics engaged, chugging and whining and straining as it began slowly to lift the SUV from the river. The nearby officers motioned to Darby to back away from the guardrail. She did and saw Noel hovering by her side.

The Explorer looked like a wrecking ball had attacked it: the roof was crushed, the front end slammed into an accordion of twisted steel. Water rushed out of the missing windows as the crane lifted it into the air, and Darby felt her stomach lift along with it. From the corner of her eye she could see Bradley having a private conversation with Stetson Man, who kept flicking glances her way.

The woods and the roaring water, the crane and the male faces – everything took on a surreal, dreamy quality. A sudden gust of wind scattered the crane's diesel fumes, the pungent, sickening odour filling her nostrils and lungs and making her feel even more lightheaded and nauseous than she already was.

Now the SUV hovered over the rapids, spinning lazily from a grappling hook. In the play of light she could make out the shape of a pale and bloated body pinned behind the crumpled steering column.

Don't look away. It was her father's voice – calm but firm. *If you look away, if you so much as shed a single tear or if they hear your voice break, they'll avoid you.*

And, in one way or another, they were all watching her to see how she was going to react. She wasn't imagining it; almost every face here was either aimed directly at her or stealing glances at her. Every man here was taking her measure. Noel was still hovering next to her, and the two men standing nearby had moved in a bit closer, assuming she was going to faint or throw up or pass out or whatever. As frightened and sick as she felt, she wouldn't let them see her break down. She would hold it together for Coop. After everything he'd done for her, she owed him at least that much.

The crane's boom swung around and then moved the SUV toward the road, river water splashing against the pavement. Now it lowered the dripping wreckage, stopping when the SUV hovered less than a foot from the ground. The deputies approached, their gloved hands gripping the mangled heap, helping to guide the still-inflated tyres on to the road so the vehicle could be examined and, afterwards, loaded on to a flatbed tow-truck that was parked behind the crane, its red-and-orange emergency light spinning lazily, like a heartbeat at rest.

The crane's engine shut off. Darby could still feel its hum throbbing in her ears. *Get ready, it's time to get ready*. As a couple of men carried over one of the portable flood-lights, she took out the pair of blue nitrile gloves she always kept tucked inside her jacket pocket.

Bradley hung back as Stetson Man made his approach. Another man materialized out of the dark, holding a cam-era, and began to take pictures of the vehicle from different angles. Several beams of light played over the SUV, the men gathering around it, searching. Darby couldn't see Coop, not from this angle – the Explorer's twisted backend faced her – but in the halos of light she could make out the wet silhouette pinned in the driver's seat. One of the officers made a sign of the cross.

Stetson Man moved to the SUV, said something quickly to one of his officers, then broke away. Now he was coming toward her. The officer he had just spoken to said something to the group of men, and, as they moved away from the Explorer, she saw several glance at her. They had been told who Coop was and who she was, and they were giving her some space so she could view the body. So she could say goodbye.

Her heart seized as Noel turned his back to the group and, his hands tucked in his overcoat pockets, leaned slightly forward and spoke close to her ear. 'You don't have to do this,' he said. 'You want, you can give me a list of Cooper's distinguishing characteristics and I can go and look, make the ID.'

Darby didn't want to look, had to look – had to see for herself. She had to know, didn't want to know.

'Just remember,' he said. 'Whatever you need, I'm here for you.'

Stetson Man was short – stood barely five-seven in his thick-soled boots – and his face was full of sympathy. 'Sheriff Kevin Powers,' he said to Noel. 'We spoke on the phone.' A quick handshake and then he turned to Darby. 'I'm sorry we have to meet under these circumstances, Dr McCormick.'

She shook his hand, her grip limp, but her voice was clear when she spoke. 'Have we met before?'

'No, ma'am, we haven't. I know your name, of course, and your reputation.' He pursed his lips tightly and sighed deeply. 'Agent Covington told me you knew the deceased well. I'm sorry for your loss.'

'Thank you, Sheriff. May I borrow your flashlight?'

'Of course.' He handed it to her, a big, powerful Maglite.

Darby tucked it under her arm, then stood as though rooted to the ground.

Keep it together, she told herself. *Keep it together so you can think. You only have one shot at this.*

It seemed to take a Herculean effort to step forward. Now she was walking, navigating her way across the road and experiencing what almost every single rape victim had told her about: the sense of being transported outside their own bodies while they were being attacked. The psychological term was dissociation. She left her body but still felt, acutely, the dread, fear and grief scrabbling at the walls, trying to climb them so they could begin their assault.

The driver's entire head and the left part of his shoulders were hidden behind a warped section of car roof. The seatbelt was strapped against him, and he was bundled inside a dark-green down parka; the down feathers, soaked from the river, made the jacket hang limply. She stared at the body, listening to the water dripping inside the car, and remembered that night at Logan when he'd hugged her, how wonderful he'd felt and how great he'd smelled. How, driving home that night, she'd wondered what it would have been like to hold him, skin to skin, but mainly wondered if she should have told him about how she'd realized she didn't want to live so far away from him any more, that she missed seeing him and working with him. How they should have gone into business together, consulting. How great they were together as a team.

And, if she could have summoned up the nerve, maybe brought up the subject of trying a life as something more than just friends.

But she hadn't told him these things and never would because Coop was inside this car, dead. She knew it was him – could only be him.

All eyes were on her, waiting. Noel Covington seemed to be caught between the urge to come over and assist or to stay put. She made the decision for him: she sidled up to the door.

Turned on her flashlight.

Then, with a sense of falling, she leaned forward to examine what remained of Coop's face.

18

With homicides, there was always some rationale at work, some basis of understanding for the violence, no matter how grisly: I shot my husband because he was cheating; I shook my baby because he/she wouldn't stop crying; so-and-so was killed because he or she was a drug dealer, or a gang-banger, or the world's biggest asshole. Homicides always came down to one if not more of the seven deadly sins: lust, gluttony, greed, sloth, wrath, pride and envy. There was always a thread to follow. You just had to find it.

But car accidents had a cruel randomness that always got under her skin. Maybe it was because physics and the laws of gravity were so detached and vicious in their killing. Darby didn't recognize Coop's face because there wasn't much of a face left. What remained had been savagely torn during the fall and then sloughed off during his time in the cold, fast-moving water. His eyes had been punctured and cut, making them unrecognizable, and the rest of his head, which rested on his right shoulder like someone catching a nap during a long plane flight, was badly mangled – the skull dented and deformed, the remaining skin bloodless and so pale it looked waxy, covered with lacerations so deep they exposed bone.

She wasn't ready to say his name. Once she did, Noel would come over, thank her kindly and then push her aside, probably having Bradley or someone else drive her back to the hotel. She was alone at the moment and she was prepared to use the time wisely – but quickly. Noel wouldn't leave her on her own for too long.

Her heart was banging against her ribcage, and she swallowed drily as she fitted her right arm and then her head through the crumpled section of window. Drops of water plopped against the dashboard and upholstery and against her scalp, like small pieces of ice. The body had been in the water for a good amount of time, the skin that was visible already showing signs of slippage. Carefully – very, very carefully – she patted down the front jacket and jeans pocket, the metallic and earthy scent of the river filling her nostrils. She couldn't reach the back pockets, so she patted the sides along the chest, then used her flashlight to look around the front seats and search through the expected detritus – pebbled fragments of broken glass, river silt and broken branches, some of them containing pine needles.

Darby backed out of the SUV and swung her attention to Noel, who was standing with Bradley and the sheriff.

'It's not him,' she yelled.

That got Noel moving. As the others followed, she examined the back seat and tailgate, finding them empty of anything worthwhile. The sad truth was she needed more time alone with the vehicle in order to take a closer look.

Whatever Noel had been expecting to see inside the SUV was apparently different from what he *was* seeing; the skin of his face flexed and tightened. If it was an act, it was a hell of a good one.

'It's not Cooper,' Darby said again. The sick feeling inside her chest didn't dissolve, but the discovery had sent up a small balloon of hope. Then it popped when she realized the cold, hard truth: Coop was still missing.

'The ear is wrong,' she said. 'It's slightly smaller than Cooper's ear, and there's no evidence of lidding.'

'Lidding?' the sheriff asked.

'It's where cartilage in the top part of the ear is folded over, or indented. A benign congenital defect. Cooper has it on his left ear, never got it fixed.' Noel, she noticed, was staring at the body. No, not staring at it but through it, preoccupied with some private thought.

Her forensic instincts took over. 'Sheriff,' she said, 'this body has been in the water for several days, which explains why most of the facial skin is missing.'

'It slipped off from being submerged in the water.'

'And from the current,' Darby said, nodding. 'He's wearing leather gloves, but don't remove them or you'll risk injuring the skin. Bag the hands right now, so no more skin sloughs off when it's time to move the body. Do you have someone who knows how to print a floater?'

'I'd have to ask the medical office, inquire about their personnel.'

'Make sure this person has printed a floater not once but several times. It's delicate and difficult work, and you have only one shot at it. If they don't have someone, I can do it for you.'

'I may take you up on that offer.' Powers flicked his gaze back and forth between Noel and Bradley as he said, 'You know who this man is?'

Bradley shook his head.

'No,' Noel said, appearing genuinely dumbfounded. 'Let's check him for an ID.'

Darby said, 'If you go poking around, you'll damage more of his skin. Wait until he's on the table, or at least out of the car.'

'We also found a suitcase,' the sheriff said. 'Let me show it to you.'

Darby handed the flashlight back to Powers and stuck her bare hands back in her jacket pockets to warm them up. Bradley stayed behind to make sure the victim's hands were properly bagged.

The sheriff took them down the wide trail made by the falling SUV. When they had almost reached the bottom, the loud rush of water thrumming all around them, he shone his flashlight on a half-buried suitcase, its wheels sticking up in the air.

Powers had to raise his voice over the roaring water. 'It was almost completely covered when they found it,' he said. 'We took the pictures before the boys carefully dug around it, to see whose it was.'

The black metallic hard-shell was dented, banged and scratched, Darby suspected, from tumbling inside the SUV before being thrown out and smashed up against one or more tree trunks until it finally landed here.

'Looks like the suitcase hit the trees there and there,' Powers said, shining the beam of his flashlight on some deep gouges on a pair of nearby trunks. Then he moved the beam back to the suitcase, where Darby saw a luggage tag. It wasn't the cheap cardstock kind, with the flimsy elastic, readily available at airport check-in counters; this one had a white plastic name card protected inside an orange-tinted PVC pouch to keep it safe from the elements.

Darby had to move around the man in order to read the writing on the card: *Jackson Francis Cooper* and his Virginia address and phone number all in black marker in his distinctively neat Catholic-school-taught penmanship. (*About the only thing the nuns were good for*, he'd told her on several occasions. *That, and reminding you just how hot hell is*.)

Noel was moving the beam of his flashlight across the snowdrifts as he said, 'So now the question is whether or not Agent Cooper was a passenger inside the vehicle. What's going on over there?' He pointed downstream at a pair of dim beams of light sweeping across the river's black, glassy surface.

'My people have been searching the banks to see if anything washed up – more luggage, clothing, what have you,' Powers said.

'Anything I can do to help?'

'Yeah. Let's get out of this damn cold and away from the water so we can talk without shouting at each other.'

Darby followed the men back up the steep hill, using nearby branches for support. Powers had the appropriate boots, the soles and heels covered by Yaktrax that bit into the ice and made his ascent easier. She had the boots but Noel was wearing a pair of black oxfords. She had to stop several times either to pick him up or to reach out to keep him from falling. As she climbed, she kept wondering if Coop had been a passenger in the Explorer. If he had been thrown from the vehicle, his body could very well be buried somewhere out here, or washed somewhere downstream.

When she reached the top, Darby was out of breath – not from the exertion but from the altitude. Bright stars danced in front of her vision and then bled into comets, and she saw Powers standing next to one of his officers, a woman, who was holding a black down jacket. It was soaking wet, as though it had just been plucked from the river below; and in the play of light Darby could see the places where the jacket had been torn, the fabric smeared with mud and silt, the front lapels stained black with blood. She saw the Patagonia label on the front and thought, *Coop's jacket.*

19

The coat was the same colour and style as the one Darby had seen at Logan Airport. Darby's body kicked into gear before her mind did, her legs marching forward. The wind, which had suddenly come to life in the past few minutes, blasted against her as if trying to push her back, saying, *No, please don't do what you're about to do.*

She looked at the inside collar and saw a big black X drawn in marker over the Patagonia label.

Why is there a black X on the label?

To let the world know you bought it at a heavy discount at an outlet, Coop had answered. *You're a girl, you're supposed to know these things.*

The female officer said, 'I checked the pockets and found this.' Then she held up a clear evidence bag holding a black leather wallet containing Coop's Federal bag and his laminated ID.

Sheriff Powers said, 'Thank you. Good job.'

Darby blinked, confused as to why the man had said this to her; then she realized his words had been directed to the female officer, who, with a nod, moved forward and walked straight past them, holding Coop's jacket.

'Be careful with that,' Darby said, not realizing until after she'd spoken that she had practically shouted at the woman. She wasn't imagining it; her voice had also drawn the attention of the nearby officers busy documenting on their clipboards and photographing all the damage to the body and the SUV.

The female officer stopped in her tracks and looked at Darby with the kind of limp and awkward sympathy given to a patient who has just received and refused to accept a terminal diagnosis. It felt like spit on her face.

'I meant the evidence,' Darby said, as if by way of explanation. 'You can't put wet evidence inside plastic. It'll turn mouldy, and the plastic breaks down the DNA.'

The young woman seemed confused, maybe even a bit frightened; her gaze bounced to her boss, in a sort of 'how do you want me to handle this' look, and Darby realized Sheriff Powers and his people weren't treating this as a homicide but as a car accident, nothing more.

Which it could very well be, she thought. But she knew Coop had come here to Fort Jefferson in some capacity for the Bureau, and she was going to do everything in her power to find out everything that they weren't telling her.

'Sheriff,' Covington said. 'Is there someplace where you and I could talk? Step out of the cold, get warmed up?'

'That's a fine idea,' Powers replied. 'Let's go to my truck.'

'Could one of your people take Dr McCormick back to the hotel? It's been a long day, and she —'

'Sheriff,' Darby said, 'did you meet Agent Cooper while he was in town?'

Powers seemed surprised by the question. 'Why would I?' he said. 'But to answer your question, no, I didn't meet him – would have had no reason to meet him, unless he was here on FBI business.'

Noel said, 'He wasn't.'

'I'm sure you're right,' Powers said. 'Because if Agent Cooper was here on behalf of the FBI, he would have come straight to my office and extended the proper courtesy, let me know he was here.'

Powers knows something, Darby thought.

Noel said, 'Where's your truck?'

'Right over there,' Powers replied.

'Sheriff,' Darby said, 'do you mind if I tag along? I have some questions.'

'So do I – and no, not at all. Agent Covington?'

'I have plenty of questions myself.'

'And some answers, I hope.'

'Whatever I know I'll gladly share with you,' Noel said. 'I don't have anything to hide, Sheriff.'

Oh, but you do, Darby thought. *I know you do, you lying son of a bitch.*

20

Darby got into the back of the truck. The tan leather upholstery felt cold and hard, and the mountain air trapped in the cab smelled of the gun oil used to clean and lubricate the deer rifle locked in the gun rack mounted behind her head.

After the sheriff turned the ignition key, he fiddled with the heating dials and then repositioned himself in his seat so he could face them, back pressed up against the door and an arm draped across the top of the steering wheel.

Sheriff Powers cleared his throat. 'We've had roughly eighteen inches of snow over the past four days, with more to come,' he said. 'If Agent Cooper was a passenger inside the SUV and got thrown from it, his . . . body could very well be somewhere down there. If he got thrown into the water, he could be further down the river.'

If there is any justice in this life, she thought, *please let him be buried somewhere underneath these rolling blankets of snow.* The idea of him dead and buried, his body frozen, was somehow more bearable than the thought of Coop alive and badly injured and screaming in pain and finding himself trapped in the river's frigid water.

Noel Covington said, 'How deep is the water down there?'

Darby surprised herself when she answered the question: 'Rapids are a max of four feet. The issue isn't depth, it's temperature.'

Sheriff Powers nodded, kept nodding. Then he said, 'If Mr Cooper was thrown into the water, it would be a blessing if he straight-up drowned. And I can say that having attended too many autopsies of people who've drowned in that goddamn river from car accidents versus people who survived and died of hypothermia.'

The grief, which had so far been regulated to her stomach, shot through her limbs and rocketed up her throat, making it feel as though it were no wider than a drinking straw. She could barely swallow, and when she took in a breath her chest felt tight, her lungs spongy.

'Those are Class 5 rapids down there – townsfolk call it the Wild Straits,' Powers said. 'It continues for about another half-mile and then merges into the Peak Valley River. If Mr Cooper got caught in the water, his body would have washed ashore downriver, in which case it's buried underneath the snow. Or he could've got pinned on something, a grouping of boulders or a tangle of tree limbs, maybe even one of the congested chutes . . .'

Darby's mind exploded with images of Coop's limp and broken body drifting through the strong, icy currents. She saw him clawing furiously and uselessly at the dark waters, desperately seeking purchase to get ashore. She felt the freezing temperature attacking his limbs, and she felt the freezing cold snaking its way toward his heart, wanting to stop it and then kill it, while his mind kept comfortably whispering, *Sleep. It's okay, just shut your eyes and go to sleep and the pain will disappear; it's okay to let go.*

'We won't find his body until spring,' Darby said. 'That's what you're saying.'

'If you're lucky,' Sheriff Powers said. 'Truth is, you may

not find his body at all, especially if it made its way into the Peak Valley River. I pray to God that's not the case. If he was alive when he washed ashore in those woods, at some point he would've passed out from hypothermia, and then you've got the problem of wildlife.'

Darby looked at the blackness beyond the truck's front window. Coop was out there somewhere, whatever remained of him. And seeing what had happened to his body and how he died, no matter how painful, was better than never finding him at all.

'Either of you take a look at the tyres?' Powers said. Then, when they said no: 'I did. Got a good close look. Treads were worn. Shouldn't have passed state inspection. That vehicle had no business being on the road, let alone on this one here. I can't tell you how many accidents and fatalities we've had over the years. Place has so many roadside crosses it looks like a damn cemetery.'

'I can have cadaver dogs here in the morning,' Noel said.

'That'll be fine. Whatever you need, Agent Covington –'

'Noel will do.'

The sheriff nodded. Then his face twisted in discomfort, as though he had developed a sudden cramp. 'I think we all agree that what happened here was a straight-up motor-vehicle accident,' he said.

I don't, Darby thought. *Not yet*.

'Reason I say that is because – and I mean no disrespect here –' Powers began.

'The Bureau will pick up the tab,' Noel said.

'Sorry to bring that up, but the town won't. It can't. The bean counters won't sign off on it, and I don't have any extra money in my department I can shuffle around.'

'We'll take care of it, Sheriff. It's not a problem. The man in the car, is there anything you can tell me about him?'

'I was gonna ask you the same question. I thought he was one of yours.'

Noel shook his head.

'I need to ask this,' Powers said. 'Was your man Cooper here on some sort of Bureau business?'

'If he was, he would have checked in with you.'

'That's the courteous thing to do, sure. Sometimes, though, agents forget, get tied up in things.' What the sheriff meant was: the Bureau is known for sticking its nose into other people's business and then lying when they get caught.

'Agent Cooper was on vacation,' Noel said.

That's a lie, Darby thought. The sheriff kept his face carefully blank.

'Came to Big Sky,' Noel said, 'to ski.'

Another lie. Coop doesn't ski – never had any interest in it.

Powers shifted his attention to Darby. 'And you flew into Montana to meet him and go skiing?'

Noel was watching her closely, she could tell.

Save his ass, or throw him under the bus?

'No,' Darby told the sheriff. 'I didn't come here to ski.'

Powers said nothing. Waited. If Noel was feeling even the least bit anxious or angry, he was doing a damn fine job of hiding it.

'I flew into Bozeman a few days ago,' Darby said. It seemed to take a great effort to speak – to string the words together. She sucked air deeply into her lungs and held it, wishing this would all disappear, knowing it wouldn't. 'Cooper was supposed to meet me there. We were going

109

to hang out for a bit, catch up, then head on over to Yellowstone together. When Cooper didn't return my phone calls or emails, I called his office, and they put me in touch with Agent Covington and –' Her voice caught; it wasn't a performance. 'And here we are.'

'Why Fort Jefferson?' the sheriff asked.

'What do you mean?'

'There's no skiing here. Cross-country, sure, we offer plenty of that. And snowmobiling and hunting. But that's about it in terms of winter activities. We're not exactly a tourist destination.'

Covington said, 'I checked Cooper's Bureau email account and I pulled his cell phone records, and I'm at a loss as to why he came to your town. Do you have any ideas, Sheriff?'

Powers propped his left elbow on the edge of the dashboard. He pinched the corners of his mouth between his fingers and massaged the edges of his bottom lip as he stared thoughtfully out the front window. The truck's temperature had gone from warm to hot. Darby unzipped her jacket.

'Melissa French,' the sheriff said. 'That name mean anything to you?'

Darby shook her head. Noel did the same, and she wondered if he was telling the truth.

'She moved to Fort Jefferson this past summer,' Powers said. 'We don't get much in the way of transplants. People who are born and raised here tend to stay here. So when someone moves into our town, it causes quite a stir.'

'Who is she?' Darby asked.

'Don't know much. She rented a house the bank

repossessed – we've got a good number of empty houses still sitting around, thanks to the housing bubble and recession from a few years back. Town still hasn't recovered . . . Anyway, this was in June of last year. Single woman, fifties, no kids, took a waitressing job at the C & J Diner downtown. Nice lady. Always came by to make sure my coffee cup was topped up. She also did a lot of babysitting, from what I hear.'

The sheriff scratched an eyebrow with his fingernail. 'This past week, I've been hearing . . . rumblings, I guess you could call it, about some outsider – a big, tall guy who sort of looked like the quarterback for the New England Patriots, whatshisname . . .'

Darby said, 'Tom Brady.'

Powers snapped his fingers. 'That's him,' he said, and cocked a finger at her. 'He was going around town asking questions about the French woman – where did she go and how could he get in touch with her. That sort of thing.'

Darby's attention was now fully inside the truck, on the conversation. Finally, a possible connection to what Coop was doing in Montana.

Noel was listening intently, but his tone was casual when he said, 'Something happen to her, Sheriff?'

'Yeah,' Powers replied. 'She quit her job, packed up and left town.'

21

Darby said nothing, thinking. Watched Noel as he said, 'How long ago was this?'

'When she left? Middle of January, I think,' Sheriff Powers replied. 'Betsey Sullivan – she would be the owner of the diner – she told me about Melissa one morning while I was sitting at the counter for lunch. I hadn't seen her for a stretch – Melissa, not Betsey – and when I asked after her Betsey told me Melissa had quit.'

It was now the 22nd of February. The sheriff was talking about, roughly, almost a five-week period.

'And you're saying Agent Cooper was going around town asking for her?' Noel asked.

'That's what I've been hearing, yeah,' Powers replied. 'Something going on?'

'I'm here to find out. Sheriff, I need to report back to my supervisor tonight about what happened here, tell her about this new information about Cooper here in Fort Jefferson, asking questions about Melissa French. I'd like your permission to go around your town and ask some questions myself, gather some additional evidence.'

'Whatever you need, you'll have our full cooperation.'

Darby heard approaching footsteps crunching against the ice and compacted snow. She turned toward the sound, to her left, and through her back window saw the woman who had been holding Coop's jacket heading their way.

Powers cracked open the window.

'Medical examiner is here,' she said. 'I told Bobby to hold off on moving the body, figured you might want to be there to supervise.'

'Thanks, Terry. Tell him we'll be there in a minute.' Powers rolled up the window, swinging his attention to Noel. 'I know you've got to do a full report, so if you want I can have the SUV moved to the helicopter hangar next to the station. Back in the old days, we used to assist Big Sky in searching for skiers who got injured on some black diamond or hikers who got lost. Copter's gone, but we've still got the hangar, and it's got heaters.'

'I appreciate that, Sheriff. Thank you.'

'Glad to help.'

'Before I go,' Noel said, 'I'd like to look through Cooper's suitcase. There might be something in there that could show us why he came to Fort Jefferson.'

'Of course.'

'Handling a floater can be a tricky business, as Dr McCormick said. With your permission, I'd like her to supervise.'

Powers looked at her. 'No disrespect, but are you sure you're up for that?'

Darby nodded.

'Okay, then,' the sheriff said, and opened the door.

Maybe Noel was indulging her grief, or possibly too exhausted to care, or perhaps it was something else entirely. Whatever the reason, neither he nor Bradley said anything when she instructed the men on how to remove the body from the car seat, or when she insisted that the officer with a camera take more pictures, and from which angles.

Once they got the John Doe out of the seat and inside

the unwrapped body bag on the gurney, Darby carefully prodded the man's pockets, hoping to find ID, but they were all empty.

'Probably fell out during the crash,' Powers said.

Or was swept away by the river, Darby thought. She and the others checked inside the SUV to be sure, and didn't find anything.

Coop's suitcase had been moved into the hatchback of an SUV owned by the sheriff's office. Darby stood at the rear of the vehicle and, her hands covered in latex, checked the outside zipped compartments. They were empty.

When she opened the suitcase, she found Coop's clothing: boxers and socks and undershirts, a couple of flannel shirts and an extra pair of jeans. She rooted through the clothes and found nothing of value. His leather toiletry bag contained a toothbrush, toothpaste, deodorant and a prescription bottle of Ambien, the popular sleeping medication used to treat insomnia.

Darby closed the suitcase, and for some reason it triggered a memory of a kind man named John Murphy, the funeral director who had gently closed the lid on her father's coffin.

'Tomorrow morning's gonna be as clear as a bell,' Powers said. 'We'll search the crash site again in the daylight.'

A few minutes later, as the body was loaded inside the back of a van, another vehicle approached, its tyres crunching the ice as it slowly made its way down the winding road, approaching them. Black SUV. Given its length and body, it looked like a Ford Expedition.

Noel waved to the driver. Then he turned to Darby and said, 'That's your ride. Come on, I'll walk with you.'

Darby didn't want to go back to the hotel. She didn't want to go to some strange room and sit alone with the knowledge of what had happened to Coop. 'The hangar the sheriff mentioned,' she said. 'I'd like to go there.'

Noel climbed the rise, heading toward the Expedition, thinking.

'And do what?' he asked, anger skirting along the edge of his voice.

'Take a closer look at the SUV. The hangar will have better lights, and I'll be out of the cold so I can take my time, make a thorough inventory.' This, she knew, was the attention you gave a homicide, not a motor-vehicle accident.

'Powers is sending some of his people there to do that – make sure the evidence is properly catalogued,' he said, taking long strides, anxious to get rid of her. 'Bradley will be there to supervise. And, to answer your next question, no, we're not treating this as a homicide.' He glanced over his shoulder, then looked back at her and said, 'Did he share the pictures with you?'

Pictures? What pictures? Darby managed to hold back her surprise. 'No,' she said, which was true. She managed not to say: 'He wanted to show them to me in person.'

Noel said nothing. Darby wondered if he had been playing her – using her grief as a way of getting her to confess the details of her conversation with Coop. Or maybe he was testing her on how much she knew, or whether in fact she knew anything at all.

Had she slipped up?

'I admire the way you handled yourself back there,' Noel said. He was speaking briskly, one professional to another. 'What I need to know is, are you still in a headspace where you can think critically? If you can't, I completely understand. But be honest, because I'm running out of time.'

'Running out of time for what?'

'Can you help me? Yes or no.'

They had reached the passenger's side of the Expedition. Noel had his hand on the door but didn't open it.

'What do you need?' Darby asked.

'A fresh set of eyes,' he replied. 'Go to Rail Mont Avenue in Fort Jefferson. Number Thirty-three. That's the house Melissa French was renting. There's a key inside the gas grille on the back porch – or there should be, if Cooper put it back. If not, get creative.'

Break in, he meant.

'I don't know what, if anything, is inside the house,' Noel continued. 'What I do know is the day after Cooper called you – Thursday, the 18th – Cooper made two stops there. One in the morning, when he took the pictures; the second time later that day, around six, well after he had spoken to you.' He searched her face for a moment. 'Didn't he tell you this?'

'About the house? No.' Which was true. 'What did he tell you?'

'I last spoke to him on Wednesday. The only information I have is the signal tracking for Cooper's two phones – his personal cell and the Bureau one. The computer managed to backtrack both signals, and they both show Cooper made two stops at the house that day.'

'After the last stop at the house, where did the signals show him going?'

'Nowhere,' Noel said. 'Both signals died at the house, at 11.53 p.m. on the night of the 18th. Either he shut both phones off himself –'

'Or someone did it for him.'

'Go there and see what, if anything, Melissa may have left behind.'

'If she left in the middle of January, we're talking roughly five weeks until Cooper arrived. If there was something there to find, Cooper would have found it.'

'Maybe. Will you at least take a look?'

'I'll need the pictures he gave you.'

'Already forwarded them to your email. My cell number is in the message. Call me.'

He fished a pair of hundred-dollar bills out of his wallet and handed them to her. 'Give that to the driver. Make sure he sticks around while you're inside the house. Take all the time you need, but under no circumstances is he to leave you there alone.'

22

Instead of getting back to the matters at hand, Noel watched the Expedition slowly climb up the icy rise, its tyres sometimes skidding and slipping. He felt his heart skidding and slipping along with it. The idea of Darby alone inside Karen's house had filled him with a sense of dread that was now bleeding over into what would become, if he weren't careful, a bone-rattling panic.

His fear for Darby's safety was irrational – the Red Ryder wasn't hiding inside the house or lurking in the neighbourhood, lying in wait, watching – but the underlying fears were solid. Karen had been missing for over a month, and Cooper was dead, his body either buried somewhere underneath all the snow out in those woods or swallowed by the river. And a John Doe had been found strapped inside the driver's seat of Cooper's rental. The only common thread linking everything together was the Red Ryder.

He's alive, and he's here, Noel thought, as he turned and moved back down the icy road. But where was the son of a bitch? Karen hadn't specified in her letter, leaving Noel to assume she had encountered the Red Ryder somewhere during her travels in Fort Jefferson – most likely at the diner where she worked. The piece of paper containing the grocery list was stained with grease and mustard and coffee. Had to be the diner, because she sure as hell wouldn't have invited him over to her place for breakfast or lunch.

The Red Ryder had written that list. Vivian could dismiss handwriting analysis as quack science, but the man who had compared the handwriting samples, Roland Bauer, was the head of the Bureau's 'Questioned Documents' section – a man who had worked several high-profile cases that had resulted in convictions. The person who had written the grocery list was the same person who had penned the thirteen Halloween cards mailed to the *San Francisco Chronicle*. *I'd stake my reputation on it*, Roland had told him. Vivian had been in Roland's office when he said those exact words, and she had nodded in agreement.

Noel's thoughts and his mounting panic returned to Darby. He found comfort in an unlikely source: Vivian.

Darby McCormick is a killing machine, Vivian had told him. *She has the highest body count of any law enforcement officer in the country.*

The panic abated, but the dread was still there, like an unreachable itch, as he made his way to Sheriff Powers, who was telling his people what he needed from them and what would happen tonight at the hangar and tomorrow morning, when the Bureau brought up the cadaver dogs from Missoula. The SUV was loaded on the flatbed, ready to go. Bradley, bundled in a coat with a hood and wearing gloves and busy making notes on a clipboard, saw him approaching and broke away from the herd.

Bradley stepped up to him and said, 'We're wrapping this up, thank God. My nuts feel like a pair of ice cubes.'

'You have any luck getting a signal on your phone?'

Bradley shook his head.

'What about your personal phone?' Noel asked.

'Barely a single bar.'

A single bar is all I need, Noel thought. 'I saw you talking to someone earlier.'

Bradley nodded. 'That was Keefe who called.'

'Keefe?'

'Guy arranging the cadaver dogs. I could barely hear him. I told him I'd call him back when I got to the hangar.'

'I need to borrow your Samsung.'

'Hotel's less than ten minutes away. They'll have a hard-wired phone. You won't get any static or interference.'

'I need to make a call right now.'

'You feeling okay?' Bradley asked as he dipped a hand into his jacket pocket.

'Never better. Why?'

'Your left eye keeps twitching.'

Noel said nothing.

'It's been twitching since the moment we stepped on the copter. You sure you're okay?'

'No,' Noel replied, and paused for effect.

Bradley came closer.

'I haven't had enough water,' Noel said, 'and I've got one pisser of a headache.'

Bradley's face beamed with a conspiratorial grin, like the two of them were in on a secret. 'I warned you about the altitude,' he said, and handed over his Samsung.

Sheriff Powers offered Noel the use of his truck to make the call, to get out of the cold and wind. As Powers handed over his keys, Noel caught the unmistakable look in the man's eyes, one he recognized from all his dealings with just about every law enforcement officer outside of the Bureau: *Bullshit me all you want, but you and I both know you have a hidden agenda. And it's only a matter of time until I uncover what it is.*

Noel was strictly an Apple guy; he didn't know anything about Samsung Galaxy phones and the Android OS. After he started the sheriff's truck, he took a few minutes to familiarize himself with Bradley's phone. Then he dialled Vivian's direct number. She would be in her office, even at this late hour, because she spent Monday through Sunday holed up there – in what she jokingly referred to as her *pied-à-terre*. Four years ago, when she turned fifty-two, she started taking Sundays off, which simply meant she spent a good chunk of the day at home on her laptop going through her emails and making notes in her planner, a three-ring leather binder the size of a phone book, so she could start off her week with some semblance of control. Control was the operative word when it came to everything Vivian said and did in her life, in and outside the office.

A single ring and Vivian picked up.

'Tell me everything, Mr Bradley. How's Noel?'

'You're talking to Noel.'

'I understand McCormick is with you.'

'Who told you that? Bradley?'

'Now don't get testy,' Vivian said, not sounding the least bit upset or embarrassed at being found out. 'I asked Mr Bradley to keep an eye on you – and I'm glad I did, as he told me the good doctor accompanied you to Fort Jefferson.'

'She offered to identify Cooper's body for us.'

'How wonderfully thoughtful of her.'

'I wanted to move things along. I'm surprised your new BFF didn't tell you.'

'Petulance isn't an attractive quality in a man, even if that man is as handsome and charming as you,' Vivian said pleasantly.

Noel heard the rattle of ice inside a glass on the other end of the line. Scotch time. Vivian allowed herself one and only one drink during the last hour of work: an exact four fluid ounces of either Glenfiddich or Macallan, whatever she had on hand, poured over two and only two ice cubes. He pictured her sitting behind the grotesquely large desk everyone referred to as 'the moat', her slender five-foot-five frame reclining back in the big leather chair she'd had specially made to relieve the pain from two degenerative spinal discs. She had grey, almost white hair that was cut short and styled like the British actress she eerily resembled, Judi Dench. Spoke like her too, in that same crisp and castrating tone.

The itching sensation Noel had felt was now creeping along the back of his skull, like an army of ants. 'Did Bradley tell you about the man we found behind the wheel of Cooper's SUV?'

'He did.'

'Is this John Doe one of yours?' Noel asked. In highly sensitive operations, Vivian liked to secretly employ the services of her retired 'friends', to make sure she was being told the full picture by the people working for her. The moment he had seen the waterlogged body, Noel was sure she had followed this exact same procedure with Cooper, to make sure he was feeding her and only her the latest information.

'Given the course of events,' Vivian said, 'I wish I *had* sent someone to watch over him. Back to the John Doe. Where is he being taken?'

'The ME's office in Missoula.'

'Good.'

'You've dealt with them before?'

'A long time ago. They weren't good then. Fortunately, they had a major shakeup last year – some ethical controversies that I can't recall off the top of my head, plus the usual bitching and moaning about backlogs – and the woman who took over, Dr Baker, came in and cleaned house. She's excellent.' Vivian knew the MEs in almost every major city. 'I'll make some calls, see if I can get John Doe bumped up to the top of the list. Still, it will be a few days.'

'I'm planning on attending the autopsy.'

'There's no need. Dr Baker is –'

'I want to be there, make sure no stone is left unturned.'

Vivian paused. When she spoke, her voice sounded strained. 'If that's what you want. But you can't bring along *your* new BFF. The good doctor has a flight to catch.'

'When?'

'Tomorrow. No need to concern yourself with the details. Mr Bradley is taking care of everything.'

Noel was looking out the window, watching the flatbed driving away with Cooper's crushed SUV. 'Darby knows,' Noel lied. 'Melissa French and Karen Decker, the Red Ryder and the handwriting, all of it.'

A throbbing silence greeted him on the other end of the line. Noel smiled, imagining Vivian sitting erect in her chair, as though a piece of rebar or a two-by-four had been shoved up her ass – the way she always reacted when she received bad news. He saw her grinding her teeth, her face flushed with anger and her tiny lips pressed together into a small button. He wished he were in her office right now, standing on the opposite side of the moat to see it, savouring the expression on her face.

'Push her away now,' he said, 'she might go public with what she knows.'

'She's brash but not stupid. She knows the trouble we can make for her.'

'You ready to call her bluff?'

'I'm ready for you to come home.' Noel heard a new and rare tone in her voice: compassion. 'I'm worried about your –'

'I'm fine.'

'Bradley tells me your left eye is twitching. Constantly.'

Noel said nothing.

'You know it's only going to get worse, which is why you need to –'

'I'll be in touch,' Noel said, and hung up. His hand was steady and he felt a stillness come over him, followed, absurdly, by an intense wave of heat, as though he were standing in one of the Army-constructed command bunkers, the dry air boiling with heat as he stared at the phone, waiting for it to ring, to bring him more news of death.

23

Coop had taken ten photos, each one an interior shot of the house Melissa French had rented, each taken between 10 and 11 a.m. on the day after he had called her from the payphone in Fort Jefferson.

The first photo had been taken from the front doorway: a panoramic shot of the downstairs, which had an open-concept floor plan. Square-shaped foyer in front of carpeted steps leading upstairs and, to the right, a closet door. To the left of the stairs, a living room with a wood stove mounted inside a stone fireplace, a sectional couch facing it and a TV. A circular maple table with four matching chairs, and behind it an island counter made of a dark granite or laminate. She pinched her fingers to enlarge sections of the picture, searching for ... what? What was she looking for? Noel said he didn't know because Coop hadn't told him – didn't have time to tell him.

And what was the reason behind his sudden change of heart back at the accident site, asking her to go to the house and look around, when up until that moment he had done everything to keep her in the dark?

Back to the photographs.

The remaining nine shots were all interiors taken mostly from doorways of bathrooms and bedrooms. Everything was neat and orderly: beds made, no mess on any of the counters. The kind of pictures a real-estate agent would load on to the company website to give a potential buyer a feel of the place. *Staged* photographs. This wasn't a lived-in space. Either Melissa had cleaned and arranged everything before she left town or someone else had done this. Darby made a mental note to check with the realtor, see if they'd hired a local cleaning company or asked a couple of employees to come in and tidy everything up.

See what you can find, Noel had told her.

But there wasn't anything to find, at least not in these ten pictures. Nothing jumped out and screamed *Look! Over here!* Coop had taken pictures of the living room and kitchen and the downstairs bathroom and the upstairs bathroom, with its old-fashioned claw-foot bath, and the two bedrooms, one of which was a child's room, with a pair of bunk beds and Disney princess decals and posters on the wall. If a crime had taken place inside that house, there was no evidence of it in these photos. And if a crime had taken place inside the house and been cleaned up by the perpetrator, how was she going to find and collect any evidence when she didn't have use of her forensics kit?

The phone's screen dimmed from inactivity. Darby looked out the window, thinking about *why* Coop had taken these pictures.

'We'll be at the house in about five minutes,' her driver said. His name was Michael and, in addition to his black Stetson and long, scraggly beard, he wore a long Texas-Ranger-style black duster. Slap a six-shooter into his hand and the guy could have easily played some cocksure gunslinger in a Clint Eastwood spaghetti Western.

The SUV's high beams sliced the darkness, lighting up

the road. Both sides were lined with tall trees, not a single streetlight or house anywhere in sight – no, wait, there was a house. It was set far back from the road, its single, dimly lit window nearly swallowed up by the forest.

'Where you from?' he asked.

'Boston, originally.'

He made a fist and tapped it against the top of the steering wheel. 'I knew it,' he said, smiling from beneath his beard. 'You've got the accent – not as bad as you hear in the movies, but I was sure I caught a hint of it.' He smiled brightly, pleased with himself. 'Who you know in Fort Jefferson?'

Darby didn't see the harm in telling him. 'Woman named Melissa French.'

His brow furrowed in thought. 'Can't say I know her – and I know a good number of people here. Fort Jefferson's real small now, about, oh, 300 people, I'd say. Could be less.'

'You live in Fort Jefferson?'

'Not any more. Well, not full time, anyway. I was born and raised here, and my parents still live on Hanover Avenue, right behind Goodies department store. I try to get down every weekend, or at least every other weekend, to check in on 'em. They're getting on in years, scared to death of pretty much everything – politicians, getting their guns taken away just as World War III is about to break out – and I hate to say it, it *is* going to happen in our lifetime, don't you think?'

'You never know.'

'How long's your friend Melissa been here?'

'Only a few months. She's new to the area. Works at the C & J Diner.'

'They make the world's best blueberry-and-cinnamon pancakes, no lie.'

Having spent a good amount of her adulthood travelling through what political pundits consistently referred to as 'Middle America', that magical stretch of heartland separating the two coasts, it always amazed her how friendly and chatty people were, how they liked to strike up random conversations with random people. She had grown up in provincial Boston, with Irish Catholic parents who kept to themselves, like everyone else in the neighbourhood. You talked to tourists only when they asked for directions (usually to the Bull & Finch Restaurant that was used in the TV show *Cheers*), and you never struck up a conversation with someone you didn't know while waiting in a line or sharing a taxi – and God help the outsider who decided to move into the neighbourhood. Friends were hard to make, unless you survived the gradual thawing that could last months if not years, to see if you and your family were trustworthy. Not a good way to go through life, but it was the life she had been given. She and Coop.

Coop.

A tide of anger and loss, hot and nearly boiling, rose within her, wanting to scald her. She turned her back to it, but she could feel the tide rising behind her, as tall as a mountain. She swallowed, sucking in deep breaths through her nose, holding them as she forced her attention outside the window.

The forest of trees had disappeared maybe a mile or so back. Now they were travelling through a wide street in the downtown area; she saw there was a pharmacy, bakery and grocery store, with ample parking for all the businesses. Straight ahead she saw an ornate wooden sign peeking out from a mound of snow, welcoming them to downtown Fort Jefferson. The limbs of the bare trees and the pavilion's railings and pillars were strung with tiny white Christmas lights that glowed like distant stars.

'Place where I picked you up,' her driver said, taking a right at a corner belonging to Buzzy's Beer. A big neon sign of a happy, smiling bee holding a beer can was mounted on the bricks above the front door. 'What happened there? Some sort of car accident?'

Darby nodded absently, thinking of Coop's wet jacket, torn and stained with dried blood.

'They call that place Dead Man's Curve – I know, not original, but the name fits. Number of people who got in car accidents there and died?' He whistled. 'You look okay, praise be. Must have a guardian angel watching out for you.'

Now they were driving past flat and empty land, as though the downtown area was the remnant of a ghost town. He saw her looking around and, either wanting to fill the silence or just be friendly and chatty, said, 'We've got ourselves a great town here, and even greater people. But, as you've probably guessed by now, there's not a lot going on in terms of career prospects – unless you see dishwashing or lawn and road maintenance in your future. Which is why I had to leave.'

Darby spotted signs of life ahead: clusters of homes together on both sides of the street – and actual road signs. Some windows burned with light, and, although the homes were reasonably close together to form actual neighbourhoods, the area still struck her as lonely and desolate, probably because she was used to living in cities.

'Went to the University of Montana for hospitality management but never finished, 'cause I decided to go to Big Sky and spend a semester skiing. But it all worked out. Got a sweet gig at the hotel that includes free skiing and free housing. Got to share the bathroom with the other guys on my floor, but hey, it's all good.'

She suspected Michael the Driver was in his late twenties or early thirties and, to use one of Coop's phrases, 'into hippy-dippy bullshit'. They hung around ski lodges and campsites, these guys who had no career ambitions beyond earning enough money to support their passions, which were skiing and drinking beer and hiking and camping and drinking beer and hunting with big coolers full of beer. They didn't live to work but worked to live, and there was a part of her that secretly envied their devil-may-care attitude to life.

The dashboard GPS spoke, announcing that their destination was a mile away.

'What time do you have to be back at the hotel?' Darby asked, digging a hand into her back pocket.

'My shift ended an hour ago. Why?'

'I've got some things I need to do inside the house.'

'Anything I can help you with?'

'No, but I may be a while. Will two hundred cover it?'

'Ma'am, for two hundred dollars, I'll roll around the snow in my skivvies and howl at the moon. Take all the time you need.'

24

Darby had grown up in a city where if you owned a single family home with a garage and a backyard large enough to accommodate a swing-set, maybe even an above-ground pool, you were considered well-off – 'well-to-do', to use one of her father's favourite phrases. Her parents owned a single family home with a postage-stamp-sized front lawn and on-street parking, the only house in the neighbourhood that wasn't a triple-decker or duplex, everything crammed together to maximize space. In the warmer months, her bedroom windows open and streetlights blazing, she fell asleep listening to the sounds of traffic and her neighbours either laughing or arguing well into the night.

So it always surprised her when she visited neighbourhoods like the one where Melissa French had lived: not a single streetlight anywhere, the only sound the steady purr of the SUV's resting engine, and the houses – all small, two-floor affairs with trucks or SUVs parked in the driveways – separated by a decent number of trees. Living here, you wouldn't have to deal with, say, standing in front of your bedroom mirror and trying on your training bra for the first time, only to turn around and see your seventeen-year-old neighbour Michael Birmingham watching you from his bedroom window and raising the can of beer he'd pilfered from his father's basement fridge in approval.

No snow on the walkway or front steps; the real-estate agency must have hired someone to shovel and plough, keep the outside looking neat and inviting for prospective buyers. Had Melissa put a stop on her mail? A quick check of the black mailbox posted outside the front door revealed she had.

Standing at the front door and looking around the neighbourhood, what little of it she could see, one thing occurred to her: the house was secluded enough to allow anyone to come and go without being detected, especially at night.

Darby was coming down the front steps when the driver's side window rolled down. Michael had taken off his cowboy hat, revealing a sweaty mess of thick curls. 'You sure there's nothing I can help you with?' he asked. 'It don't feel right just sitting here doing nothing, given what you paid me.'

'I'll holler if I need you. Until then, just sit tight.'

He nodded, not happy about it, seemingly in that rare group of men who believed in working for each and every dollar. The window went back up and out of the corner of her eye she could see him watching her as she made her way to the backyard, wading through a good three feet of snow, the top layer a frozen crust.

As she trudged along the side of the house, the Expedition's headlights lighting her way and casting her shadow across a rolling blanket of undisturbed snow, Darby wondered if Melissa French was some sort of high-level informant for the Bureau. That would have explained the secrecy surrounding Coop's visit, but it didn't explain why Coop had been chosen to do the visiting. Coop was a lab rat; he specialized in fingerprints. You sent lab rats into the field when you wanted evidence examined – not to speak to or hunt down an informant. That was a job for the handler. Coop had no experience working with informants.

She saw no tracks or footprints in the backyard or on the back porch; the snow remained undisturbed. Darby climbed the porch steps, her thighs already burning with fatigue from the awkward and strenuous walk, and then used her arm to swipe away the snow covering the top of the grille. She flipped the lid open and, using the light from her phone, saw a strip of black duct tape fastened to the inside hood.

Darby peeled away the tape and found the key. It worked perfectly on the back-door lock.

Inside the house, stale and cool air. The bank had turned the heat down to its lowest acceptable setting to keep the pipes from freezing. She fumbled along the wall until she found the light switch. *Flick* and canister lights came to life. She was standing in the kitchen she'd seen in the pictures.

Darby brushed the snow from her jeans, which were now damp, and then froze when she grabbed the last pair of gloves from her inside jacket pocket. Coop had stood in the exact same spot where she was right now – had breathed in the same stale air. The thought brought her close to tears. She blinked them back, but a few slipped past and rolled down her cheek.

Go ahead and let it out, an inner voice urged. *No one's watching you now, and no one's going to come in and catch you.*

No. Once she allowed the floodgates to open, she

could forget it. She wouldn't be able to think about anything other than Coop, and he was depending on her to finish whatever he had started.

Swallowing and deep breathing and more deep breathing, and after a few minutes she was . . . not ready, but as close as she was going to get to it.

Phone in hand, Darby looked at the pictures Coop had taken of the kitchen, comparing them to what she saw here.

The countertops, made of black speckled granite, were clean and tidy, just like Coop's picture. Sink and drying rack empty, just like the picture. The glass carafe in the coffee-maker was empty, just like the picture. Nothing had been moved or removed, as far as she could tell.

Darby tucked the phone back inside her jacket pocket and then wandered around the kitchen, living area and downstairs bathroom, looking, searching, touching.

The dishwasher was empty. The cupboards held dishes and glassware but no canned or boxed food – no food of any kind. The pair of plastic garbage cans underneath the sink were empty. The freezer was empty and the refrigerator was empty. The downstairs bathroom didn't have a medicine cabinet, but the vanity drawers were empty. The linen closets held folded blue towels and rolls of toilet paper. Coop hadn't taken pictures of any of these things, so there was no basis for comparison.

Had Melissa purged the food and dumped it before leaving? Darby hoped cleaners hadn't been through here. They would have scrubbed the entire house to make it perfect for future real-estate showings.

Darby thought back to that moment with Noel, when

he'd asked her to come here. He should have given her everything he had on Melissa French – every single file and note. Instead, he had sent her here on some half-assed attempt to find a needle in a haystack. She wasn't a goddamn psychic.

Darby took out her phone and compared Coop's pictures to everything she saw in the downstairs rooms. She didn't know what else to do.

It was like playing a game, looking at the pictures and then at the rooms to see if something was missing or misplaced or possibly different in some way. Concentrating, though, was hard; she was exhausted and worn-out and hungry, and her mind kept returning to Coop, his Patagonia jacket and the mangled SUV and the John Doe behind the wheel – a man Noel claimed he didn't know. She worked as methodically as she could while Noel's words from earlier echoed inside her head: *I'm running out of time.*

When she finished with the downstairs rooms, she glanced at her watch. Almost forty-five minutes had passed.

Darby peeled back the curtain and saw that Michael had turned off the Expedition's headlights. The windows were tinted, so she couldn't see her driver, but the SUV was definitely running; plumes of exhaust streamed from the tailpipe, scattering in the wind.

What if Melissa *had*, in fact, packed up and left? Informants – if Melissa was one – split all the time. Came and went. The Bureau investigated, sure, but they didn't go balls-to-the-wall unless the informant was absolutely critical to an ongoing investigation or a case that was about to go to trial.

But if something had happened to her . . .

Melissa wasn't the key player at the moment; Noel was. Noel had told her he was running out of time and hadn't explained why. He had sent Coop here and hadn't explained why. Noel was holding back critical information from her and he had asked her to come to the house to take a look around and find, what? What was he expecting her to find?

Enough of this bullshit, Darby thought, and dialled Noel's number.

It went straight to voicemail.

Leave or stay?

Darby headed upstairs, the thick crimson runner along the steps masking her footfalls.

25

The bathroom separating the two bedrooms had a medicine cabinet. Darby opened it. Empty shelves. The drawers for the vanity were empty, but the cabinet held toilet paper and a bottle of liquid soap. Blue towels were piled on the shelves of the linen closet. No personal items – not even a box of tampons or maxi-pads.

The spare bedroom was fully furnished and didn't have any clothes in the drawers, and the closet was empty. Empty was becoming the key word here. The only room that had a trace of personality was the master bedroom, with its thick quilt, sturdy oak furniture and twin bookshelves, which were packed with religious hardcover and paperback books and an assortment of religious knick-knacks and bric-a-brac: well-worn copies of the entire 'Left Behind' series wedged behind a pair of stone praying hands; a wooden cross and a plastic statue of the Virgin Mary; and prayer cards sticking out of copies of *God Loves You*, *The Road of Light* and *A Room at the End of the World: My Journey from Disbeliever to Believer*. There was also an entire series of Christian romances featuring plain-looking women on the cover who had, after suffering tragic accidents and personal misfortune, found solace in hunky but appropriately clothed men. Yikes.

Again, she searched through the photos, enlarging different areas. Again, she found it difficult to concentrate, and she gave in quickly to her frustration regarding Noel, who, she was sure, had sent her here on a fool's errand.

One more time, she thought. *Go through the house one more time.*

Darby put the phone away, went back downstairs and roamed through the rooms.

An hour later, she once more found herself in the upstairs bedroom, sitting on the bed between the two bookcases, rubbing her eyes with the heels of her palms.

New locks and deadbolts had been installed on the front and back doors: Maximus locks, considered the best in the business. Not the sort of thing you'd expect to find inside a residential home, as the company catered to commercial businesses. If Melissa French was one of those paranoid types looking for the best locks money could buy, she may have jumped on the Internet and found the Maximus company and decided on their locks, given their high user ratings. Not ordinary but not *unordinary* either.

What *was* out of the ordinary was finding a bedroom doorknob with a key-operated lock. What was extraordinary was finding a deadbolt behind the bedroom door. Not only did the woman want to lock the door to prevent anyone from entering while she wasn't home, she wanted to prevent anyone from entering her bedroom each night when she went to sleep.

What kind of person installed a key-operated lock and a deadbolt in a bedroom door?

Head stuffed and frustration growling in her stomach, Darby didn't have much need to pay attention to the road. Twenty, maybe even thirty minutes had passed before she realized Michael the Driver wasn't taking her to a hotel in Fort Jefferson.

'I work at the Moonlight Mile Lodge in Big Sky,' he said with enthusiasm. 'It's a pretty sweet place – and I'm not just saying that because I work there.'

It *was* pretty sweet – and surprisingly large. Not as big as the Overlook Hotel in the movie version of *The Shining* but something fairly close to it, a big, imposing and sprawling structure, the front area, protected by a flat room, long and wide enough to accommodate the passengers in one if not two buses. There was plenty of activity even at this late hour: cars parked everywhere, people leaving and people coming to stay. The staff handling the luggage and opening the doors were all young men that, like Michael the Driver, wore matching black shirts and jeans, a Stetson and a black duster. The lobby, with its warm tiled floor, fireplaces and lodge-type furniture, had a life-sized bronze bear in the centre.

Two young blonde women were working the front desk: they wore matching blue sweaters adorned with snowflakes. They were dealing with an older man with a long white beard who was complaining about the water in his room. As Darby approached, she heard one of the girls say, 'We're having problems with the filtration system.'

One of the women, chubby and wearing braces, turned to Darby and smiled brightly, as though she were greeting a fellow sorority sister at a key party. Darby gave her name and the young woman said, 'I have everything right here, waiting for you. Mr Covington called ahead, told us you were on your way and to make sure we had everything ready. Your bags are already in your room.'

Then, when Darby took out her wallet, she said, 'We don't need your credit card and licence. Mr Covington took care of everything. You're on the second floor. Room Two-seventeen.' She handed Darby an envelope holding two keycards.

'Is Noel Covington or Phil Bradley staying here?' Darby asked.

'Let me check.' The woman turned to the computer. The other one smiled politely, her tiny silver nose ring glinting underneath the overhead lights.

If Noel or Bradley was staying here, she would try to find a way to get into the agent's room, see if any information had been left behind – files, messages, whatever – that could help to shed some much-needed light on who Melissa French was and why she was so important to the Bureau.

The chubby woman shook her head. 'They don't have a reservation with us.'

'Did a Jackson Cooper stay here? This would have been last week.'

'Let's see . . . No, he didn't stay with us.'

'Thank you.'

'Elevator is directly behind you. The kitchen is open for another hour. Mr Covington told me to tell you to order whatever you want and charge it to the room. Enjoy your stay.'

Darby wanted a hot shower and longed to sleep under warm sheets and to close her eyes; but she didn't feel like being locked inside a strange room, alone, coming to grips with Coop's death. She started to walk around the hotel because she didn't know what else to do, or where to go, the grief moving inside her like a bat trapped in an attic.

The hotel had its own bar, located at the far end of the building, but it was too crowded and noisy, with a band playing bad country music. She spotted a lounge not far from the hotel's front desk, a quiet place that served coffee, sodas, sandwiches and, after ten, allowed guests to purchase wine, bottled beer or to choose from a limited but decent selection of hard alcohol. It was nearly deserted, save for an elderly man sitting at one of the oval tables, working diligently on what appeared to be a Sudoku puzzle.

The person manning the counter was a woman getting on in years: hearing aid, her face deeply furrowed, makeup applied somewhat haphazardly. She wore the same black shirt and jeans as Michael the Driver and the boys out front. Darby ordered a Knob Creek, double neat, and carried the glass with her to a pair of leather club chairs and matching couch arranged around a long coffee table made of logs, all of it facing a massive flagstone fireplace and hearth that took up almost the entire wall.

Darby sat on the couch. The logs behind the firescreen still had some life left in them and gave out a decent amount of heat.

'Good,' Noel Covington said. 'You're still up.'

26

Darby felt a tremor of surprise move through her. She had left Noel a message saying she had found Sentinel Maximus locks, including a deadbolt, installed in Melissa's *bedroom* door, but had found nothing in relation to the pictures Coop had taken. Noel hadn't called her back or texted, and, given the lateness of hour, she'd expected to hear from him early tomorrow morning, when he would call to tell her what time the cadaver dogs would arrive.

Now he was standing here in his overcoat, his suit and tie replaced by a zippered grey hoodie, black nylon running pants and fluorescent yellow sneakers. There was a tightly coiled anxiety in his posture, his expression and his eyes; it radiated off him like waves of heat. His left eye twitched, then stopped after he blinked it away. He looked like a man holding a bomb, terrified of doing or saying the wrong thing.

'Those are by far *the* ugliest sneakers I've ever seen,' Darby said. 'They come with batteries?'

His boyish grin reminded her of Coop. She felt a piercing loss and then it melted away, behind the bourbon.

'My shoes and pants got soaked when we were out in the woods,' Noel said. 'I was hoping we could talk.'

'That depends.'

'On what?'

142

'Is Bradley with you?'

'No. He went to Missoula, to take care of the paper-work.'

'Then grab a drink and pull up a chair.'

He came back with two glasses of bourbon. After he'd draped his jacket on the back of one of the club chairs, he sat next to her.

'Melissa French,' he said. 'How much did Coop tell you?'

Darby said nothing. Keeping quiet on the details of her conversation with Coop – not that she had anything specific – was the only leverage she had over Noel. But he didn't need to know that.

'Okay,' Noel said when she didn't answer. 'You don't trust me. You figure that once you tell me what you know, I'll send you packing. Fine, I get it. Melissa French? Her real name is Karen Decker.'

Darby felt a tingle in the back of her skull that spread down her neck and spine.

Her expression must have changed, because Noel said, 'So he *did* tell you about her.'

'No,' Darby said. 'Not a single thing. This is the first time I've heard the name.'

'But clearly you recognize it.'

'That depends.'

'On what?'

'The only Karen Decker I know is the one who was an early victim of a serial killer from the late seventies called the Red Ryder.'

'What else do you know about her?'

'She was a teenager when she was vacationing with her

family in Vallejo, California, when the Red Ryder pulled up behind their station wagon, came out and shot them with a 9-millimetre Luger with a pen-light taped underneath the bottom of the barrel. He drove away and then decided to come back, saw her running away and shot her several more times.'

'If Coop didn't share this with you, how do you know all this?'

Darby now knew why Coop had called and asked her to come to Montana. 'Coop knew I'd done my Ph.D. dissertation on the Red Ryder,' she said. 'He was one of the first known case studies in sexual sadism – was, and probably still is, considered *the* most intelligent, skillful and organized sexual sadist on record. He attacked thirteen couples and families.'

'Thirteen that we know of.'

'After each attack, he sent Halloween cards with these creepy Victorian images pasted on them to the editor of the *San Francisco Chronicle*, not only claiming responsibility for the murders but also providing a bloody swath of clothing he'd cut from the victims.'

'After he shot Karen Decker and her family,' Noel said, 'he called 911 and told the operator what he'd done and where they could find the bodies. He used a knife on the mother to cut away a strip of clothing from her shoulder and, even though she was already dead, stabbed her twenty-two times in the face and chest.'

'I remember what he wrote in the Decker card. It said, "I am the man responsible for shooting the family at the Vallejo campground. I liked shooting the girl the most. I want to kill every pretty thing." The last card he sent to the *Chronicle* contained only one word: *Goodbye*. They never heard from him again.'

'He stopped after the last family: Kay Byram, a single mother, and her fifteen-year-old daughter Jennifer. He stabbed them.'

'And Jennifer survived, just like Karen.'

'Just like Karen,' he repeated blankly.

'Both girls were terrified that the Red Ryder would find them, so they went into hiding. I heard rumours Karen had gone into Witness Protection.'

'You would be correct.'

'And Jen Byram?'

'WITSEC? No. But she definitely went into hiding. Wherever she is now — whoever she is — I couldn't tell you. She did a fantastic job covering her tracks. Karen, though, left the programme about seven years ago.'

'Voluntarily? Or was she kicked out?'

Noel mulled over the question for a moment.

'About to be kicked out, I think,' he said. 'Karen had a lot of fans. We all felt for her. WITSEC gave her a lot of chances, and so, *so* many opportunities to start over anywhere she wanted. And Karen ... she blew each and every one. But, to answer your question, technically speaking, she left of her own accord.'

'And then you tracked her down to Fort Jefferson.'

'No. No one was looking for her.'

'Then how did you find her?'

'She reached out to me.'

'WITSEC falls under the US Marshals,' Darby said. 'You're FBI.'

'That I am.'

'What's the Bureau's interest in Karen Decker?'

'We don't have one.'

'And yet here you are.'

He nodded. 'I'm here because I owe her a tremendous debt. Karen Decker,' Noel Covington said, 'is my sister.'

27

Noel saw genuine surprise on Darby's face.

Was she putting on a performance for him?

It was possible, sure, but he doubted it. Since her arrival in Bozeman, his gut had repeatedly told him that Cooper hadn't shared any details about his sister, the Red Ryder, WITSEC, none of it. Noel had sought Cooper out not just based on his expertise in fingerprints; he had heard through various sources over the years that Cooper was someone trustworthy, a man who, when he gave you his word, meant it. Dependable. Cooper had pulled him into his office and promised to keep the case material and anything else he wanted private and confidential.

So then why had Cooper asked her to come to Montana? Surely he had to have told her *something*.

Darby had leaned forward quickly, spilling some of her bourbon on the thigh of her jeans. She barely noticed. 'You're *him*,' she said, staring intensely at him, like a virologist who was about to unlock the genetic sequence to a deadly disease. 'The one from the newspaper pictures.'

Noel had been a little over two years old when the picture had been taken. Being so young, he had no memory of it, of course. But he had seen the photograph on the Internet sites and books devoted to the Red Ryder: a patrolman cradling a tow-headed boy dressed in a white onesie worn underneath a pair of mustard-coloured overalls, his clothes dirty, his face and chubby cheeks and arms scratched and bloodied by brambles. A reporter for the *San Francisco Chronicle* had written the best title: 'The Boy Who Lived'.

'You're Paul Decker,' Darby said.

'Well, at least until I was six.' Noel offered up a weary smile. 'My father's bachelor uncle took us in after our parents were killed. Nobody knew Uncle Dave was in the early stages of Alzheimer's; he did a fantastic job of hiding it. Four years later he couldn't hide it any more. The state got involved, and that's when close friends of my uncle stepped in – a couple named Noel and Regina Covington. They took us in and legally adopted us. Well, at least me.'

'They didn't want your sister?'

'She didn't want them. Karen was eighteen by then, a legal adult, and she was convinced the Red Ryder was going to come after her. Kept running away from home. So Regina reached out to a family friend, this woman named Vivian Whitney, who worked for the marshals' service. Vivian moved Karen into WITSEC and became Karen's handler.'

Noel nearly drained his glass. 'But you don't want to know that stuff,' he said. 'You want to know everything that happened that night.'

Darby probably already knew the broad strokes; everything was well documented in dozens of books and hundreds of newspaper and magazine articles. The haunting scene had been acted out in excruciatingly gory detail in the Red Ryder movie, which had won an Oscar for best cinematography.

'Go ahead and ask,' he said. 'Everyone does.'

'I'm not everyone.' Darby stared at him a beat and then

finished her drink. 'Did Karen find the Red Ryder? Is that what you're trying to tell me?'

'I don't know. Maybe.'

'Wait. You didn't ask her?'

'Didn't have the chance. Karen contacted me by letter.'

'When?'

'She mailed it early last month. She didn't include her phone number, but she *did* include evidence: a crumpled piece of paper. I gave it to Cooper to examine for prints, because he's the best there is.'

'He got a match.'

'I wish. He pulled some pretty impressive latent prints, but the ridge quality on the paper was for shit. The hand-writing on the paper was another matter. It matched the Red Ryder's.'

'What kind of probability are we talking about?'

'The guy who examined it is the head of "Questioned Documents". He told me he'd stake his reputation on it. But handwriting isn't enough – we need evidence. Like fingerprints. So we decided to send Coop here to talk to Karen under the guise of a tourist. Didn't want to make a big Federal show out of it in case the Red Ryder knew about Karen, that she'd found him, and was watching her.'

'Which is why you didn't involve the locals.'

Noel nodded. 'We call them, tell them that Melissa French is Karen Decker and she has credible evidence of the Red Ryder's identity and location? Forget it. Word gets out – and word always gets out, as you and I both know – and you've got a media circus. So we decided to keep the circle small, see what information we could get from Karen.'

'Only she wasn't here when Coop arrived,' Darby said.

'And that's what's bothering me.' He took out his phone, tapped a finger a couple of times across the screen. 'Here,' he said, and handed the phone over to her.

Noel had taken a photo of the letter his sister had written to him.

'When did you get this?'

'The letter was postmarked from Big Sky, Montana, on the 4th of January,' Noel said. 'It arrived on my office desk while I was on vacation.'

'Now we're in February. Coop left for Montana on Sunday, the 14th – Valentine's Day – so we're talking roughly a six-week time period from when the letter was mailed until Coop arrived. Did you or Vivian call her?'

'No. We didn't have her number, and we couldn't find any numbers belonging to a Melissa French in Fort Jefferson.'

'So maybe she got sick of waiting and did, in fact, give her notice and leave.'

'You read the letter. Does that sound like a woman who would pack up and leave?'

'Has she done this sort of thing before?'

Noel sighed. Stared down in his glass. 'Yes,' he said. 'She has. More than once.'

'What about her bank records?'

'The bank took its sweet time approving the paperwork for our request. They finally allowed us access a few days ago. Anyway, I reviewed her statements going all the way back to when she first opened the chequing account. That's all she had, no debit or credit cards. Each statement follows the same pattern from month to month. Her money from the diner is automatically deposited. Karen would leave in just enough money to cover her rent and utilities, then withdrew the rest as cash. Cash is king when you're on the run and don't want to be found.

'Another interesting thing,' Noel said. 'The bank she used is the same one that owns the mortgage on her house, this small bank in downtown Fort Jefferson. I talked to the manager over the phone. Her rent is due on the first of the month. In her account, one of the customer service reps made a notation that Melissa – Karen – would be leaving at the end of January. Not a big deal as far as the bank was concerned, because she hadn't signed a lease: she rented on a month-to-month basis.'

'When was the notation made?'

'Monday, 4th of January.'

'By letter or phone call?'

'Phone call,' Noel said. 'They don't keep recordings of the calls, so I have no idea whether it was Karen who called or not. And the phone number listed in her file belongs to a burner. We've been trying to track its signal for almost a week and can't find it.'

'And, again, you don't think she got sick of waiting and left.'

'Like I said, has she done it before? Yes. Only this letter . . . it felt different. She was convinced she'd found the Red Ryder and begged me to help her. Maybe she was, you know, making preparations *to* leave while waiting to hear from me. Or maybe –'

'What?'

'Karen was diagnosed with MDD.'

'Major depressive disorder.'

Another nod. 'In the letter she said she was on her

medication,' he said. 'But if she got sick of waiting, like you said, and it triggered her depression, I'm worried . . . She's tried to kill herself before. Four times.'

Darby nodded. Took a moment to take it all in.

She checked her watch.

'You feel up to taking a ride?'

'Sure,' Noel said. 'Where we going?'

'To your sister's house. I want to check on something – something that's been nagging at me.'

'What?'

Darby thought about it for a moment. 'I think it's better if I show you,' she said.

28

There was no need to go to the front desk to see if one of the hotel staff could drive them to Fort Jefferson: Sheriff Powers had lent Noel a car from the motor pool, an SUV with a faulty heater, the sheriff's logos painted in forest-green on both sides of the doors. The heater, Noel told her as he slid behind the wheel, would shut off for no apparent reason.

Within minutes of pulling away from the lodge, they were driving on the same lonely roads she'd seen earlier on her way here, no streetlights, everything flat. Lonely.

'Bradley,' Darby said. 'How much does he know?'

'About Karen and the Red Ryder? Nothing. Like I said, we made the decision to keep that information contained, until I come across hard evidence that proves the Red Ryder is alive.'

'Then what's Bradley's role in this?'

'When we were in Bozeman and found out about the car crash, he was ordered to come up here and do the investigation and paperwork.'

'Why him and not you?'

'Because Vivian wants –'

'Your sister's former handler.'

Noel nodded. 'She wants Bradley to handle Cooper's accident.'

'I thought you said you're a Fed.'

'I am. I'm a liaison between the Bureau and WITSEC. The marshals don't have access to the same forensic talent the Bureau does, so my job is to wrangle the appropriate forensic resources for marshal-related cases. Vivian is my boss for as long as I'm the liaison with the marshals' service. My job – my role here in Montana – is to see if I can find any potential information or evidence that shows the Red Ryder could still be alive and in Fort Jefferson.'

'You have evidence – the handwriting on that bit of scrap paper,' Darby said. 'You told me the head of "Questioned Documents" said –'

'Vivian thinks it's junk science. I disagree, but she wants something more definite, like a fingerprint, before she allocates additional resources.'

Handwriting wouldn't be enough to secure a warrant, sure, but it certainly wasn't junk science. Take, for example, the handwriting on the luggage tag: there was no question that was Coop's handwriting. It was difficult – not impossible but extremely difficult – to duplicate someone's handwriting.

'I also think she believes nothing is going to come of this,' Noel said. 'Like I told you earlier, Karen has done this sort of thing before – packed up and moved on. Vivian's pretty much washed her hands of her. Given what Karen has put her through – put us through – I can't say I blame her.'

Darby nodded and stared out the window, the hum of the tyres soothing against her ears. The exhaustion of the day had set in, and when she closed her eyes, wanting to rest for a moment, she was thinking again of Coop's dented suitcase sitting in the snow. Why was it still nagging at her?

Because she had been hoping to find something inside it instead of Coop's clothes and toiletries?

And why hadn't Coop been wearing his seatbelt? He had buckled up every time they'd gotten into a car.

'I need you to level with me,' Noel said.

'About what?'

'Cooper. If he didn't tell you anything specific, what are you doing here?'

'I came because he asked.'

'I've been straight with you. Now it's your turn.'

Darby sucked in air through her nose and held it for a moment before opening her eyes and exhaling.

'He didn't get into specifics,' she said. 'Just told me he would feel better if I were here.'

'Why?'

'He didn't tell me. I think he wanted me to come here because something spooked him about either Karen or the Red Ryder or both – and, like I said, he knew I'd written my dissertation on him. I think he wanted me here because if something went wrong, he knew I'd have his back.'

'I told him he could trust me.'

'How well do you know him?'

'Not as well as you, obviously.'

'But mainly in a professional context, right?'

'Mainly, yes.'

'That makes you an untested quantity. I'm not. He knows if something happened to him, I wouldn't stop digging until I found the truth, because that's what I do. I create my own agenda. You can't because you have to report to people.'

'That doesn't mean he couldn't –'

'You're not autonomous,' Darby said. 'At some point, you're going to have to leave. I'll leave when I want and not before then. If Vivian or that shithead Bradley gets in my way, I will bury them. That's not an idle threat.'

'I'm very well aware of your reputation.' Noel cocked his head at her and smiled. 'Everyone in the Bureau is.'

29

Darby wasn't aware that she had fallen asleep until she felt a hand on her shoulder, gently shaking her awake.

'We're here,' Noel said, and killed the engine.

She had fallen into such a deep sleep that for a moment she had no idea where *here* was, or the name of the man with the handsome face and the kind, warm eyes sitting next to her. She sat up and rubbed her eyes, and everything came back to her in a rush, Coop an empty space in the centre of her chest.

She was about to open her door when Noel said, 'I need to ask you a question about Karen.'

'Okay.'

'For the moment, let's assume the Red Ryder is, in fact, still alive. Let's also assume he discovered that Melissa French was Karen Decker, and that she had found him. What do you think his next move would be?'

'If he was smart, he'd get out of town because he'd be thinking the police would be coming to talk to him. But Powers didn't mention anything of the sort. Then again, we didn't ask him.'

'True. Let's put the police part aside and focus on what we know, which is that Karen is gone. If we assume the Red Ryder is behind it – that he abducted her, made it look like she just packed up and left –'

'Which may have happened.'

'I know. But if it *didn't* happen – if he abducted her – he wouldn't kill her right away, would he?'

'You're asking me if Karen could still be alive.'

'Yes. That's exactly what I'm asking you.'

Darby said nothing. The car's cooling engine ticked in the silence.

'You told me the Red Ryder is a sexual sadist,' Noel said. 'My understanding is that sexual sadists like to . . . preserve the moments with their victims. Make the torture last as long as possible, make it as painful as possible.'

'The Red Ryder shot and stabbed his victims. He didn't abduct them.'

'I'm sensing a *but* here.'

'A highly intelligent and organized sadist like the Red Ryder wouldn't stop killing, but he would need to change his methodology.'

'So if he found out that Melissa French was Karen Decker, it's possible he might have taken her somewhere and tortured her for information: how she found him, who else knew, et cetera.

'And this place he'd take her, it would be where he knew he wouldn't be discovered. Neither he nor his victims.'

'It's possible.'

'I think it's more than possible, Darby. The idea of being able to torture one of his former victims would be too great an opportunity to pass up – a massive, once-in-a-lifetime opportunity, wouldn't you agree?'

'I think that going down this road will drive you insane. Don't forget: she could have gotten sick and tired of waiting for you and then decided to pack up and leave.'

'You're right. But thank you.'

'For what?'

'For being upfront with me about the other stuff.'

Noel had already grabbed the key from the grille at the back of the house. They went in through the front. The same cool, stale air greeted her. Now that she was moving, she was awake, but her head was beginning to pound and ache a bit from the booze and altitude and from not having had enough water. She found the light switch for the upstairs hallway. She headed up, about to reach the landing, when she glanced over her shoulder and saw Noel still standing in the foyer, taking in the rooms.

Then she remembered: this was Noel's first time inside Karen's house. This was the first time he'd been this close to his sister in seven years.

Darby took out her phone and found the picture she wanted. She studied it for a moment, then found the light switch for the bedroom. The weak light from the glass fixture mounted on the ceiling above the bed allowed her to see the room well enough.

Nothing had changed since her visit only a few short hours ago. The queen bed was still sitting between a pair of wall-built bookcases that stood facing each other like sentries; the closet door was still closed, everything neat and clean except for the depression she'd left on the quilt from where she'd sat. The idea that she was standing inside the room of one of the Red Ryder's early victims – and one of only two survivors – gave the air an electrical charge that had all her senses on alert.

She went to the bookcase to the right of the bed, the

one holding the assortment of religious books, while Noel hovered in the doorway, watching. The item she had come here to find wasn't here.

She motioned for Noel to join her. As he came to her, his shoes clicking across hardwood, she used her fingers to enhance a section of the bookcase.

'Coop took pictures of the bedroom,' she said, working the phone. 'I've blown up a section of this bookcase.'

Then she turned her phone to him: it showed a black orbital ball with a camera fixed inside a white plastic base, SAMSUNG written across the front. The camera sat on top of the stack of 'Left Behind' paperbacks, a Fisher-Price baby monitor sitting on a corner of the shelf.

'This Samsung baby camera? It's a wireless model that links to a separate LED screen,' Darby said. 'I recognized it because I bought one for a friend.'

'Okay.'

'The camera was here when Coop took the picture. Now it's not here.'

'But the baby monitor is here,' Noel said.

'That Fisher-Price thing? It's one of those cheap plastic twenty-dollar models you buy at Walmart so you can hear your baby cry. It has nothing to do with the Samsung camera. Totally separate unit, and now it's missing.'

'The sheriff told us Karen – Melissa – did a lot of baby-sitting. Maybe a neighbour came by and grabbed it.'

'You mean she borrowed it.'

'Exactly.'

'So if it belonged to a neighbour and she borrowed it, why not leave it downstairs by the door or something? Why bring it to her bedroom – and why place the camera on top of these books so the lens is pointed at the other wall? Doesn't that seem odd to you?'

Noel didn't answer. But the disappointed expression on his face told her he'd had much bigger hopes for this midnight trip.

'Help me look,' she said.

'For what? I don't know what you're looking for.'

'Neither do I. That's why we're looking. Let's start with that bookcase.'

The camera had been pointed at a bookshelf on the opposite side of the bed. That bookshelf was a mirror image of the one behind her: a face-frame made of one-inch-thick pine and six long shelves painted white, with a load-bearing centre of wood that ran horizontally through the middle. She examined the shelves and saw the brad nails, the pocket-holes and holes for counter-sink screws.

'This was a custom job,' she said. 'Someone who's a carpenter built this.'

Noel was running his hand over the crown moulding. Darby was looking at the strip used to decorate the vertical board. It wasn't nailed down.

The one on the other side of the bed used finishing nails.

Darby grabbed the board. It didn't budge.

'This one's glued,' she said.

'Great. We'll lodge a complaint with the carpenter, tell him he scrimped on the materials.'

The back wall of the bookcase looked like it had been made with MDF – medium-density fibreboard. It was inexpensive but sturdy. She wrapped a knuckle against it, heard a hollow sound return.

She placed a hand flat against the board and pushed.

Felt it give.

'Back up,' she told him, and, when he did, she lifted a leg and placed the sole of her boot against the board and then kicked it once, twice, three times, until the board broke free and her foot went through to the other side.

It took her a moment to free her leg. After she did, Noel moved in front of her and used his hands to push the board some more, the wood straining, snapping. When he had enough room, he took out his phone and then threaded the arm holding it past the opening and inside, giving him a view of whatever was beyond the bookcase.

Darby's pulse was racing. 'What do you see?' she asked.

'A gate latch with a pull wire. It's connected to an eyelet. Hold on.' He threaded his way back out of the hole and then stood and reached up to the top-right-hand corner of the bookcase. Darby heard a *click*. 'Button for the latch,' he said.

Noel grabbed a corner of the shelf and pulled.

The bookcase came free from the wall.

30

Darby didn't know what to expect, but that didn't prevent her mind from racing with possibilities ranging from the perfectly reasonable to the perfectly ridiculous: a hidden crawlspace holding a safe and a cache of drugs, guns and bound cash in thick stacks of hundred-dollar bills; a make-shift panic room in which they'd find Karen Decker passed out or probably dead from dehydration; a husband's collection of hardcore, violent S & M porno magazines and films on VHS and DVD; the shrine of a serial killer who had shot thirteen couples and families with a Luger, killing thirty-two people and then sending a final Halloween card to the *San Francisco Chronicle* with one word written inside it: *Goodbye*.

What she hadn't expected to find was a spiral staircase. She hadn't expected to find a hidden world built between the walls of this suburban home in Nowhere, Montana. The walls were stuffed with pink fibreglass insulation and the floor was covered in plywood and, hanging from a nail pounded into a stud and facing her, was a framed needle-point picture sewn with green yarn and picking out Psalm 91:1: 'He who dwells in the shelter of the Most High will rest in the shadow of the Almighty.'

Noel was standing by her side. She heard the click in his throat when he swallowed as she tucked her nine back in her shoulder holster and moved to the entranceway carved behind the bookcase. The light from the bedroom parted some of the gloom; she could see the staircase's black metal railing and its black steps twisting out like a fan and circling down into the waiting darkness below.

Noel's voice behind her: 'Look at this.'

On the plywood backing used for the bookcase and almost directly eye level with her she saw a plain beige plastic crucifix glued next to a peephole that had been installed inside an electrical socket.

A bare bulb in a lighting fixture was mounted on an exposed 2 × 4. She yanked on the chain. Nothing happened. She removed the bulb and found out why: it was dead. She didn't have to ask Noel to grab one from the bedroom lamps; he had already headed off.

Phone in hand, Darby pressed the flashlight app. She turned it up to its maximum brightness and pointed the light over the staircase, looking down. She saw a cramped area down there too, the floor covered with sheets of plywood, the same pink fibreglass insulation packed into the walls – and some other things.

'There's a refrigerator down there,' she said. 'One of those small ones college students use in their dorms.'

To the left of the staircase she found that another space had been created behind another set of walls – a narrow lane just large enough for someone to slip through sideways. She took a few steps in, stopped and looked around as Noel returned.

'This place is a custom job,' he said as he screwed in the bulb. 'You don't get this kind of space between the walls of a normal house – you have to factor this space in before you start digging.' *Clink* as he pulled the light-chain once. She didn't see the light turn on behind her. *Clink* again and then he said, 'The electrical socket must be broken.'

'Jesus.'

'What?'

Darby moved back to him. 'The mirror installed in the bathroom,' she said. 'It's the same two-way glass used in police stations. I can see inside the entire bathroom.'

The colour had drained from Noel's face. He was disturbed not just by the discovery of this creepy and odd space that had been deliberately constructed behind these walls, but by what this space represented: that someone had stood in here and watched their wife or kids or both sleep and shower and go to the bathroom, everything approved, apparently, by Jesus. Darby had found crucifixes glued to the edges of the bathroom glass.

'Your phone,' she said. 'You have one of those flashlight apps downloaded on it?'

'No. Why?'

'Because my battery's got less than ten per cent left.'

'Let me check the SUV. Stay right here until I get back.' Darby opened her mouth to speak, but he continued before she managed to say a word. 'No, I'm not asking you to do that because you're a woman or because I don't think you can't take care of yourself. I know you can, okay? But it's smarter to have someone watching your back, and you know it.'

'I was going to say that if you strike out with the flashlight, there are some candles in the kitchen. I remember seeing them in one of the cabinets above the stove.'

'Matches?' he asked, slightly chastened.

'Don't need them. Stove is a gas range. I'll stay right here and try not to faint.'

Noel darted off into the bedroom and down the hall. She could hear his footfalls rushing down the steps, and, as she listened to the front door open, she wondered if Coop had found this place and, for reasons she didn't know and possibly would never know, hadn't been able to tell Noel.

The front door opened.

Was this secret chamber somehow connected to the Red Ryder?

Had Coop found it?

And the John Doe strapped behind the wheel of Coop's rental – could he be the Red Ryder?

The front door slammed shut. Footsteps pounded their way up the stairs and she wondered if both the killer and Coop had died in a car accident. Where had they been going – where had the Red Ryder intended to take Coop?

Darby stared below, into the darkness.

What the hell is this place?

31

When Noel returned, he was holding not a flashlight but a hexagonal-shaped object made of bright, hard plastic mesh.

'Battery-operated LED road flare,' he said. 'Four settings. Unless you want strobe lights, I suggest using this one.' He pressed the button twice. A bright-orange emergency light began to spin lazily across the floors and wall, making her feel as though she had boarded some dark carnival ride. 'If you don't want to use this, I can grab a candle from the kitchen.'

'This'll work,' Darby said.

This was their first time working together, so she needed to lay down some ground rules. 'Only one person should go down. It'll lessen the chance of disturbing any potential evidence.'

'I've done this before, you know.'

'But not with me. I need to think, and I can't do that if you're behind me or hovering near me, asking me questions, giving me a running commentary.'

'I'll be standing right here. Holler if you need anything.'

The heels and hard soles of her leather harness boots clanged off each metal step. Darby took them one by one. It would have been easier – and quicker – if she had held on to the curved metal banister, but she didn't want to disturb any potential fingerprints in case this place turned into a crime scene.

Darby held the battery-operated flare in her left hand, up by her shoulder, the revolving orange light splashing across the insulated walls as she slowly made her way down and down. She felt a bit like one of the characters she'd seen in the old black-and-white Gothic horror movies she'd watched on a TV with rabbit ears when she was young: the damsel in distress dressed in a white gown and barefoot and terrified as she wound her way down one dusty corridor after another inside a large castle, heading to an antechamber where she would suddenly come face to face with the supernatural creature that had been hunting her.

Her heart pounded with anticipation. Dread. The day had been long, and she felt emotionally drained, and her thoughts skidded with exhaustion inside her head. She didn't have the energy to push them aside. There was one thought she couldn't escape: the feeling that Coop had not only discovered this hidden chamber but had walked down these very same steps, looking at the exact same things and most likely thinking the exact same thoughts.

The stairs ended and she found herself in a tight, claustrophobic space. The area directly off the stairs was a bit longer, maybe six feet wide, large enough to accommodate the small refrigerator and, next to it, a small plastic bucket, the kind used in a home office or in a bathroom. The black bucket was stocked with empty soda cans and tiny candy wrappers from the chocolates people usually handed out for Halloween: Three Musketeers, Baby Ruth, Butterfinger and Mr Goodbar, which had somehow survived for over a century, although she had never seen anyone eating one in her entire life. *Odd, the things that occur to you when you're full of dread*, she thought.

And she had good reason to be: directly in front of her and flush against the bottom wall was a 6 × 6 steel door. It was locked with not one but three eight-inch-long slide bolts.

The refrigerator sat to the left of the door, but it wasn't humming. She looked in the back and found that it wasn't plugged in. Kneeling, she opened the fridge door.

The shelves were empty.

Darby got back to her feet. She could feel Noel above her, hovering, watching. The air was cool and smelled of insulation and wood.

To her left, she found lanes between the walls like the one she'd seen above. There was just enough room for her to shuffle her way sideways through them. She quickly explored each one now, thinking about what Noel had said earlier – that whoever had built this house had specifically designed this space between the walls as . . . what?

What sort of a person – or persons, she didn't know yet – would want to spy on his or her family? And what was waiting for her behind the small steel door off the bottom steps?

Another thought occurred to her: did this home belong to the Red Ryder? Had he built it and lived here? If so, how had Karen found it – and why in God's name would she willingly decide to move in here?

No, Darby thought. *That doesn't make any sense*. If Karen had somehow discovered this house belonged to the Red Ryder – that he had built it and raised a family here, or maybe had been raised here – Karen wouldn't have deliberately moved into it.

Or would she?

Another question: had Karen even known this space existed?

The narrow lanes between the walls on the bottom floor had beige plastic crucifixes glued next to peepholes, just like the one she had seen on the plywood back of the bookcase. The downstairs bathroom had the same sort of glass as the upstairs – a two-way allowing the viewer to watch someone undetected. Darby's stomach roiled at the thought.

'Everything okay down there?'

Noel's voice from above, and it felt like a razor blade against her skin.

'I'm fine,' Darby said, agitated. 'If I need anything, I'll let you know.'

She returned to the bottom of the spiral staircase, the orange LED lights revolving back and forth across the walls and floor and glaring at her from the steel door, like a warning. She got down on her knee, her heart kicking inside her chest, and she was gripped with terror, as if she were about to open the door on a secret she didn't want to know – something that, once discovered, would not only change the way she viewed herself but also the people she loved the most.

Those three people were dead. Two were already buried, the other one waiting to be found, God willing, and given a decent burial.

Darby slid one bolt. A scrape and then a dull boom echoed inside the walls.

What the hell could be in there?
She slid back the second bolt.
Did Coop see this place? What was in here?
The final bolt.
Scrape and *boom* and she thought: *Is that why he was killed? Because he found this secret place?*

32

Noel kept walking around the top of the steps, trying to find the best angle for keeping an eye on Darby. The best view he got was the one he had right now: leaning somewhat perilously over the banister and staring at her back and the back of her head and her hand, which was sliding back the first of three deadbolts belonging to what looked like, from all the way up here, a steel door. The hand holding the battery-operated road flare was steady, the revolving orange LEDs jumping up the walls like flames from hell.

Darby slid back the last deadbolt. Now she used a finger to grab the edge of the door, and, as she pulled it open, he thought of what she'd told him earlier about Karen, how the Red Ryder may have kidnapped Karen and taken her someplace where he could slowly torture her over hours, days, weeks. The image triggered another panic attack, this one so powerful it felt like his heart was being squeezed inside a vice with pointed teeth, and if someone had offered him a match and a gallon of gasoline he would have taken it and willingly set himself on fire to make the pain stop. Darby opened the door.

Recoiled as dozens and dozens of tiny pieces of paper spilled out on to the floor.

He didn't reach for his nine; he was already holding it. He didn't ask what was going on, just watched as she held open the door with her right shoulder and then inched her head past the entranceway, taking the light with her.

He counted off the time in his head. *One Mississippi. Two Mississippis . . .*

By the time she moved back from the entranceway, eighteen seconds had passed. The door closed, slapping against the wall with a dull thud that echoed all the way upstairs. She didn't turn and climb up the steps; she stood with her head bowed, taking a moment, he guessed, to collect herself. Noel thought he could hear her breathing but he wasn't sure.

Instead of greeting her when she came up the staircase, he quietly pushed himself away from the banister and moved into the bedroom, where he slid his nine back into his hip holster. Outside, the trees rustled. Blood roared through his head and pounded like a war drum against his ears.

When she returned, Noel couldn't read anything in her face. Her legs were steady but she didn't know what to do with her hands.

'Two sets of remains. Just bones and dried skin,' she said, her voice clear but stripped of emotion. She swallowed, then sucked in a deep breath, her attention drawn inward for a few seconds before her eyes focused back on him. 'Could be more. It was hard to tell with all the candy wrappers.'

Candy wrappers?

A sharp cry exploded from a speaker somewhere behind him.

They both started, turned and saw a colourful light dancing on the baby monitor, which had suddenly come to life, Noel thinking, *No, not suddenly, it was on the whole time because it runs on batteries and he was listening to us the whole time – is listening to us and maybe watching us too.*

From the speaker came a loud groan, deep and guttural – a man's voice, no question. Noel was about to tell Darby about a case where a perp had tapped into the frequency of a baby monitor and listened in on the family, and that these frequencies had a limited range – they were usually confined to the radius of the house – when Darby exploded out of the room.

Noel chased her across the hall. 'He's got to be close,' he began.

'I know.' Darby raced down the staircase, taking the steps two at a time. Noel's gaze was locked on the front door when she said, 'He's probably parked somewhere on the street.'

She threw open the door, and when he followed her outside the cold night air felt like a slap against his face. He chased after her as she ran up the driveway, the only thing besides the streets not covered in snow, amazed at how fast she was. When he caught up with her in the middle of the street, he sucked in air, the cold feeling like shards of glass blowing through his lungs, and saw the nine in her hand, the tactical light mounted underneath the barrel turned off.

The street was dark; no cars were parked anywhere nearby.

Beats of silence as their eyes flicked through the darkness, listening.

'He's here,' she whispered to him. 'He's watching us right now, deciding whether to run or to stay put and –'

Someone crashed through the woods on their right, snapping branches as he fled. Darby had turned on her tactical light and was aiming the beam at a wall of snow at least five feet high, when Noel heard a man scream, a plaintive howl that sent his mind spinning back in time to a winter morning in Kirkuk, where a man had knelt in the road cradling the remains of a child, his plaintive, hysterical howl louder than the gunfire and radio chatter and soldiers shouting orders; loud enough to wake even God himself from His eternal slumber.

23rd of February
Tuesday

33

The neighbourhood looked completely different in the creeping morning light. The houses – at least the ones Darby could see from the living-room window – appeared nearly identical in structure to the one she was standing in, the only difference being the choice of exterior colours. The flat land lying underneath the eggplant-coloured sky looked naked and vulnerable.

Sheriff Powers sat in one of the four high-back maple chairs arranged around the circular table inside Karen Decker's rental home – Melissa French, to everyone in Fort Jefferson. He'd put on his uniform before coming here. Noel sat across from him, his legs crossed and his hands folded on his lap, his expression grave. The clock hanging on the wall near the wood stove ticked off each second. It said 4.46 a.m.

'Okay,' Powers said, staring down at the table, where he'd placed his hat. His face was pale, and the hand moving back and forth across his thin lips wasn't steady.

The sheriff had just returned from the chamber, shrine, whatever, secreted behind the walls in the heart of the home. When Noel called him, he told the sheriff to make sure he brought a few high-powered flashlights with him.

When Powers saw what lay beyond the steel door, he recoiled in horror, just as she had.

Noel, though, had taken in the horror with a cold eye,

his adrenalin already having been spent by what had happened outside, the way the man had screamed, like someone who'd had the most precious thing in his life ripped from him. *Was it the Red Ryder? Who else could it be?*

'Okay,' Powers said again, and laid his palms flat against the table, as if they were aboard a ship that was heaving against stormy tides that refused to relent. He kept blinking, no doubt trying to wash away the images of the mummified remains of two young women, possibly teenagers, sitting upright in a sea of candy wrappers and empty soda cans and Hi-C juice boxes that went up past their waists. The girls had been gagged and bound with rope and duct tape and handcuffs. One of them had a noose wrapped around her throat.

'I've never . . .' Powers didn't complete his thought. He turned his head to Darby, who was standing with her arms folded across her chest, her shoulder leaning against the wall near the living-room window, where she had been looking outside at the snow and thinking of Coop. 'What about you? Have you ever seen something like this?'

Darby shook her head. 'Not inside the centre of someone's home,' she said, her gaze flicking toward the wall off the kitchen, near the back door. The two girls were behind it.

'And you're sure someone was watching you?' Powers said.

'We didn't see him but we definitely heard him,' Darby said.

'Twice, you said.'

Darby nodded. They had told the sheriff about what had happened outside and what they had heard in the bedroom, on the Fisher-Price baby monitor. She hadn't examined it beforehand – hadn't stopped to consider that batteries were still in it and the monitor was turned on and working. She knew she had made a mistake, maybe even a critical one, but there was no point in wishing for a different outcome.

Sheriff Powers said, 'And you have no idea who this person is?'

Well, Sheriff, we think he's the Red Ryder – you know, the infamous serial killer from the late seventies and early eighties who killed thirty-two people and then decided to retire. I'm sure you've heard of him. Oh, and incidentally, the kitchen chair you're sitting in belongs not to Melissa French but to Karen Lee Decker, one of the Red Ryder's victims – one of two women who survived. That's right, she was living right here in your town because she was convinced she'd found the Red Ryder.

Darby shook her head. Powers looked to Noel, who did the same.

She was about to ask questions about who had built the house and request a list of missing persons but stopped herself. She had no jurisdiction here – absolutely no authority. Noel could offer support services and lab resources, but that didn't mean the sheriff had to say yes.

Powers leaned back in his chair and placed a hand on the table. 'What's the FBI's interest in Melissa French?' he asked.

Noel didn't look to her, kept his attention focused on Powers. She and Noel had discussed at length what they would tell Powers before calling him.

'We don't have one,' Noel said.

'You, sir, are not a good liar. And you –' Powers swung

181

his attention to Darby. 'Are you going to stick to your story about Melissa French? That you have no idea who she is?'

'I've never met her, and Coop never mentioned her name to me,' Darby replied, which was true. 'I hadn't heard her name until you mentioned it when the three of us were sitting inside your truck.'

The sheriff's cold smile was full of irony. 'And why is it that I don't believe you?'

'Because you have trust issues that stem from childhood?'

'Here's what I think,' Powers said. 'I think the two of you are working on something together. I think you, Dr McCormick, for reasons you can't or won't tell me, decided to break into this house in the middle of the night.'

'I didn't break in,' Darby said.

Powers snapped his fingers. 'That's right,' he said coyly. 'You told me you conveniently found a house key underneath the welcome mat by the front door.' He smiled. 'Then you went upstairs, where – again – you conveniently found a hidden entranceway located behind a bookcase.'

'That's what happened.'

Powers drummed his fingers on the table. 'It's all so wonderfully convenient, don't you think?'

'I think you're forgetting the fact that the remains of two young women are buried behind the walls of this house,' Darby said.

'That fact is front and centre in my mind, Doctor.'

'I called you,' Darby began.

'*And* Agent Covington,' Powers said. 'My guess is he arrived here well before I did. Am I right?'

'One hundred per cent. In case you forget, one of his agents – my friend – is missing.'

The sheriff looked at her, confused at her choice of the word 'missing'. Looked at her as if he wanted to say, *Don't you mean dead?*

'This key,' Powers said. 'May I see it?'

Darby's eyes shifted to Noel, and the sheriff said, 'See, that's what I'm talking about right there. You need his permission, 'cause he's the one pulling the strings on this.'

The sheriff rose to his feet, the chair skidding behind him. His hair, thick and black and parted razor sharp on the side, was damp. Darby saw beads of perspiration on his smooth forehead, and his cheeks were rosy with anger.

'I don't know what's going on, but I don't want no part of it,' Powers said, but there wasn't much strength in his voice – a good sign. He didn't want the nightmare that had been thrown into his lap. He might be willing to accept outside help. 'Right now, I've got the remains of two women sitting in a home in my town.'

Noel cleared his throat. 'Sheriff, we can offer you the services of our lab and our –'

'I've had just about enough of your help.' The man's jaw trembled with anger.

Darby didn't blame him. Two interlopers had come into his town and dumped a big, steaming pile of shit on him. Powers was, first and foremost, an administrator; he always had to be mindful of figures when it came to allocating resources. Two sets of remains, maybe more, found inside a hidden room inside a hidden chamber hidden behind a bedroom-wall bookcase – it was a forensics nightmare that, even if done correctly, would take at least a week of people working in shifts around the clock. That kind of overtime probably wasn't in the man's budget, which meant he had to go hat in hand to whoever controlled the purse strings and beg for money. That wouldn't go down well come re-election time – unless Powers identified the remains *and* found the killer.

And he would have to do all of this under a media microscope. This kind of story, with all its grisly details, gave reporters wet dreams.

Powers said, 'An agent of yours is dead, and for that I'm truly sorry. I'll extend you every courtesy so you can find him and bring him home. But, as for what happened here, behind these walls? Me and my people will take care of these girls, make sure they get the respect and treatment they deserve. Now get out, the both of you.'

34

Noel didn't speak until they were inside the SUV, after he'd shut the door. The front windshield was covered with frost, and their breath plumed in the air, fogging up the glass.

'Well,' he said, his voice empty, 'that went pretty much as expected.'

When Darby spoke, her voice was just as empty. 'Surprised he didn't ask for his loaner back.'

'What, you think he wants to be stuck in a car with us right now, playing chauffer?'

'Given how pissed off he is, I think he'd want us to hand over our jackets and shoes and socks before making us walk back to the hotel.'

Noel nodded, either in agreement or because he felt the need to do something. Their empty words had nothing to do with the sheriff and everything to do with what happened inside the bedroom. Someone had hacked the baby monitor and listened in on them.

Noel turned the key in the ignition. 'The way that guy screamed in the woods,' he said.

Darby could hear it now, roaring inside her ears, that howl of outrage.

'We have no way of knowing if the man we heard was, in fact, the Red Ryder,' she said.

Noel leaned back against his seat and folded his arms

across his chest as the car warmed up. 'We also don't have any proof it *wasn't* him,' he said. 'Then again, what are the chances that it was someone else *besides* him?'

Unlikely, Darby thought.

Before calling Powers, they had discussed whether or not to share the information on Karen Decker, her letter and her belief that she'd found the Red Ryder here in Fort Jefferson. In the end, Noel had made the decision to keep the matter confidential until they came across some piece of evidence or some thread to follow. Right now, it was best to keep the matter contained as much as possible.

'That place we found, the killing chamber,' Noel began. 'Those girls weren't killed in there. If they were, the decomposition – the odours would have permeated through the walls and into the house. Someone would have complained.'

'Not if you were the one who'd killed them and you lived there alone.'

'True. But, given what I could see' – she hadn't entered the chamber, not wanting to disturb any evidence – 'I couldn't see the usual staining and such as you'd see with decomposition. That chamber, room, whatever, it's . . . a sacred space. My guess is he took each of them someplace quiet and private – where he knew for certain no one would ever be able to hear them scream, and where no one would smell them when they decomposed. After nature had taken its course – when they were practically mummified – he brought them to this house.'

'His house,' Noel said.

'We've already discussed this.'

Noel waved his hands. 'I know, I know, we don't know

for certain the Red Ryder lived there at one point in time – at least not yet,' he said. 'But, Jesus, how many other people in Fort Jefferson do you think have a secret room behind a bookcase that leads to a room containing two dead bodies?'

'I hear you. But I don't think we should – okay, let's assume he did *live* here at some point. What are the chances of your sister coming to Fort Jefferson and renting the *same* home that had once belonged to the man who had tried to kill her?'

Noel didn't answer right away. 'Slim,' he said reluctantly.

'*Very* slim, to the point of being next to impossible.'

'Still, coincidences *do* happen in our line of work.'

Darby didn't answer. Not because he could be right – coincidences did happen, more than she liked to admit – but because she reached the point of exhaustion where her brain felt like it had turned to soup.

'Let's go to the diner and grab something to eat,' she said. 'See if Betsey Sullivan is there, talk to her.'

Noel nodded, lost in thought. 'The girls . . . you said you believed he took them someplace private before he transferred them to his house – excuse me, this house. That means he has a place somewhere in town or nearby. Karen could be there right now.'

'Maybe.'

'But you don't believe it, do you?'

'Hard to say. Right now, I'm concerned about the talent level here – the people I saw last night examining Coop's rental, how they went about documenting everything . . . I'm not sure they've got the skills for something like this.'

'Agreed. The smart play will be for Powers to call the

state lab, get their people to come here and do the work. They've got the skill set, and, if anything goes wrong down the line, he can point the finger at them.'

'The Bureau would make a much better scapegoat.'

'And we have much deeper pockets to finance this sort of thing,' Noel added. 'But if Powers doesn't want us here, there's not much we can do. And if he does ask us for help – forensics, whatever – I still have to run it up the flagpole.'

'Where it will be shot down.'

'Not necessarily. The marshals bent a lot of rules for Karen, because everyone truly cared for her. But she left, and WITSEC isn't going to advertise that fact. They don't want any press, and Vivian will want to keep a close eye on what's going on now, so she can prepare herself, prevent any potential bad publicity.'

'Once Fort Jefferson starts digging, they'll find out who Melissa French really is.' *Or was*, Darby added privately. She didn't believe the woman was still alive but kept the thought to herself.

Noel backed out of the driveway.

'Just so we're clear,' she said, 'I'm not leaving Fort Jefferson.'

'Wasn't expecting you to.'

'You may want to relay that to your buddy, Bradley. If he approaches me and tries to drive me to the airport, he'll be taking his next meal through a straw.'

'I think you need to get some sleep.'

'I'm serious.'

'Wasn't suggesting you weren't. But he's not going to find you.'

'Oh?'

'I booked you a room at our hotel. He thinks you're staying there. He doesn't know you decided to ditch us for some fancy lodge in Big Sky.'

'And if he calls around?'

'Let him. He won't find you. I've taken care of it.'

The light in the sky wasn't any brighter. It was like the sky couldn't decide whether or not to release it. Like maybe it wanted to swallow the light and leave everything below the sky in darkness.

'I'll give Powers some time to cool down before I take another run at him,' Noel said as they drove across the street. 'At the end of the day, he needs us.'

Darby was looking out her side window, at the next-door neighbour's house. The downstairs lights were still off, but the bedroom facing Karen's home – the light was on there and she saw a young girl with blonde hair standing in the window, looking at the SUV.

Her eyes met Darby's.

The girl made the sign of the cross.

'The cadaver dogs,' Darby said.

'They'll be here at nine thirty. The moment I find out, I'll –'

'You're not going to find his body.'

'It's a lot of ground to cover, and it's going to be tough because it's all packed in snow. But if he's there, I promise you I'll find him.'

Ground to cover. For some reason the words triggered the image of Coop's suitcase just sitting there, its luggage tag –

She straightened a bit in her seat, tensing.

Noel caught it. 'What's wrong?'

35

'The luggage tag on his suitcase,' Darby said. 'You remember it?'

Noel nodded.

'The tag was encased in clear plastic,' she said. 'We both saw the writing.

'You told the sheriff it was Cooper's handwriting.'

'It is. No question in my mind. Only Coop wrote out his full name – Jackson Francis Cooper. Francis is Coop's father. Guy left when Coop was six. Left him and his sisters and mother high and dry. Family had to go on welfare.'

'Okay,' Noel said, his voice hesitant. Wary.

'When Coop turned eighteen, he legally changed his name from Jackson Francis Cooper to Jackson Cooper, no middle initial. He doesn't use a middle name because he doesn't have one. It's not on his driver's licence or passport. He never used it on any forms at Boston PD, and I bet if you check any FBI forms he filled out, any tax returns, you'll find the exact same thing.'

Noel said nothing.

'Call the Massachusetts Probate and Family Court if you don't believe me,' Darby said. 'Ask them to pull the papers.'

'I believe you.'

'Another thing: Who ever puts their full middle name

on a luggage tag? A middle initial, maybe, but your full middle name?'

'You think Cooper was trying to send you a message.'

'I'm thinking the accident we saw was staged to look like a car accident. It conveniently happened on a road well known for accidents during the winter, the SUV inside a river with a Class 5 rapid that pretty much ensured that all the evidence was washed away, and we found a John Doe behind the wheel and Coop nowhere at all.'

'But we did find his suitcase and his coat,' Noel said.

'We did. But what if they were left there so we thought he was dead? That his body had gotten caught in the river?'

'Okay, so how does our John Doe fit into this?'

'Misdirection,' Darby said. 'The Red Ryder wants us and Powers to think this guy is responsible for what happened to Coop, maybe even your sister. I will guarantee you this much: when they run John Doe's fingerprints through the database, they'll come back with a match. This guy will have a criminal record for sexual assault against young women or children.'

'You think the John Doe is connected to the remains we found in the house?'

'I think he'll have some sort of connection to the house. Whatever it is, don't be surprised if Powers uses it to close the case.'

Noel nodded, listening, thinking.

'Another small but important detail – at least as far as I'm concerned,' Darby said. 'Coop always wore his seatbelt. It's a state law in Massachusetts. We grew up with it; it's second nature to us, you just do it.'

'If the whole thing was staged by our friend, then why not just dump Cooper's body somewhere so we'd find it?'

'I've been asking myself the same question.'

'And?'

'You told me Coop knows about the Red Ryder and your sister.'

'I told him everything.'

'So Coop's an information resource for him.'

'Like my sister is,' Noel said. 'Or was.'

'Coop knows about the handwriting, the letter your sister wrote to you, all of it. Coop wouldn't be willing to give out that information, but under the right . . . conditions, he might.'

'If the Red Ryder has or had them somewhere,' Noel said, 'it suggests he's local. That he didn't pack up and leave because he decided to stick around and keep an eye on things, see what develops before he makes his next move. Guy would be, what, between sixty and seventy right now?'

'About that.'

'I'll put someone on to looking at white men in that age range who live in town.' Noel swiped his elbow along the corner of his mouth. 'You think he could still be alive? Cooper?'

'It's what I want to believe.'

Noel nodded, Darby grateful when he didn't ask any more questions.

Darby felt her exhaustion as though it were a living, breathing thing. She carried it with her as she got out of the car and followed Noel, who looked like he was dragging himself, across a sidewalk scattered with rock salt.

The downtown area was so quiet it looked on the verge of extinction. The C & J Diner was a corner storefront, its windows filmed with dirt, the building it was in and the whole area in desperate need of a good scrubbing, followed by a facelift. Inside, it was about as big as a classroom, and everywhere Darby looked she saw beige Formica counter-tops and thick white mugs and plates that brought back memories from her childhood, a time when things were built to last.

The diner was at full capacity, occupied mostly by men, most of them old and carrying the years in their faces. When Darby stepped inside, she saw nearly everyone look up from their phones and newspapers or away from the pair of TVs hanging on the walls to take a good look at her and Noel, study them for a moment because they were strangers, and strangers didn't pass through a place like Fort Jefferson unless they needed or wanted something.

All the tables and booths were occupied, but there was space at the counter. Darby took the stool next to a guy who was somewhere north of seventy, his bloated cheeks covered in white stubble and his unwashed checkered flannel shirt reeking. Could he be the Red Ryder?

The man working behind the counter, clearing away the dirty plates, was also up there in years. He was lithe, neat and trim, and wore a pair of rainbow suspenders over a black T-shirt. What about him? Could he be the Red Ryder? How many old men were living here in Fort Jefferson?

Noel didn't have to ask for Betsey Sullivan; she was working the counter, the woman looking like a middle-aged Snow White, with her short black hair and smooth, almost translucent skin. She was all smiles when she poured their coffee and took their order, the smile faltering a bit when Noel asked about Melissa French.

'You two are, what, family? Friends?' Betsey asked. She had a soft, soothing voice that was difficult to hear over the clack and clang of dishes and silverware.

Noel showed her his badge, not making a big display of it.

'What kind of trouble she in now?' Betsey asked.

The big, mouldy-smelling man next to Darby got up with a grunt. He grabbed his coat and hat with his big hand from the adjoining stool, Darby suddenly having the insane need to follow him, find out who he was, where he was going. Then he said, 'Thanks for breakfast, Bets. Have a good one.'

'Don't forget to take your medicine, Dad.'

He waved over his shoulder as he lumbered off. He grabbed an orthopaedic cane leaning against the wall as Noel looked to Betsey and said, 'What did you mean by "What kind of trouble is she in *now*?" What kind of trouble was she in before?'

'Well, she never got into specifics . . .'

'But?'

'But she had some scars on her wrists that made me think she had tried to kill herself. She never talked about it. That, or why she limped. A couple of times I saw these really awful surgical-type scars along her neck and arms. She never talked about it with me, and I never asked questions because it's none of my business, and because Melissa was real private. And a great worker. One of the best I've ever had. What kind of trouble is she in?'

194

'Don't know,' Noel said. 'She's missing, and we're trying to find her.'

'That's too bad. Her family must be really hurting.'

'She ever talk about them?'

Betsey shook her head as she refilled their coffee. 'She told me they'd written her off,' she said. 'Told her that she was worthless. The mother, not the brother.'

Whatever Noel was feeling, Darby thought he was hiding it well.

'That's who I thought he was at first,' Betsey told them.

'Pardon?'

'The guy who came around last week looking for her. Tall guy with blond hair who looked like he could bench-press a car. He said he was a friend, though, some guy named . . . Jack, I think?'

Noel nodded. 'Yes, he's a friend. That's why we're here, to help find Melissa. What else can you tell us about her?'

'Not much. Like I said before, she was real private. Didn't much like talking about herself, her past or where she'd come from. I can tell you she worked hard, she went to church, and she picked up some extra money babysitting.'

'Names?' Noel took out his notebook.

'Shelly Reece. She lives over on Carter. Number Twenty-two, I think. That's the only one I know, off the top of my head. Oh, one other thing. The day she gave her two-week notice, Melissa seemed real sad. Like, heartbroken. Couple of other people here noticed it too, but Mel waved it off, said it was nothing.'

'She say anything to you?'

'I asked, of course, more than once because I liked her

and, quite frankly, didn't want her to leave,' Betsey said. 'The only thing she told me was she *had* to leave. She didn't get into specifics, and I didn't pry, 'cause it was none of my business. I hope you find her, Mr Covington. And when you do? Please tell her that Betsey from C & J says hello and that she's a good person. Make sure you tell her I told you that.'

36

Fortified by food and coffee, Darby felt infused with a new energy and clarity. Noel did too, and they decided to go to the real-estate agency, to see if they could find out any information on the house Karen had rented.

Darby had been expecting some rinky-dink operation manned by a single secretary inside some downtown storefront, the employees a couple of overweight hausfraus with out-of-date hairstyles, bad makeup and wearing the kind of plus-size clothing that a normal department store would refuse to stock because the styles and colours were so ugly.

She had been right about the secretary part: Sampson Realty had one, a young, shy woman with an overbite who couldn't have been a day older than twenty-five. The real-estate company, though, operated out of a two-floor redwood-stained home located on the edge of the neighbourhood where Karen lived. According to the pictures gracing the wall just beyond the main door, two other realtors worked there – both young, fit guys in their early twenties, Darby guessed. The owner, Pamela Sampson, was the complete opposite of a hausfrau: short and thin, with sharp, angular features and a Mediterranean complexion, her distinguishing characteristic a hairline that began two, maybe three inches above her thick eyebrows, which had been meticulously shaped.

The secretary told them Pamela Sampson and the others were already out showing properties and wouldn't be back until sometime that afternoon.

The secretary was a mousy girl who wore too much makeup for a woman so young. Her name was Caitlyn, and she was very conscious of her overbite when she spoke. She lived in Fort Jefferson. When Noel asked about the property Melissa French had rented, Caitlyn looked visibly nervous – had looked that way, Darby thought, since she and Noel had entered.

'I . . . I can't talk about that place,' she said.

'Oh? And why's that?' Noel asked kindly.

'Because I'm not supposed to.'

'I think you can,' Noel showed his Federal ID.

Staring at the badge, the young woman placed her hand on a small gold crucifix she wore on a chain. Then she looked around the room as if hoping someone would come in and rescue her from this conversation.

Darby was looking around the room too, at the messy desks and potted plants that needed watering, especially the big peace lily sitting on the front counter, when Noel said, 'Is there something wrong, Caitlyn?'

'It's just . . .' Again she swallowed. 'A man came in here last week asking questions.'

'Big guy, blond hair?'

She nodded, Darby noticing the sweat that had formed along the girl's hairline.

'He had some questions about the person living there,' Caitlyn said.

'Melissa French,' Noel said.

'Yeah. Her. He was just trying to get some information

on her because they were friends, and he was concerned when she, you know, just got up and left. Pamela – that would be my boss, Pamela Sampson – she came out and took him into her office and they talked, but after he *left*? She yelled at me. In front of everyone. Said that I'm not to share information with anyone, for any reason. Said if I did, I'd be fired. And I *need* this job. You don't know how hard it is to get a job in this town, what you have to go through.'

Darby took out her phone and tapped a finger across the screen as Noel said, 'We're alone, Caitlyn. I give you my word that I won't –'

'That's the thing,' Caitlyn said. 'We're not.' She nodded with her chin to the security camera mounted on the wall in the corner of the room. 'So, as much as I'd *like* to talk, I really can't. Besides, I don't really know much about the property. You should talk to Pamela. She's been here for, like, forever, and she was the one who showed the property. She could tell you more about Melissa French and the Andersons.'

'The Andersons?'

'The previous owners.'

'Where are they living now?'

The young woman shrugged. 'They moved, like, five years ago? Here's Pamela's card. Her phone numbers are on the front.' Caitlyn handed them a card each.

Noel said, 'Where's your boss now?'

'Showing properties out in Great Bear.'

'How far away is that?'

'About an hour away.' Caitlyn wouldn't meet their eyes. She looked around her desk and the room, anywhere but at them. Looked like she wanted to shut her eyes and do some deep breathing, calm herself down. 'She told me she'll be back around one or two. I can have her call you then.'

'Please do.' Noel gave his card to her. 'Thanks.'

As they left, Darby looked over her shoulder, and through the glass door saw Caitlyn watching them, her face twisted with worry as she rubbed the crucifix between her fingers.

They were driving away when Noel said, 'What just happened back there?'

'Could be nothing. She struck me as jittery the moment we stepped inside, one of those girls who's constantly jumpy. Anxious. You?'

'Maybe. But she seemed . . . scared.'

'Shit.'

'What?'

'I forgot my phone. Left it on the counter.'

When Darby went back inside, Caitlyn was talking on the phone to someone.

'Thank you, I'll tell her you called,' she said, speaking quickly into the receiver. Then she hung up.

Darby smiled politely. 'Forgot this,' she said, picking up her phone. She had left it in front of the peace lily plant, where Caitlyn couldn't see it.

Driving away, she told Noel she had left her phone behind on purpose. She had set it to record and played it now.

Over the speaker came the sound of Caitlyn dialling a number. Seconds of silence and then they heard Caitlyn say, 'They just left. I told them everything you told me to say . . . Yes. Yes, I understand – oh, shit. Shit. She's coming back.' The sound of the bell on the front door could be heard, and then Caitlyn said to the person on the other end of the line, 'Thank you, I'll tell her you called.'

Darby stopped the recording. She stared out the window, thinking.

'This is the part where one of us should say something clever,' Noel said.

'You got a line handy?'

'How about "The game's afoot"?'

'I like that. Now, if we could find out who she called . . .'

Darby knew what Noel was thinking: that in order to access the woman's cell phone records – any phone records – he would have to go through a lot of legal red tape. It would take time – time they didn't have.

'I'll take care of Caitlyn,' she told him.

37

War has many rules, but only two are critical to your survival. The first one is that you live behind your rifle and your pistol and your bullet-proof vest, the last protecting your heart, which is pumping blood into your vital organs. The second is that you use everything at your disposal to protect yourself, to keep you safe and, God willing, deliver you back home to your family.

He wasn't at war right now – at least not the kind where he had groups of people, sometimes an entire city, wishing him dead. He didn't have IEDs hidden in the road he was driving on or inside a parked car or in a heap of trash as high as a wall and stinking like a morgue stuffed floor to ceiling with corpses, the air-conditioning and refrigeration units turned off. He didn't have to worry about some barefoot or sandal-wearing Iraqi boy coming toward his Humvee, smiling nervously and holding dripping slices of watermelon the colour of blood, a suicide vest strapped underneath his robes.

When he pulled into the driveway belonging to the Green Valley Motor Lodge – a group of low brown buildings made of dark timber stacked together and looking like a pile of shit with windows in it – he was seized with panic, imagining people rushing out from behind the buildings and through the doors and from behind parked cars, all of them brandishing guns, readying to fire. When that didn't happen, his brain told him to search the area for hidden IEDs, while the voice he had relied upon in Iraq, one that had saved his life several times, too many times, told him to throw the car in reverse and get the hell out.

Darby was staring at him. He could feel the sweat popping along his forehead.

'You feel okay?' she asked.

'Tired. No, exhausted.' He smiled wearily. 'Second rule of combat is to grab sleep whenever you can. I want you to take the car and drive back to Big Sky.'

'I'll crash here.'

'This place is an absolute shithole.'

'I've stayed in plenty of shitholes.'

'My FOB – Forward Operating Base – I lived in while I was stationed in Iraq was cleaner. And I never found pubic hairs in my towel.'

'You've got me beat there. I'll head to Big Sky.'

Noel threw open the door and got out. As he made his way round the front bumper he imagined not his head locked in crosshairs but hers, someone ready to pull the trigger. He knew he was being foolish and irrational, but the feeling didn't go away. Dug its roots in and sharpened its pointed teeth, to get ready for fresh meat – his. This thing in him only wanted to feast on him, his brain.

There's only one way out, the thing said. *Grab your gun and stick it in your –*

'I'll be there when the dogs arrive,' he said.

She stood in front of him, her gaze searching his face. 'What?'

'You're sweating,' she said. 'And your left eye is twitching.'

'I had malaria. It acts up every now and again when I'm tired. It'll pass.'

Her eyes were as cold and unforgiving as the winter morning. He was about to run through the rehearsed script he told everyone when this moment happened, when she brushed past him and walked around the car.

Noel wanted to run back and tell her to get out, have her stand inside the motel while he examined the SUV, searching it for an IED. Again, he knew he was being irrational – most of all because if an IED had been planted in it, it would have already gone off. But the Red Ryder didn't deal in bombs, he dealt in guns – handguns, which he fired up close, creating a canvas that he could watch and admire, like a painter who had finished administering the final masterful brushstroke.

Noel was about to open the front door to the motel and step into the lobby, with its shaggy carpeting and panelled walls displaying cheaply framed pictures of grizzly bears and hunting parties, when he inhaled the cold morning air smelling of pine and suddenly felt invigorated, the way he did back in Iraq when he was in his early twenties, all balls and will, ready to take on the world and fix it. He let go of the door and then ambled toward the parking lot, which was mostly empty.

A home at the end of the world, he thought, reaching into his pocket.

Vivian was used to answering her phone at all hours of the night. 'Noel,' she said, her voice clear and strong even though it was shortly before 5 a.m. in Virginia.

He told her about how Darby had discovered the

hidden chamber inside the home Karen had rented, the skeletal remains he'd seen, the hacked baby monitor.

'The sheriff,' Vivian said after he finished speaking. 'You think he'll change his mind?'

'I don't.' Noel told her about the young woman's telephone conversation at the real-estate office.

'Okay,' Vivian said after he finished. 'I'll see what I can do on my end, see who she called.'

'I'm more concerned right now about the sheriff.'

'We can offer our help. He doesn't have to accept it.'

'Or we can take over the investigation.'

'I'd rather not go down that road.'

'Two dead women.'

Vivian said nothing.

'Darby thinks there could be more inside the chamber area, whatever it's called,' Noel said.

'Buried in candy wrappers.'

'Yes.'

'Did she take a look inside?'

'No. Darby didn't want to go in there, disturb any potential evidence.'

'Smart girl.'

'And one of the best in her field.'

Vivian said nothing.

'I think the Red Ryder is here,' he said.

'I think you mean *was*. If that was him you heard in the woods last night – if he's somehow linked to that house your sister was renting – don't you think he'll go underground or, better yet, take off somewhere?'

'Maybe. But I'm not running.'

Vivian said nothing.

'I need to put an end to this,' he said.

Vivian's voice was so low, almost a whisper: 'I know you do.'

'So help me.'

Vivian sighed.

'One condition,' she said.

'No.'

'You don't know her.'

'Darby stays.'

'She'll throw you to the wolves without a second thought if it means saving herself or Cooper.'

No, he thought. *That's what you would do.*

38

When Darby opened her eyes, it was quarter to four in the afternoon. Being winter, the sun was already gone, the breathtaking, snowcapped-mountain view from the bedroom now lost behind a sky as black and thick as paint. The bare trees below were strung with tiny white lights, and outside she could hear the crunch of footsteps moving back and forth across compacted snow and the muted conversations of people returning from a day of skiing, the dinner plans they were making for that night.

The bedroom opened on to a suite featuring a kitchen and a rustic living room with a gas fireplace. Her phone sat on the kitchen counter, next to the sink. She'd missed two calls, two voicemail messages had been left.

The first was from Rosemary Shapiro. In a strained, raspy voice, she asked Darby to return her call. Earlier, before she hit the sack, Darby had sent an email asking Rosemary to see what she could find on the young woman named Caitlyn who worked at Sampson Realty. She had also asked for information on the house that Karen Decker had rented.

The second, from Noel, was about the cadaver dogs. They had finished searching the area around the accident site and had failed to find Coop's body.

The news didn't come as a surprise to her. She believed – and still did – that the accident site had been staged, that the Red Ryder (because who else could it be?) had forced Coop to write his name on the luggage tag so his suitcase would be easily identified. During that moment, Coop had written out his full name, including the middle name he had legally removed, to send her a message, which was . . . what? That he'd written his full name under duress? That the accident site was not what it appeared to be? If so, message received.

The Red Ryder wanted the police to find Coop's suitcase and for them and the FBI and anyone else who came along, including her, to think Coop had been ejected from the SUV and thrown into the water, his broken and mangled body conveniently carried away by Class 5 rapids that dumped into a river known for swallowing its dead.

Where was Coop right now?

Was he still alive?

Darby's head pounded from last night's bourbon, fragmented sleep and also, she guessed, from the sudden change in altitude. She grabbed a glass from the cabinet and filled it with water from the kitchen faucet.

The tap water had a pungently sweet and tangy taste that reminded her of Sweet'n Low. She didn't gag, but her stomach quickly protested its arrival. Fortunately, when she opened the refrigerator, she saw that the shelves were stocked with bottled water. She drained one, then started another on her way to the bathroom, drinking the rest of it as she turned on the shower.

The water coming out of the showerhead was black.

Darby stared at it, confused and slightly sickened, wondering what could have caused the water to turn black. Then she remembered passing by the front desk last night – a guy with a Santa Claus beard was complaining about the water in his room having a weird odour, colour and taste, and the chubby-faced girl with the braces said something about a malfunctioning filtration unit. Apparently her room had been affected too.

Great, she thought.

The black water faded to a brownish tint then disappeared; the water was now running clear. She stepped inside the shower and within a few short minutes she was surrounded by the pleasant odour of the hotel's almond-scented soap and shampoo, the man known only as the Red Ryder devouring her thoughts and attention.

Karen Decker had disappeared.

Had the Red Ryder taken her?

Had he taken Coop? Could they both still be alive?

If they were, they were in pain.

A lot of pain.

Darby turned off the shower, her skin prickling in fear and her hands shaking as she sluiced water away from her face and hair, knowing she could not – would not – stop until she found the Red Ryder and killed him.

39

'I remember Melissa French very well,' said Pamela Sampson, the head of Sampson Realty. 'I don't get too many out-of-towners coming here looking to buy or rent, let alone people from out of state.'

'How'd she contact you?' Noel asked.

'By phone. Called up and asked if she could look at some properties we had for rent.'

'How many?'

'Gosh, that was . . . eight months ago?' She fingered a string of pearls, staring out the window behind her desk, the parking lot lit by a single floodlight.

Noel sat in one of the two chairs set up in front of her immaculately organized desk in her immaculately organized and clean office. She had insisted on sitting next to him. She told her secretary to hold her calls.

Pamela Sampson turned back to him and, with a slight grin, said, 'You know, I'm really not supposed to be talking to you.'

'Why's that?'

'The sheriff, it seems, is angry with you. Doesn't want me talking to you or your friend about Melissa French or her property, pretty much anything.'

That's interesting, Noel thought.

'Want to tell me why?' Pamela Sampson asked.

'What did he tell you?'

'Oh, he didn't get into specifics. But I'm hoping you will.' Her grin grew wider, playful, maybe even a bit flirty, he thought. 'This is pretty exciting stuff.'

'You first.'

She had a great smile.

'Four,' she said. 'I'm pretty sure I showed her four rental properties. I can get you the listings, if you'd like.'

'I would appreciate it. Thank you.'

She stood, looking elegant in her black heels and black suit, and when she popped her head out the door and asked the girl named Sheila manning the phones to print out the property listings, Noel sat thinking about Bradley at the hangar with Cooper's rental vehicle, working on it with the two men who had come up this morning to do the forensics and paperwork.

Noel rubbed his eyes. He had managed to grab three hours of sleep, but it had been restless, fragmented by dreams he couldn't for the life of him remember and broken by his jumping at every little sound – the creak of a floorboard outside his room, the heat knocking its way through the motel's old pipes. He'd start awake, his sidearm already gripped in his hand. He had wrapped his hand around it before he lay down on top of a forest-green comforter painted with regal family crests, as though the comforter had been purloined from the royal bed of a prince or a king.

'Is she in some sort of trouble?' Pamela Sampson asked when she retook her seat. 'Melissa?'

'What makes you think that?'

'Well,' she said, smiling nervously, 'maybe it's because an FBI agent is sitting inside my office asking questions about her, for one.'

'That's a clue, sure.' Noel picked up the bottle of water she'd given him.

She chuckled softly. 'The guy who came in here looking for her – Caitlyn didn't give him any specifics. Not that she knew much of anything. I think she was flirting with him. Anyway, I spoke to him, this Jack fellow, and I told him I didn't know much of anything, which was the truth. It's not like she would have left me any forwarding information.'

Noel drank some of his water.

'He came in, said he was a close friend of Melissa, from out of town. Came to ski in Big Sky and stopped by to see her and saw the "For Sale" sign at her place, asked if I knew where she'd gone, if I had any contact information – which raised red flags, because how good a friend could he have been if Melissa didn't give him any info? I told him he should go to the bank and ask them. They might have a forwarding address.'

'Freedom Banking.'

She nodded. 'Have you talked with them?'

'I did,' he said. 'They didn't have much information either.'

'That man, Cooper, are you looking for him too?'

'In a manner of speaking.' He didn't see the harm in telling her because the news was going to get out sooner or later. 'He was a Federal agent. That's why I'm here.'

'If he was a Federal agent, why didn't he just tell me? I would have given any information I had – not that I had any to give.'

'He was here on vacation and not working in any Federal capacity, so identifying himself as an agent to get information would have been unethical, not to mention against regulations.'

'Ah. So why the questions about Melissa, then, if you don't mind my asking?'

'I can't really get into details with an active investigation.'

'Sorry. I've always been a nosy busybody.'

'The house Melissa rented,' Noel said, getting her back on track. 'May I have a list of the previous owners and occupants? Who built the house?'

'Sure,' she replied, a bit wary, probably trying to figure out why he had asked for such a thing. 'The previous owners of the house were Gregg and Kim Anderson. Gregg had been unemployed for a while, and with his benefits about to run out he and the family decided to split and leave the bank holding the note.'

'And go where?'

'Your guess is as good as mine. They lived there a good, oh, seventeen years or so. I'll see what I have listed on my computer, but the best way to find out everything about the house, including the owners, is a property-title search company. I can recommend a few names.'

'Thank you,' Noel said, although he wouldn't be using any of them. He already had people at his office compiling information on the house.

Pamela stared out the window again, her hands folded on her lap. She bounced her foot for a moment – not nervous, he thought, just thinking. He sensed she was the kind of woman who had difficulty sitting still for more than five minutes.

'I remember . . .' Her words trailed off. 'You know,' she said, waving a hand. 'Never mind, it's nothing.'

'Tell me anyway.'

'I was just thinking I bet she does that a lot. Melissa.'

'Does what a lot?'

'Packs up and moves,' Pamela said. 'Day I took her to look at the properties, we spent, I dunno, maybe two hours together. She was perfectly polite – asked a lot of questions about the town, what it was like living here, how did I like it – you know, the typical stuff. When I asked her questions – where you from, married, kids, all that – she'd give me these real short answers and very subtly would shift the conversation away from her. I got this sense she was . . . it was like she had a lot of sadness locked up inside her. Like she was the kind of person who, if she talked about it, it would really screw with her head, or something. I'm probably reading too much into it, to be honest. I like playing armchair shrink. I watch way too much *Dr Phil*.'

'That's the saddest thing I've ever heard.'

Pamela snorted. 'I can tell you this much,' she said. 'Based on all my years of doing real estate, there's no question in my mind Melissa was one of those people who liked to move around, try on different places to see which one, you know, fits. She was the type who can't put down any roots. Like if they do, they'll quickly wither away and die.'

40

Darby was on her way back to Fort Jefferson, to meet Noel at the police-owned hangar that housed Coop's rental vehicle, when she returned Rosemary's call. As she dialled the number, her mind tumbled back to the blonde girl she'd seen staring down at her from the window of a neighbouring house. It was a school day, so it made sense she was up at such an early hour, but why was she watching them? There had been no flashing police lights or commotion, nothing.

Rosemary picked up and, as usual, started talking at warp speed. 'Honey, how are you doing? Talk to me, tell me everything.'

'I'm doing –'

'I haven't been able to sleep since you called, I'm so sick over what happened to Coop, oh my God you must be feeling awful. What can I do? What do you need? You shouldn't be there alone, which is why I'm going to come out there and join you. Where are you staying again?'

While Rosemary was someone you could count on during your darkest hour – she would drop whatever was going on in her life to help a friend – her incessant stream-of-consciousness talking and her emotions, which careened as wildly and unpredictably as a pinball, could be life-draining and, at times, soul-crushing. The last thing Darby wanted was for her to come out to Montana.

'I appreciate that, Rosemary, but if you really want to help me I need you to stay right where you are. Did you pass along that email I sent you to your PI?'

'I did. My man Booker came up with a lot of interesting shit. He – wait, are you someplace where you can talk freely?'

'I'm alone. Tell me everything.'

'We need to talk some legal matters first. That paperwork the Bureau was supposed to send over first thing this morning? I never got it.'

'Why?'

'Excellent question,' Rosemary said.

'Did they drop the charges?'

'I don't know – and I've been calling every single contact I have, pulling every string. I don't like it. You may want to talk to Noel Covington.'

'I will. Tell me about the Caitlyn girl who works for Sampson Realty in Fort Jefferson. What did your PI find?'

'Her full name is Caitlyn Ann Lee,' Rosemary said. 'She's twenty-three and single, no kids, lives at 22 Simmons Road in Fort Jefferson – with her parents, I'm guessing, since the house is under their name. John and Camilla Lee. No college degree, just a high school diploma. No criminal history. She's pretty vanilla – nothing jumps out.'

'I'm more interested in her cell phone records.'

'She doesn't own one – at least not under her name.'

'I saw her talking on a cell phone. What about her parents?'

'No cell phones, but they do own a landline. Just local calls.'

So Caitlyn Ann Lee had been talking on a disposable cell phone.

Why would a 23-year-old girl own a burner?

'What about that address I gave you?' Darby asked, referring to the house Karen Decker had rented.

'A woman named Melissa French rented the property for a few months, up until January of this year. Before that, a couple named Gregg and Kim Anderson lived in the home for roughly seventeen years before bailing on their mortgage. They're currently living in Seattle, Washington.'

'I'm more interested in the original owners.'

'I can tell you the house was built in 1955. As for the original owners, my PI can't find anything on any of the databases. Your best bet, he said, would be to go to the county records office.'

'Okay.'

'I also asked my PI to do some digging on the two Feds you're with, see if we could find any dirt in case they decided not to play nice,' Rosemary said. 'Bradley's pretty boring – at least on paper – but one look at his mug and you know he got hit with a major case of fugly. I bet his hand falls asleep when he's pulling his pud. Now the other one, Noel Covington?' Rosemary whistled. 'Yummy, yummy, yummy, I'd want him bouncing on top of my tummy.'

'I'll pass that along.'

'Don't bother, he's too emotionally and psychologically damaged. Major case of post-traumatic stress disorder. He enlisted in the Air Force at nineteen, then went to a bomb school in Florida. Graduated, flew over to play in the sandbox with Ali Baba. Did two tours and when he came home he had problems adjusting to normal civilian life.'

'How did you get access to his medical files?'

'We're all bytes and data streams scattered inside the cloud or whatever they're calling it now. Oh, and he was adopted.'

'Birth family?'

'Closed adoption, so I don't know. Why? Is it important?'

'No. Just curious.'

Rosemary suddenly burst into sobs.

Darby straightened in her seat. 'What's wrong?'

'You. You're what's wrong,' Rosemary said. 'The love of your life is dead, and for you it's business as usual.'

'Coop and I were just –'

'Don't hand me that bullshit. I saw the way he looked at you, and the way you looked at him. You loved him, and he loved you. God put the perfect man in your path and you ignored it. Why? Why would you do such a thing?'

But Rosemary wasn't expecting Darby to answer. 'That's all you can ever hope for in this life, for a man to love you and have your back,' she said. 'God gave you the perfect man and you kept turning your back on him and kept letting him walk away. You kept letting him walk away.'

41

The airplane hangar had been built within walking distance of the rambling farmhouse that had been gutted and converted into the Fort Jefferson sheriff's office. The search-and-rescue helicopter was long gone, and the hangar had visible pockets of rust along the walls, the concrete floor cracked and crumbling in a few areas. But it had six powerful wall heaters that were being fed by the same outside generator supplying the electricity. The warm air inside the hangar smelled damp and carried the metallic odour of the river.

Noel tried hard to concentrate on what Bradley was telling him about the status of the forensics on the Ford Explorer, how the boys he'd called early this morning from the Missoula office had brought up a portable fuming tent, assembled it over the SUV and pumped it full of cyanoacrylate. They collected a whole bunch of fingerprints but found none on the steering wheel, not even a *smudge*. Granted, the John Doe had been wearing gloves when he was pulled out of the water, so his hands could have rubbed some prints away as he drove, but *all* of them?

The boys from Missoula – there were two, Dale and Peters, stocky middle-aged men who wore permanent scowls – were finishing up work on the SUV, writing up their reports. When they weren't looking at clipboards or through a camera lens, they were stealing glances at the door, their expressions anxious, like they were waiting for someone to walk in and start firing.

Noel's attention drifted back to this morning, how he'd jumped at every sound, thinking the Red Ryder was now coming for *him*. It wasn't an outrageous thought. If the Red Ryder had kidnapped and tortured both Karen and Cooper, as Darby believed, it was possible they might have, in anger or fear or extreme pain, told him that Noel Covington, the brother of Karen Decker, was now a Federal agent. Would the Red Ryder try to kill him from a distance or get up all close and personal?

And what about Darby? What if he went after her?

'Sound like a plan?' Bradley asked.

Noel turned to him, confused. 'I'm sorry, could you repeat that?'

'What I was telling you about the evidence.' Bradley chin-nodded to the folding table in front of them. It held Cooper's suitcase and his clothes. They'd been hung out overnight to dry and were now folded, bagged into evidence. 'We're going to take it to Bozeman, process it there.'

'Do me a favour and process the luggage tag first, see what prints you get off it.'

One of the side doors opened. Sheriff Powers stepped inside, bringing a blast of cold air in with him.

The man, unsurprisingly, wasn't happy. But Noel detected something else fuelling his unhappiness: perhaps he'd been ordered to apologize and play nice. Noel wondered if Vivian, working behind the scenes, had called in favours or applied the appropriate pressure on the appropriate people to get Powers to cooperate with the Bureau or, even better, hand over the reins of the investigation.

'We've identified our John Doe,' Powers said.

Noel's eyebrows jumped in surprise. 'That was fast,' he said.

'Last night, I sent a couple of my people to Missoula with Mr Bradley here, to make sure John Doe's clothes were properly collected. My guy said he saw a tattoo on the John Doe's right thigh, near his groin.'

Bradley said, 'A red heart encased in a gold heart. It's a tattoo we've started seeing on a lot of paedophiles. I told your guy that.'

'You did. And that was very helpful, 'cause it helped to narrow our initial search. Two guys in the state have that tattoo, according to their files. So we pulled their prints and compared them to the gentleman we found behind the wheel and got a match. His name is Toby Dennis, a resident over in Beacon Point. His flavour was girls between the ages of ten and fifteen – the younger, the better. Been in and out of prison, was living in a camper his brother had given him. We'd had a few run-ins with him – peeping-Tom stuff, a couple of instances when he'd tried to lure a girl into his car – but he knew better than to go sneaking around in my backyard.' Powers looked directly at Noel when he said those last words.

'We appreciate your sharing this information with us,' Noel said.

'I can't tell you how happy that makes me, Mr Covington.'

'How old is he?' Noel asked.

'Dennis?' Powers scratched the corner of his nose with his thumb. 'Seventy-three, I believe. Could be a few years older, though.'

Roughly the same age the Red Ryder would be, Noel thought. 'You find anything in his background that connects him to the house Melissa French rented?'

'A direct link? No. But I can tell you he was born and raised here in Fort Jefferson and once upon a time worked construction for the J. C. Mountain Group. They built pretty much everything in this town. That's all I've got, Mr Covington. The moment I find out anything else, I'll be sure to email you. Have a safe trip back home.'

Before Noel could speak, Bradley stepped forward. 'We'll be out of your hair first thing in the morning,' he said, and shook the man's hand. 'Thanks for all your help, Sheriff.'

42

Noel felt a white-hot heat in the centre of his brain, about to go supernova. Instead of reacting, he walked over to the passenger's side of Cooper's SUV.

Darby told him that Cooper, had he been inside the car, would have buckled up. He reached through the twisted opening and checked the seatbelt.

It wouldn't lock.

He tried two more times before he gave up. Either it was broken, or it had been tampered with, to make the accident seem authentic. Or maybe he hadn't been given the chance to buckle up. Maybe he had been forced into the back seat.

Maybe he hadn't been inside the car at all.

Noel turned his attention to Bradley and said, 'Who's shut down the investigation?'

'Step outside with me for a minute,' Bradley said.

'I need to make a phone call first.'

Bradley stared at him for a beat and then walked away.

Noel dialled Vivian's direct number. When she didn't answer, he hung up and called her cell. Again, no answer. He didn't leave a message.

He found Bradley outside, standing near the east side of the hangar, where the wind wasn't blowing. It wasn't even six and it was full dark, no stars. Bradley took out a pack of Marlboro Lights and offered one to Noel.

Noel shook his head and stuffed his fists inside his overcoat pockets as he began to pace.

'I allow myself one smoke at the end of the day – two, when I close a case,' Bradley said. 'I plan on smoking two tonight, because my job here on the accident is done.'

Noel felt his left eye twitch. He rubbed at it with the heel of his palm, and he could feel himself sweating underneath his clothes, his shirt sticking against his skin.

'When did she do it? Vivian?'

'When did she pull the plug?'

Noel nodded.

Bradley pinched a cigarette between his chapped lips. 'Couldn't tell you,' he said, taking out his lighter. 'She didn't speak to me directly. My boss spoke to her. She thanked him for our help with the search and for finding Cooper's vehicle, and told him that, for all intents and purposes, the FBI's job here is done. That's what my boss said when he called me this afternoon, told me I'd be coming home at the end of the day or first thing tomorrow morning.'

'So he agreed with Vivian,' Noel said flatly.

'It's over. The cadaver dogs struck out this morning, and I finished the exam and paperwork on the rental car. There's nothing left to do, not unless we happen to find Cooper's body in the next twenty-four hours.'

Tell him that Cooper may still be alive? No. That won't change anything.

Noel rubbed at his eye again, thinking about the small pill case of Xanax tucked inside his inner jacket pocket. A white pill half the size of a pencil eraser and the twitching and anxiety and stress would all float away – and his brain along with it.

Bradley sucked deeply on his cigarette. 'I owe you my gratitude,' he said.

'For what?'

'For your service.' Bradley exhaled a long stream of smoke. 'You did, what, two tours overseas?'

Noel said nothing. He knew Bradley already knew the answer. Vivian had told him, he was sure of it. *Keep an eye on him*, Noel imagined Vivian saying to Bradley. *Noel suffers from PTSD and chronic depression. The chemical cocktail we've got him on works, but it'll vanish like a fart in the wind the moment he's under extreme stress — and you'll know when that is because his eyes will start twitching. He won't be able to sit or stand still. He won't sleep. The moment you notice any of these signs, Mr Bradley, you're to call me.*

'My nephew did a tour in Iraq,' Bradley said. 'Saw a lot of action in someplace called Hawija.'

Noel had been inside the town – a hateful place of blast craters and dead dogs and walls of garbage surrounding a crowded marketplace of booths and stalls selling fruit and electronics, the air reeking of body odour and burning trash and diesel exhaust. He had seen this mostly through the armoured-glass windows of a Humvee, the biggest threat not the hidden snipers on the rooftops but the crowd itself, hundreds and hundreds of people packed on the street and surrounding the Humvee and refusing to move despite the honking of the horn or the American soldiers and the top gunner screaming and threatening to shoot if they didn't move, Noel always tensely watching for that moment when the sea would suddenly part to reveal an attacker, usually a kid, the grenade already having left his hand.

Bradley said, 'After he returned home, his wife – his soon-to-be ex-wife, I should say – she said she'd wake up a lot of nights and find him sitting on the stairs in the dark holding a rifle, a couple of handguns on the step beside him. He told me he wanted to protect his family – they have two kids – from home invaders, burglars, whatever. He kept seeing danger where none existed, and we, his family, had to step in and help him out.'

Noel stood near the back of the hangar. The only light he could see came from the windows belonging to the converted farmhouse now being used as the sheriff's office. From this distance it looked like a houseboat floating on a flat sea.

'Why are you telling me this?'

Bradley took another long drag from his cigarette. 'I don't know what's going on here beyond looking for Cooper's body and finding out if he could have died in a car accident,' he said, then exhaled another stream of white smoke. 'At first I wanted to know. Then, when I heard about what you and the Doctor pulled last night at the house that Melissa woman rented, what you found there – that's when I decided I wanted to be left in the dark. And I want to stay there. You know why?'

'It doesn't matter.'

'I'm going to tell you anyway,' Bradley said. 'Collecting a paycheque every two weeks is what makes me happy. To get that paycheque, all I have to do is what I'm told, and I can go fly-fishing during the summer, take my nephew and niece and their kids with me, or take them skiing or out to dinner or to some Caribbean island. A lot of people, they wake up every morning wanting to put on a cape,

226

tackle the injustices of the world. Me? I want to be able to go to a restaurant and order the shrimp cocktail *and* the best steak on the menu. Don't care about much else beyond that. It's not that I'm not capable. It's that I don't want to.'

'Again,' Noel said, 'why are you telling me this?'

'Whatever's going on here, I'm no longer a part of it. First thing tomorrow, I'll be on the road, on my way home – with McCormick in the car. In handcuffs.'

'What?'

'The Bureau has decided to go ahead with the assault charges.'

Shit. 'Does Powers know about this?' Noel asked.

'I haven't told him – don't plan on telling him.'

'So there's no warrant.'

'Not yet. But if I don't find her by, say, late tomorrow morning, then I wouldn't be surprised to find out one was issued. That broad is not well liked. So, the real reason you're here, whatever it is, if you want her help, you'd best hide her, keep her out of Fort Jefferson. Like I said, I've been ordered to find and arrest her. Same deal with the two guys inside the hangar.'

'Back there with the sheriff, you said I was going home.'

'That's what my boss told me, yeah, you've been ordered to pack it in. I'm guessing Vivian has told you.'

'Not yet.'

'Anyway, I thought you deserved a heads-up.' Bradley took a final drag off his cigarette and then tossed it on to the ground. 'Thank you for your service,' he said again, stubbing out the butt with the heel of his shoe.

43

The neighbouring house looked like an almost exact replica of the one Karen Decker had rented, except it was painted white instead of tan, and came with an attached two-car garage. The house had the exact same black shutters and the same four concrete steps with a pair of wrought-iron rails and a black mailbox hanging to the left of a solid white door.

All the lights were off inside Karen's house, but all the lights were on here, the windows facing the street glowing from top to bottom, when Darby pulled up into the driveway and killed the engine. She got out, and, as she walked toward the house, the ticking of the SUV's cooling engine filling the frigid air, she saw one of the upstairs lights wink off.

Darby rang the doorbell. The chime was loud and seemed to go on forever. After it died, she heard approaching footsteps, small and light, the kind she associated with a child or a small adult.

The door cracked open, hesitantly, then another two or three feet before it stopped. The face that appeared in the gap belonged to the girl she had seen in the small hours of the morning.

Darby smiled. 'Hello.'

The girl said nothing. She stood defiantly, no surprise or curiosity in her face about the stranger standing on her front doorstep, as though her presence had been expected.

'My name is Darby. I'm an investigator. May I speak to your parents?'

'They're not home.'

Darby could see into the living room. It led to the open kitchen area, a table set up in the exact same area as in Karen's home, only this table was rectangular, with six high-back seats. They were pulled away from the table, away from the plates still holding half-eaten portions of mashed potatoes with gravy, chicken and green beans, their water glasses still full.

'When will they be back?' Darby asked.

'That's none of your business.'

The girl was eight, maybe ten years old. She had blue eyes and her hair was so blonde it was almost white. She wore it in a ponytail that lay flat against the shoulder of a black angora sweater, the hem of which came past her knees. The air inside was warm and smelled of food.

Darby's phone rang. She ignored it and said, 'Is there someone else I could speak to? Maybe your grandparents?'

'You don't belong here,' the girl said, and slammed the door shut so suddenly Darby started.

A deadbolt was thrown into place. Darby stared at the door, blinking, listening for voices. She didn't hear any, then moved her head closer to the door and thought she heard something but couldn't be sure.

She was about to stick her card in the doorjamb when she decided to go to the SUV and wait. If the girl were telling the truth about her parents not being home, they would have to return at some point.

Darby checked her phone. Noel had left her a voice-mail, asking her to call him back immediately.

Settling back behind the wheel, she dialled his number, studying the house. All the upstairs lights had been turned off, and she thought she saw the flutter of a curtain, maybe a shade, as if someone were watching her, waiting for her to leave.

Caitlyn Lee had already left for the day, according to the man who answered the phone at the realtor's office, so Darby plugged the address Rosemary had given her into her phone's GPS and fifteen minutes later pulled into the driveway of a ranch house with black shutters and blocks of ice weighing down the front gutters. A silver Toyota Tacoma truck that had seen better days was parked underneath a carport, its roof covered with frozen snow packed so high it was a wonder the carport hadn't collapsed.

The lights were on inside the house. Darby knocked instead of using the doorbell.

No one answered the door.

Someone was home and she wasn't leaving until she'd spoken to Caitlyn – or discovered where she was and tracked her down. She rang the doorbell and knocked again, hard, and when no one answered she tried the doorknob and found it unlocked.

Darby opened the door. She didn't step all the way inside, just put her foot on the threshold and poked in her head, the air warm and smelling of potpourri. There were bowls of it everywhere, and in the tiny kitchen off the small living room she saw an opened bottle of wine and two glasses, one half full, sitting on the coffee table next to a Scrabble dictionary, the board game tucked neatly inside the box.

The house phone rang – a cordless unit mounted on the wall underneath a crucifix with a ceramic Jesus hanging on the cross. The artist had captured his agony and spared no expense in depicting the blood leaking from the nails and his crown of thorns, the deep gash along his side left by the soldier's spear.

The phone stopped ringing. 'Hello? Mr and Mrs Lee? Caitlyn?' she called out as the answering machine built inside the phone clicked on. 'I need to talk to you. My name is Darby McCormick.'

No answer.

Shit. She'd have to try again later.

Darby was easing the door shut when she heard the beep of a recording followed by a man's voice leaving a message: 'You're very pretty,' he said, his voice monotone. Unemotional. 'I like killing pretty things.'

44

Noel was driving a four-door KIA sedan, with heated black leather seats. While it didn't have that new-car smell, the interior was meticulously detailed. A pair of rosary beads hung from the rear-view mirror.

He had insisted on picking her up. He didn't get into specifics – just asked her in a tone that was both urgent and angry to park the sheriff's borrowed SUV in the driveway of Karen's home and stay out of sight until he got there, which would be in five minutes or less.

'He called,' Darby said after she shut the door.

'What?'

'The Red Ryder. While I was at the Lee house.' She told him what happened. 'He was watching me.' *And probably still is*, Darby added to herself.

'That's evidence,' Noel said. 'We can give that call to the lab, ask them to compare –'

'There's nothing to compare it to. The Vallejo police didn't record phone calls back then.'

'Right.' Noel sighed, rubbed at his face. 'Right, I forgot. Still, we should get the recording.'

'Agreed.'

They drove back to the Lee house. The lights were still on, the truck was still parked underneath the carport and, behind it, was a battered Honda Civic. The trunk was open, the interior packed with plastic grocery bags.

The woman who came out of the house looked and dressed the way Darby guessed a retired nun would: bone-white hair and orthopaedic shoes with a heavy wool skirt and sweater. She was overweight – obese, really – and clutched the railing as she moved down the steps, taking one at a time.

Noel introduced himself. The woman was Camilla Lee, Caitlyn's mother.

'We'd like a moment of your time,' Noel said. 'But first, how about we help you with these groceries.'

'God bless you, that would be wonderful.'

Then, when they were inside, the bags loaded on to the kitchen counter, Noel and Darby both looked at the phone, its red message light blinking.

Darby took the lead. 'Mrs Lee, do you know where Caitlyn is?'

'Out with her friends, I would imagine. She's very social.'

'What's her cell phone number?'

'She doesn't have one.'

Actually she does, Darby thought. *A burner.*

The woman looked slightly embarrassed. 'We don't own any,' she said. 'We're on a very tight budget here.'

'I understand.'

'Is Caitlyn in some sort of trouble?'

'No. I'm just trying to get in contact with her. Have you listened to your messages yet?'

'Not yet. Why?'

'I was wondering if we could listen. I think Caitlyn may have left a message for me here.'

Camilla Lee blinked in confusion behind her thick glasses. 'On our house phone?'

'I'm sorry for the confusion. May we just listen? It will only take a moment.'

The woman waddled over to the phone and pressed the 'Play' button.

Beep.

'Patty, it's me. Bob Pinkerton's truck broke down again, and I promised him I'd help get it back on the road before morning. I won't be home for supper.'

Another beep and a computerized voice came on and said, 'End of messages.'

Darby's brow furrowed as the woman said, 'That was my husband, John. He's a mechanic.'

'May I look at your phone?'

'Okay.'

Darby pressed the 'Play' button and held her finger down on it, to play any old messages that had been left on the machine.

Beep.

The answering machine's robotic voice came on and said, 'No new messages.'

Silence. Darby could hear blood pounding in her ears.

'Where are my manners?' Camilla Lee said. 'Can I offer you water or a Sprite? It's the store-bought brand but it tastes just like the real thing.'

45

Darby didn't speak until they were on the road.

'The son of a bitch must've gone inside the house after I left and erased it.'

'Okay.'

She turned to him. 'You don't believe me?'

'Of course I believe you,' Noel said, and then lapsed into thought.

Darby looked around the car. 'This doesn't look like a rental,' she said.

'More like a loaner.'

'But not from the sheriff.'

Noel shook his head. 'Bradley,' he said, and then he told her about what happened inside the hangar and his private conversation with Bradley, who'd had his car brought up that morning by one of the guys he'd asked to come to Fort Jefferson to do the forensics and paperwork on Cooper's Ford Explorer. As he talked, Darby noticed they were heading back to Big Sky; he had already programmed the lodge's address into the dashboard's navigational system.

Darby remained quiet while he spoke, concentrating on his words, surprising herself by not feeling angry. Maybe because Rosemary had already given her the heads-up about the Feds still pursuing the assault charges, allowing her time to digest the reality of her situation. Maybe because being shut out of an investigation by some pencil-pushing nitwit who was more interested in saving money than doing the right thing wasn't anything new to her.

But the Feds wanting to arrest her *was* new.

Darby had forced her thoughts back to what had taken place at the neighbour's house when Noel checked in with her. 'How are you feeling?'

'Not surprised,' she said. Now it was her turn to share. She gave him a rundown of her encounter with the next-door neighbour.

'What do you think that's about?'

'I have no idea. But this place . . .'

'What?'

'It's odd.'

Noel nodded in agreement. 'Small town, small minds.'

'We need to talk to the kid and the parents. I'm sure they knew Karen in some capacity – maybe she babysat the kid. We should go back there and wait for them to show up.'

'Too risky.'

'For me,' she said. 'Not you.'

'That's why I'm going to drop you off at the lodge. Then I'll come back and see what I can find out.'

'I can't believe this,' Darby said, but there wasn't any anger or heat in her voice, just a sad weariness at the politics involved.

They decided to get something to eat, but the closest restaurants were in Big Sky. The road ahead of them was pitch black, no lights except for the car's high beams. Darby felt like she was crossing an immense black sea, no port anywhere in sight.

She stared out the window, thinking, minutes ticking by . . .

She said, 'Let me talk to her.'

'That girl? You just said –'

'No. Vivian. The puppet master.'

'It won't change anything.'

'What's her problem with me, anyway?'

'Honestly? I don't know.'

'Noel, she must have said *something* about me to you.'

He chewed on that for a moment.

'You're not going to hurt my feelings, if that's what you're worried about.'

'I was telling you the truth before when I said I didn't know. She doesn't trust you. Said you were morally dangerous – her words.'

'What's that supposed to mean?'

'I'd say she doesn't like you.' Noel smiled tightly, hoping to interject a moment of levity. It didn't work.

'Give me her number,' Darby said, digging into her pocket for her phone.

If she were riding next to Coop right now, he would tell her calling was a waste of time. She would insist, and he would remind her to be careful and watch her mouth, knowing she wouldn't, getting frustrated, then mad when she didn't.

'She won't take your call,' Noel said. 'But if she sees my name flash across her caller ID . . .' He took out his phone and she watched him quickly thumb-key in the four-digit password to unlock it.

Noel hit the redial button. 'Enjoy,' he said, and handed her his phone.

Vivian didn't answer her office number. She wasn't answering any of her numbers. Darby didn't leave any messages.

She dialled the main line and asked for Vivian's secretary. The man who answered identified himself as her personal assistant, his voice young. Eager.

'She can't come to the phone,' the assistant said after Darby had given her full name. 'What's the best number she can reach you at, Miss McCormack?'

'McCor*mick*. Darby.' She gave him her cell number. 'I'd like to leave her a message, if I may.'

'Yes. Absolutely.'

'Tell her she's a coward.'

A pause on the other end of the line.

'Did you get that?' Darby asked.

'I did. Yes.'

'Excellent. Have a wonderful day.'

Noel took the steep and narrow road leading up to the lodge.

'You missed your true calling,' he said.

'Oh, yeah? And what would that be?'

'Diplomacy.'

Something Coop would say. Darby allowed herself a small smile. It vanished when she saw the four patrol cars parked in front of the lodge, their lights flashing.

46

Bradley, Darby thought, straightening in her seat. The son of a bitch had changed his mind about giving them a free pass and decided to call the locals in Big Sky. That, or he had already planned this ahead of time, told them they'd be arriving in his KIA.

She had another thought, one that seemed crazy on the surface but wasn't: Vivian was tracking Noel's cell signal – not with high-tech government stuff but with one of those ridiculously cheap and simple apps or programs where all you needed to do was enter someone's number and you could see on a map *exactly* where this person's phone was, stationary or moving. Vivian saw where they were heading and called the locals for support.

But even if they had asked the police to get involved, the locals wouldn't have been waiting for them to pull up to the lodge. They would have intercepted them at the bottom of the road or, preferably, somewhere along the highway, away from civilians – and they wouldn't have brought along a fire truck or an ambulance, both of which she saw parked underneath the enormous flat roof covering the front entrance. There wouldn't be crowds of people gathered outside, huddled together, their faces anxious as they spoke to one another, trying to figure out what was happening inside the lodge.

Noel pulled up against the far end of the walkway.

Darby got out, saw a local cop heading their way to tell them to move. Noel already had his ID out.

'What's going on?' Noel asked.

'Don't know, sir,' the cop replied. 'They told me to keep the area clear.'

The lobby wasn't in total chaos but she saw guests and staff speaking in anxious whispers as police radios crackled, their attention locked on a corner to the right of the front desk, where Darby saw the two young girls who had checked her in the other night. The thin one with the mousy hair had her arms wrapped around her wool sweater, her face drained of colour as a patrolman spoke to her. The other patrolman standing there – taller and broad-shouldered and holding a notebook, his back to the crowd – was struggling to remain patient, waiting for the blonde chubby girl with the braces to stop her sobbing so she could answer his questions.

Noel flashed his ID to the big cop.

'Body up on the roof,' Big Cop said. 'Maintenance man found him.'

'Description?'

'I don't know any details.'

Access to the rooftop, the cop told them, was by the main elevator across from the reception desk. Darby entered it with Noel. When the elevator doors opened, Noel exited first, Darby followed a moment later, Noel already having turned right, toward the patrolman stationed by the emergency-access door leading into a stairwell. It was alarm-operated, Darby noticed.

Up two flights of stairs, her footfalls echoing inside the metal stairwell like small gunshots. She felt the cold air, heard it whistling above her; saw her breath steaming as she reached the final set of stairs, the outside voices growing louder.

The roof was flat and made of gravel. Darby heard the stones crunching underneath her boots as Noel, far ahead of her, raced across the rooftop, toward the cops, firefighters and EMT workers gathered on the platforms ten to fifteen feet above them, their flashlights crisscrossing through the darkness. She saw four platforms, one for each water cistern.

A ladder was mounted against a wall in front of her.

The man in charge was the one who was plainly dressed: bald, fifties, a potbelly bulging underneath a winter coat. Darby recognized him from the Bozeman office but had forgotten his name.

Noel didn't flash his ID. He looked at the man and said, 'Deputy Chief Davies.'

'Agent Covington.' The man's gaze cut back and forth between Noel and Darby. 'What brings the *two* of you here?'

'I was just about to ask you the same thing,' Noel said.

'Big Sky is a part of Gallatin County, which gives me jurisdiction. Your turn.'

'We're looking for a missing Federal agent.'

'That business in Fort Jefferson?'

Noel nodded. 'Dr McCormick is a friend of Agent Cooper. She's staying here, at the lodge. I was dropping her off.'

'And what happened between the two of you in Bozeman is, what, just water under the bridge?'

'It was a misunderstanding. Where's the body?'

'Cistern Number Two. Guests were complaining about low water pressure and black water in taps and showers, and the maintenance man came up to investigate.'

'Can I see the body?'

Davies considered the question. 'You promise to share?'

'You've got my word,' Noel said.

'Okay, then,' Davies said, and offered Noel his flashlight.

47

Cistern Number Two was ten feet tall and about five feet wide. Access to the top was by ladder.

Noel put the flashlight in his jacket pocket and climbed, his breath steaming in the cold air and the wind biting against his skin and scalp. The stars provided him with a decent amount of ambient light.

He stopped when his head poked up over the lip of the cistern. He didn't see any water.

As he reached for his flashlight, he saw Darby, Davies and a couple of men – detectives, he assumed, given their casual dress – gathered along the bottom. Darby was the only one who wasn't looking up at him.

Noel climbed the final rungs and looked down into the cistern. It was about a quarter of the way full of water. He turned on the flashlight and moved the beam across the water, stopping when it locked on the face.

Davies cupped his hands over his mouth and shouted, 'Is that your missing person?'

Noel stared down at the water, a part of him wishing he were halfway around the world right now, back in Iraq, back in a country with a sun that wanted to melt your skin and an enemy that wanted to blow your head off your shoulders or remove your limbs with a roadside car bomb. Life had been so much simpler over in sand country; there, the enemy had a face. Noel knew who wanted to kill him, and why. Here, the enemy was faceless, didn't care about political agendas or causes. Here, the enemy was singular, existed solely to torture and kill the people you loved, and then retreated back to the shadows, where it rejoiced and thrived and gained power while you mourned, clawing at your hair and wishing you'd never been born.

Darby's voice now: 'Noel?'

'No,' he shouted into the air, the wind. He was looking at his sister, at her lifeless eyes, knowing she couldn't hear him and wishing she could. 'I'm sorry.'

Noel took his time coming down. Not because his legs were shaky or because he was feeling upset or wanted to cry, because he wasn't feeling anything. He was deliberately taking his time because he needed to think about what he was going to say, how to play it. He wanted – no, needed – an open line of dialogue with Davies, who probably outranked the Fort Jefferson sheriff. Davies could be an ally. Problem was, Davies was probably still holding a grudge against him for that mess back in Bozeman.

'There's a woman's body in there,' Noel said, sounding and feeling detached from his surroundings, from what was taking place.

Davies narrowed his eyes. 'The maintenance man said it was a man.'

'She has short blonde hair, so I can see why he might've got confused. And he probably didn't take a close look – just saw the body and got down the ladder as fast as he could.'

Davies studied Noel's face carefully when he said, 'Do you have any idea who she is?'

'I don't. But you might want to check with Sheriff Powers over in Fort Jefferson.'

'I know where he is.'

'There's a woman named Melissa French who supposedly left town.' Noel could feel Darby's gaze practically drilling into the side of his face. 'That woman in there might be her.'

'Anything else you need to tell me?'

'Yeah. The house that the French woman rented? We found two bodies in the centre of the house – call Powers, and he'll fill you in. In the interim, tell me what Dr McCormick and I can do to help.'

48

Darby's face was still red from the cold when she rounded the corner and saw three maid's carts in the hallway. One was parked outside her room. It was well after 7 p.m., and she ached all over from the cold and working with the cops on the roof. All she wanted to do right now was to sit in her room, unwind for a bit, and then use her computer.

The young kid tasked with cleaning her room had a shaved head and wore the same black shirt and jeans as the other employees. He smiled thinly. 'Sorry for the late visit,' he said, removing a fresh garbage bag from his back pocket. 'The staff got tied up and we're way behind because ... you know, on account of what happened today. I'm sure you heard about it.'

Darby sighed. 'Yeah.'

'I'm almost done, but I can come back if you'd like.'

'No. Go ahead and finish.'

'You sure?'

'Positive. Take your time.'

He brightened a little. 'Oh, and thanks for that nice tip you left. Very generous of you.'

'You're welcome.'

Darby grabbed her MacBook and went to check on Noel, who had booked himself a room at the lodge.

He didn't answer his door. She was about to call to see where he was when she decided to head downstairs, to the bar. It was practically empty, which didn't come as a complete surprise. A lot of people demanded to be switched to other hotels or simply cut their vacation short. The ones who stayed were given a discount rate along with gift certificates and drinks vouchers for the other restaurants and bars in the ski village.

She ordered a double bourbon, neat, then realized she hadn't eaten — and she had to eat. She quickly looked through the menu, ordered a cheeseburger with a side salad, and, as she carried her glass to a booth in the far corner, with its window view of the village, the bare trees strung with tiny white Christmas lights, she wondered how Noel was coping with the death of his sister.

Everything she'd seen pointed to suicide. Darby had examined the body after it had been loaded on the gurney. The cold water had preserved the woman's features and there was little bloating. Borrowing a flashlight, she examined Karen Decker's hands and found no defensive wounds. There were no cuts along her head or scalp. It all suggested suicide by drowning. Karen Decker had a history of suicide attempts, and homicide by drowning was rare.

And Karen had left a suicide note: the words 'please forgive me' written in black permanent marker across her Montana driver's licence. Her purse had been found at the bottom of the cistern.

An investigation of the lodge's nearby parking lots turned up Karen's vehicle.

Suicide was the logical conclusion.

So why is it still bothering me?

The last time she'd seen Noel was an hour ago, when he was inside the lodge's security room, helping the locals to sift through the camera footage to see how Karen had managed to access the roof. They had started with the date Coop arrived in Montana and then worked their way backwards through the DVR footage, hitting pay dirt when they viewed camera footage from the night of the 2nd of February.

Darby had already watched the security footage twice, along with Noel, who made a show of looking at his watch and then telling Davies that he had to excuse himself to make some phone calls.

Davies was good about sharing. When Noel asked for copies of the DVR footage in case the woman's suicide was connected to his missing agent, Davies agreed to send him copies. Noel told her privately that he would forward copies to her.

Darby opened her computer and accessed her email. Noel had received the files from Davies and sent them on to her. She played them now while she drank her bourbon. There was no need to adjust the volume, as the cameras didn't record audio.

The first file was footage taken from the lobby camera. At 2.32 a.m., a woman entered the lodge wearing dark jeans, L. L. Bean duck boots and a dark-green winter parka – the same clothes Karen Decker had been wearing when her body was pulled from the cistern. In the video, she had her hands stuffed in her pockets, and her head was covered by a hood with a fur trim. She walked quickly with her head bowed. Her face wasn't captured due to the camera angle.

The second and final video was taken from inside the elevator.

The camera was mounted on a rear corner of the elevator's ceiling, the camera angled so it had a full view of the doors and the control panel.

Karen entered with her head bowed and immediately turned to the control panel. She studied it for several seconds, as if confused about where she needed to go. Or maybe she was gathering the courage for what she had planned.

The doors slid shut. Eighteen seconds passed before she pressed the button for the top floor. Then she leaned forward and rested her forehead against the brushed aluminium wall above the control panel, and for the next eighteen seconds she shook uncontrollably – crying, Darby guessed. She had no way of knowing for certain, but she saw what looked like tears drop against the floor.

When the elevator stopped, Karen still appeared to be crying.

The doors slid open, and she hesitantly nudged her way toward the waiting hallway – then suddenly stopped, standing on the threshold between the elevator and hallway, as if straddling two worlds, unsure of what to do or where to go.

Thirteen seconds passed before she made her decision: she exited the elevator and entered the hall of white walls and dark-green carpeting. As the elevator doors slid shut, Darby saw Karen turn right, the direction that led to the end of the hall and the door for the stairwell that provided access to the rooftop.

The video ended.

There were no cameras in the hallway.

Entry to the rooftop required a keycard. Somehow

Karen had gotten her hands on one; it was found inside her purse. The serial number on the keycard showed that it belonged to an employee who had lost it near the end of the previous month – a nineteen-year-old kid named Randy Scott, who lived in the lodge-owned apartments. Randy hailed from Connecticut and told police he had never been to Fort Jefferson.

So how did Karen get her hands on the keycard?

Darby played the elevator footage again.

Why is this still bothering me?

Answer: Because I can't see Karen's face.

49

Vivian still wasn't answering any of her lines. Noel left her the same message on each one. 'Karen's dead,' he said. 'I sent you the two videos.'

He wouldn't be returning to Fort Jefferson tonight, so he booked himself a deluxe suite, which, ironically, was located directly underneath the part of the roof where Karen's body had been found.

When he entered the room, surveying its rustic interior and ample space, he found himself oddly hungry. Famished, really. He wasn't surprised or repulsed; the human body, no matter what it endured or was forced to endure, would always constantly demand three things: water, sleep and food, and usually in that order.

The room-service menu offered deluxe cuisine for its premier guests, along with bottle service: name your poison and we'll provide it. Instead of having the usual roadside club sandwich, cheeseburger or Cobb salad, he ordered a prime rib, prosciutto-wrapped asparagus and a bottle of Hendrick's gin.

'And don't forget the cucumber slices,' he told the young-sounding woman taking his order.

'Sir?'

'You can't drink a proper gin and tonic without cucumber slices. Didn't you know that?'

The woman chuckled. 'No, sir, I didn't.'

'You shouldn't. It's completely useless information.'

The hotel had repeatedly assured him that the room given to him was serviced by a different cistern; it was safe to drink the water and to shower. Noel had no intention of drinking the water, but he was going to shower, and did.

Standing under the hot spray, he wondered if pieces of his sister were inside the water, splashing against his face and hair and sluicing down his body and dropping to the tiles, where they circled the drain. He wondered if parts of her were captured in the steam he was breathing. Probably not, but he tortured himself with it, pretending that was the case, to feel something – rather than the nothing he did feel. The knowledge of finding his sister dead should have caused some monumental internal shift within him, but he moved numbly from one task to the next – washing and towelling himself off, then brushing away the coating of the day's coffee, which felt lacquered to his teeth and tongue.

Standing inside the bedroom, the towel wrapped around his waist, he remembered he didn't have a change of clothes. He'd left everything in Fort Jefferson.

He didn't want to put his clothes back on. It would be like putting back on that person. He liked this new person now standing naked in the bedroom, exposed and completely vulnerable – the way, he imagined, a baby felt when it came out of the womb: terrifyingly alive, every nerve ending exposed, all senses on red alert, yes, but new. Untainted. The future paved with roads of unlimited possibilities and success.

The closet held a robe, but it was on the smaller side,

and since he'd never liked robes anyway he slipped back into his trousers and tank undershirt and walked barefoot into the adjoining kitchenette and living area, with its gas fireplace. He had just figured out how to start it when his dinner arrived.

The food was tasteless. He ate everything quickly, without any enthusiasm. After he finished, he fixed himself a gin and tonic and took it and his laptop to the living area. He didn't sit on the leather sofa or club chair. Instead, he sat on the floor facing the fireplace, his legs stretched out, his back propped up against the sofa.

Noel opened the laptop. Now that he was alone, he could watch the security videos of Karen and deal with his emotions.

He had refilled his glass three times and he still felt nothing.

His phone rang. It was 9.45 p.m.

Vivian's tone was measured and even. 'Where are you?'

'Big Sky. You should come out here and visit. Absolutely stunning. It really is God's country.'

'Have you been drinking?'

'I'm having a Hendrick's gin and tonic, in your honour. Exactly five cucumber slices and one lime wedge, the way you like it when you're vacationing on Nantucket. I'm raising my glass to you right now. Here's to you. Wishing you nothing but good health and good fortune.'

'I watched the videos.'

And breathed a big sigh of relief, I bet. Noel thought back to that grimy interrogation room in Idaho, Karen arrested and telling them she just wanted to die. *Then die*, Vivian hissed. *Die and be done with it.*

'Tell me about Karen.'

He told her.

Vivian remained quiet after he finished. He knew what she was thinking about right now – the question she so desperately wanted to ask.

Finally, she did. 'Did you tell the police?'

Noel didn't answer. Chewed on an ice cube as he watched the fire.

'Did you tell the police who she was?' she asked.

'I did not.'

Vivian's sigh of relief was palpable.

'But,' he said, 'I plan on doing so first thing tomorrow morning.'

'I don't think that's wise.'

'Karen was in the water. Rotting.'

Vivian said nothing.

'People were *drinking* her,' he said. '*Showering* in her.'

'I know you're upset. I am too, which is why I'm going to fly out tomorrow. We'll handle this together.'

'He's here. The Red Ryder.'

'We'll look into what happened to Karen tomorrow, after I get there.'

'He called Darby.'

'What?'

'He called her – she was at someone's house and he called and left a message. He said, "You're very pretty. I like killing pretty things."'

'I want to hear this recording.'

'Can't. He went back and deleted it.'

'He went back and deleted the recording.'

'That's what I said.'

'So there's no evidence of it.'

'Nope.'

'Did you hear it?'

Noel knew where she was leading him. 'She didn't make it up,' he said. 'Why would she make up such a thing?'

'Because she wants to be a part of this investigation – even though there's not going to be one, at least at our end. The Bureau will be reaching out to Fort Jefferson, see if the sheriff there wants their help, maybe send a couple of profilers his way.'

'The Red Ryder is here and he called her.'

'Let's talk about this tomorrow. Until then, don't do anything rash, okay? Promise me that.'

'I will if you get on the phone with the Bureau and make them drop the charges against Darby.'

'I can't do that.'

'Can't or won't?'

'Noel,' she said, incredulous, 'this is the *Bureau's* decision. I had nothing to do with it, and there's nothing I can do –'

'Make it happen or I'll go public with the Red Ryder, Karen, everything.'

'Do you *really* want to attract that sort of attention to yourself?'

'You mean *you*. You don't want all of WITSEC's dirty laundry going public. That'll really screw up your chances for the big seat, won't it?'

'If the media find out who she really is – and how she died – if they start digging around, they'll find out everything: that she was a junkie and an alcoholic, that she was a prostitute and had multiple abortions, all of it. That's how she'll be remembered.'

'Are you threatening –'

'They'll find out about you too,' Vivian said. 'They'll discover how you changed your name, and everyone will know who you are. If that happens, I can't protect you. No one can. Once the genie is out of the bottle, you can't put it back in. Are you ready to live that kind of life?'

'Call off the attack dogs.'

'Is she there with you right now? McCormick?'

'Do it. That condition is non-negotiable.'

Vivian sighed. 'Okay. Let me see what I can do.'

He pulled the phone away from his ear and pressed his thumb down on the phone's power button as her tinny voice echoed over the tiny speaker. 'Don't go public yet, not until I come out tomorrow and we've had a chance to speak –'

The phone died, and she was gone.

Noel tossed the phone aside and felt an encroaching darkness. But he wasn't scared. This darkness was both familiar and familial. This was the darkness that had greeted him when he went on his first bomb run in Iraq; it had flooded his veins and lit up his brain as the Humvee sped down a moonlit dirt road and he saw his terrified face reflected in the window; when he was doing what they called 'the long walk' to an IED or when he was sending the robot to look at one while trying to dodge enemy fire and snipers trying to get a clear shot at his head. The darkness always swept through him with the quickness of an oil spill in an ocean, screamed at him during the heat of battle, or whispered to him while he was asleep, or gathered around a campfire set up at the forward operating base after another mad, mad day among the sand people. He heard it now as someone knocked on his hotel-room door: *You're not supposed to be here, breathing this air, feeling this sun. None of it's real. You're living a borrowed life. You're supposed to be dead.*

50

Noel opened the door and saw Darby standing beyond the threshold, wearing dark jeans and a white collared shirt with leather boots.

Her face changed when she saw his, then she took in his bare feet and trousers and tank undershirt and said, 'Were you about to shut down, call it a night?'

Noel shook his head and backed up. 'Come on in,' he said. She did, and then, as he shut the door: 'Did you eat?'

Darby nodded. She didn't ask him if he'd eaten; she was looking at the empty plates stacked on the dining trolley.

'I eat when I'm under stress,' Noel explained – not that she had asked for an explanation. But the empty plates looked like a celebratory dinner instead of simply a meal. 'First rule of combat. Eat whenever you can, sleep whenever you can.'

'I forget to eat, usually, when I get wrapped up in something.'

'I've got a bottle of gin. The good stuff. Want a drink?'

'Absolutely.'

As he went about collecting what he needed, he noticed she was wearing the exact same clothes she'd worn all day yesterday, although the jeans and shirt didn't have any blood on them.

'When did you have time to get your clothes cleaned?' he asked, opening the ice bucket on the trolley.

'I didn't. Spare set.'

'You keep an identical set of clothes?'

'Four sets, actually. Wear the same ones every day.'

'Like Steve Jobs did?'

Darby nodded and slid her hands into her back pockets. 'I don't like waking up having to think about what to wear,' she said. 'These clothes are comfortable, I can wear 'em to work, then out, whatever.' A grin tugged at the corner of her mouth. 'I like routines.'

'You'd make an excellent soldier.'

Darby smiled. She had one hell of a smile. Kind that when it was aimed at you hit you straight through the heart, made you feel like you had become the centre of her universe.

'What?' he asked, handing her a glass.

'My father used to tell me I'd make the world's *worst* soldier.'

'Because you don't like taking orders.'

'Taking orders is fine,' she said. 'Following orders that are stupid or complete bullshit? That never made any sense to me. If I'm going to put my life or career or reputation on the line for someone or something, I sure as hell get a say in whether or not I want to do it.'

Noel carried his glass with him to the sofa, surprised when she sat next to him, tucking one leg underneath her thigh so she could face him.

Noel watched the gas-fed flames licking the fake logs. She took a sip of her drink and from the corner of his eye he saw her wince slightly.

'Little heavy-handed on the gin,' she said.

He looked at her. 'This from someone who drinks her bourbon straight.'

'Only way *to* drink it.'

'Bourbon straight up, prefers to wear the same outfit every day and doesn't hesitate to jump into the fray. Cooper was right.'

'Right about what?' she asked, her voice strained.

'He told me you were not only the single most interesting woman he's ever met in his entire life but the single most interesting person.' He held her gaze. 'He's right.'

When she looked away, to the fire, Noel sensed her discomfort – not from his compliment, which he meant. She didn't have low self-esteem or hold a negative image of herself. Her discomfort, he knew, came from thinking about Cooper, wondering if he were alive or dead.

Darby turned to him. 'How are you holding up?' she asked, tucking her hair behind her ear.

'The truth?'

'Always a good place to start.'

'The truth is I feel . . . I don't feel. Anything.'

'You're in shock.'

'No,' he said calmly. 'No, that's not what this is. I've been in shock. This is . . . Karen was my sister. That night –' He paused for a beat and slid his attention to the jumping flames. 'When the firing started, her first instinct was to protect me. She threw her body on top of mine, took the bullets and saved my life. When he came back, she pushed me to keep running and then she ran in the opposite direction so he would see her and follow her. She didn't want him to find me. She was still thinking about me – *only* thinking about me.'

Noel drank deeply from his glass, relishing the cold and pleasingly burning tingle of the gin sliding down his throat.

'He shot my father first, Karen said. One shot to the head and his brains exploded inside the car. My mother was screaming, Karen said, and he shot her three times in the face. By the time he turned the gun on my sister, she was already on top of me. He unloaded the rest of his clip into her back.'

Noel didn't want to talk about the rest of it. Never had, to anyone. He probably wouldn't have continued if the person sitting next to him were anyone but Darby McCormick. For well over three decades, the best and brightest minds within the FBI had tried to find the serial killer they called Traveler. Darby McCormick had found him and killed him. She had found and killed several others because she was bright and dedicated and relentless; because, as Cooper had told him one night over drinks, she didn't back down from a challenge or a fight. *Not once*, Cooper had told him. *Not as long as I've known her.*

'Karen had gotten me unbuckled from the car seat,' Noel said. 'We were out of the car, in the parking lot. No streetlights there – no lights anywhere at all, just pitch black. Quiet. She saw headlights coming back down the road. She knew it was him by the erratic way he was driving – knew that he was coming back for her, to make sure we were all dead.'

Every time Noel thought about this moment, he succumbed to the same childish wish every human being experiences at one time or another: the desire to be able to go back in time and correct a moment. If he could replace the two-year-old boy with the man he was now – a man who could not only dismantle bombs but knew his way around a rifle and a pistol; a man who could box and

261

wasn't afraid to get hit or shot – this older and stronger Noel could have helped Karen. He could have saved her and his parents. He wouldn't be trapped in this alternate universe in which he was living, where he felt panic upon reaching every corner and wondered why God had spared him that night and also allowed him to survive the sun-baked streets and marketplaces in Iraq, where almost every person wanted him dead.

'I was already running away, the way two-year-olds do,' he said. 'I was running back toward the campground, not that I knew where I was going, and Karen was hobbling away in the *opposite* direction, to try to lure the Red Ryder away from me. When he pulled back into the lot, he didn't use the spotlight this time. He had a pen-light taped under his pistol. She saw it when she looked over her shoulder, and then he fired. That was the shot that almost severed her spine.'

His eye had started to twitch again. 'He found me,' Noel said. 'Karen said he was dragging me across the road by my hair. I was screaming my head off, trying to fight him – I have no memory of it, only Karen's word. He dragged me over to Karen and said, "I'm going to take your baby brother with me. Then, when I'm on the high-way and reach eighty or ninety, I'm going to throw him out the window." Then he left her there to die.'

He felt the all-too familiar tightness building inside his chest, as though a nest of snakes had been released within him, their scaled bodies wrapping around his lungs and cutting off air, squeezing his heart like a fist – the begin-nings of a panic attack.

'I don't know if I was with him when he drove to a gas

station about a mile away from where we were parked. The place had closed for the night, and he used the pay-phone there to call the police. Told them he wanted to report a family in a station wagon who had been shot and gave them the exact address. I'm guessing he dropped me somewhere near or close to Highway 92, because that's where I was found the next day – I'd almost been hit, I'm told, because I was crossing the road.'

Noel took a long pull off his glass.

'I always wonder what he did to me during that time I was inside the car with him,' he said. 'Why he decided to let me go instead of throwing me out the window.'

51

Noel could see Darby looking at the fire too, wanting to make it easier for him to talk, he supposed.

'Karen, my parents . . . I don't have any memories of them,' he said. 'Karen was pretty much out of the picture by the time I was old enough to understand I had a sister, and when I met her – every time I met her, it was like I was sitting down with a stranger. I never really knew her, or my parents. They were my family, but after that night . . . I've always felt like he'd stolen memories from me. All these years, I'm mourning ghosts because it's what I'm supposed to do, you know?'

Darby nodded encouragingly, listening.

'Whatever Karen asked of me, I've either done it or tried to do it. But, as time wore on, it felt like I was doing it out of a sense of obligation. Now that it's over, I . . .'

'You feel guilty for having survived,' she said. 'Again.'

Her words felt like a kick to the stomach. The truth often felt that way.

'I was on the phone with Vivian right before you came over,' Noel said.

'She called you back?'

'After she found out about Karen? She most certainly did.' He saw that her glass was empty. 'You want a refill?'

'No. I'm all set for the moment. Keep talking.'

But he didn't want to talk. He never saw the benefit of

talking about himself with shrinks because they loved to pick apart your words. And the pill-pushers didn't want you to talk. All they wanted was to write prescriptions that sent him to a chemically induced half-life state where he felt like he had one foot in the real world, the other in some purgatory in which he was a zombie, his brain dead.

Darby, though, was neither. She was simply someone who understood the complicated wiring of the human brain.

He licked his lips, looking at his empty glass. He wasn't drunk but on his way to it – and the booze had liberated something in him, a need to unburden himself. He'd always joke with his therapists that if they *really* wanted to get their patients to open up they should have a well-stocked bar in the waiting room.

'I feel –' Noel sucked in air through his nostrils and exhaled loudly. 'The truth? About Karen? I feel relieved. So *fucking* relieved.'

'I know how you feel.'

He opened his mouth, about to call *bullshit* on her, that she was giving him lip service; then he remembered something he'd read in her file, an event she had endured when she was a teenager: she had been home alone one night while her mother was at work and someone had broken into her house and tried to kill her.

Darby watched the fire. 'My mother was a nurse and she had to work a lot of night shifts at the hospital,' she said. 'I was home – I was fifteen at the time – and someone broke into my house and tried to . . . I think he came there to abduct me. Anyway, I managed to escape to my mother's bedroom, where I locked the door. Then I heard the doorbell ring.'

'Your friend, whatshername, Melanie something.'

'Melanie Cruz.'

She was about to ask the question and he said, 'It was in your file.'

'So you know he took Melanie instead of me.'

Noel nodded. *And she was never seen again*, he added privately.

Darby looked at him, her eyes full of the same sad understanding. 'It's normal, what you're feeling,' she said. 'Knowing that doesn't make it any easier to carry. There were times early on – Christ, there were weeks when all I did was wish someone would come along and carry it for a while, you know, give me a break so I could rest up.'

'What do they call that? Wishful thinking?'

'That, or magical thinking. Indulging in it is what traps you.'

'What did you do?' Noel asked, surprising himself. He never talked about this except with a handful of soldiers who had become close friends. He never expected to talk about it with a civilian – and a woman, no less. But Darby was a soldier. He was sure of that.

Darby considered the question. He stared at her artlessly perfect profile in the firelight. She was ridiculously beautiful – definitely not the sort of woman you'd picture running all over the country chasing madmen. For some reason he thought back to that moment yesterday evening when he told Darby to take the seat at the front of the helicopter, Bradley shooting him a look like Noel had stolen something from him. Beauty made many men envious and jealous. Treacherous. But beauty could also help you forget about the present and the past, allow you to get lost in the possibility of a life where you woke up every day greeting the sunrise instead of dreading it.

'It doesn't change,' she said.

'What doesn't change?'

'The outcome. No amount of wishing or fantasizing about how, if you could go back in time to the event, you would do such and such and save the person's life and emerge the hero – no amount of praying or talking about it in therapy – there's nothing you can do to change the outcome. It's fixed. Done. Over. The only thing you have control over is your choices, whether you want to accept what happened and carry it, or choose to ignore it. I always chose to carry it, because it gave my life shape and purpose. At the end of the day, our choices are what define us. Our ability to choose is the only control we have.'

Darby put her empty glass on the coffee table beside her and stood.

He didn't want her to leave. Wanted her to stay, keep talking.

'You sure you don't want another drink?' he asked.

'No. I definitely don't want another drink.'

Noel got to his feet, trying to hide his disappointment. 'Darby –'

She leaned forward and kissed him.

52

Almost every woman Noel had slept with preferred – or wanted – to be the submissive. He always made the first move, and once things moved into the bedroom he wasn't shy about telling them what he wanted, how he wanted to be touched and where, when to stop. When he looked back at his sexual encounters (as he often did), he seemed always to choose women who were overly eager to accede to whatever he asked for or wanted.

So it took him completely by surprise when Darby made the first move. She kissed him gently, her hands resting against his chest as she explored his lips. Her lips were soft and full and slightly cold from the ice in her glass. He could taste the gin and lime on them and on her tongue, inhaled the smell of the shampoo in her hair and the clean scent of soap on her skin.

Her hands slid up his chest and moved around to his neck, to the back of his head, where she clutched his hair between her fingers and pressed him closer to her, kissing him more aggressively, hungrily, like she had finally discovered whatever it was he had willingly stolen from her, and now her body was tensing, preparing to fight to get it back. He felt himself hardening against his pants, and when she moved her lips away he said, 'Do you want me to stop?'

'What I want,' she told him, smiling, 'is for you to stop talking.'

She pulled off his undershirt, nearly ripping it. He felt the heat from the fire on his skin, and when she went to work unbuckling his trousers he moved his hands to the buttons on her shirt.

'No,' she said. 'Let me do it.'

When his trousers slid down his legs and pooled around his feet, he thought she was going to take a few steps back and undress herself in front of him, maybe take his hand and lead him to the bedroom. Instead, she manoeuvred him to the floor, in front of the fire. He lay back against the soft carpet and after she straightened he watched as she stood above him, unbuttoning her shirt. She wasn't wearing a bra, and when she slipped out of her jeans and he saw she wasn't wearing underwear, a part of him wondered if she had planned this moment before coming to see him.

Under normal circumstances, he would have been flattered. Under normal circumstances, he wouldn't have cared. But today was anything but normal; he had found his sister dead inside a water cistern, and he was sure Darby had been thinking about Cooper these past hours, wondering – imagining – that he too was lying dead somewhere.

Suddenly Noel found himself in the supplicant role.

She was more muscular than he'd thought – not in a masculine way but incredibly and unbelievably fit, barely any fat on her. In the light from the fire he saw her muscles move and constrict as she straddled him.

When he went to touch her, she grabbed his wrists, surprising him by her strength. She forced his hands above his head and pushed them underneath the bottom of the leather club chair and said, 'Keep them right there,' and then she straightened and reached behind his back, her fingers fumbling against the fabric of his boxers, searching for the waistband, staring down at him like she was daring him to move. He didn't, kept his hands right where they were, gripping the wood frame of the chair, even when she mounted him.

Her eyes widened slightly and a small gasp escaped her throat. Noel, again surprised by her strength, felt her thighs tighten against him, and his mind flashed back to the *Wonder Woman* comics he'd read as a kid, the heroine one of a long line of warriors from some Amazonian tribe of tough, powerful women capable not only of conquering men but, if they so chose, devouring them.

She swallowed. 'Give me your hands.'

He did. She placed them on her breasts and began to move up and down, slowly. When she found her rhythm, she let go of his hands and leaned forward, placing her hands on his shoulders, her fingers digging into the meat of his skin. When she suddenly straightened and arched her back, her arms reaching around her and hands gripping his knees and digging into his skin, her pelvis grinding against his like she desperately needed him to release something to make her whole again, he realized what he had already suspected: she was imagining Cooper beneath her, not him.

Darby whipped her head to the side, her long hair spinning behind her head and spilling across her shoulders. 'Noel?'

It took him a moment to find his voice. 'Yeah?'

Darby looked deeply into his eyes for the first time.

'I don't do cuddling,' she said.

24th of February
Wednesday

53

Darby came awake lying on her side, in a tangle of sheets and cooling air, Noel breathing softly beside her.

She hadn't planned on staying the night. After the living room, they had moved into the bedroom for a repeat performance. Afterwards, she had allowed herself to fall asleep because the bed had a king mattress. Only a king offered a clear line of demarcation, straight down the middle, giving both parties ample room to stretch out and, most importantly for her, to sleep without being touched.

Darby rolled on to her back. She felt strangely relaxed.

So why was she wide awake at – she checked the night-stand clock – 4.28 a.m.?

She wondered if the Red Ryder was awake right now.

Darby folded her hands behind the back of her head and stared up at the ceiling, seeing the video of Karen entering the elevator and punching in the number for the top floor. She had been found inside the water cistern, and the maintenance man and the cops said there was no way Karen could have pushed aside the cistern's top by herself because she was too small, not strong enough.

Karen had entered the elevator alone.

But was it her? You couldn't see her face on the videos.

Where was Coop?

Could he still be alive?

She saw Karen Decker's bloated body floating inside the water cistern. Her pulse raced and she felt sick and clammy all over.

Darby slid out of bed, not wanting to wake Noel, wanting him to sleep, knowing he needed it. Good. He hadn't stirred. She walked barefoot across the carpet and quietly closed the door, and, as she went about collecting her clothes from the floor, she thought back to the one-night stands from her college days, her girlfriends sharing how they'd tiptoed through some guy's dorm room or shared apartment and slinked out in the middle of the night or the early-morning hours, praying to God they wouldn't run into someone they knew, mortified when they did. She never understood or shared their feelings. Why should she feel the least bit embarrassed or ashamed for wanting to have sex? *She* was the one who chose. Not the man. Her.

Noel's phone was on the kitchen counter, charging.

Darby picked it up. When the screen came to life, asking for the four-digit password, she punched in the same numbers Noel had during their drive to Big Sky. She walked past the living room and quietly opened the sliding glass door and stepped out on to the terrace that was barely big enough for one person, the sky still dark but the world below her, with its snow-compacted trails leading to the village and the ski lifts, lit by the small white Christmas bulbs strung around the bare branches of the trees.

The mountain air was cold enough for her breath to

steam. She knew her way around an iPhone and found Vivian's contact info easily.

Vivian Whitney had six numbers. Given the early hour, Darby started with the woman's home number.

Two rings and then a crisp and concerned voice answered the phone: 'I'm here, Noel. What do you need?'

'This is Darby McCormick.'

'How did you get Noel's phone?'

'I borrowed it. He doesn't know I'm calling you.'

'For some reason I doubt that. You slept with him, didn't you?'

'I want you to get these bullshit charges against me dropped.'

'I guess Noel didn't tell you I work for the US Marshals. The Bureau is the one pursuing the assault charges. Frankly, I'm surprised you're not in handcuffs already. Now, if you'll excuse me, I have to make some calls.'

'Why are you so threatened by me?'

'Please,' Vivian scoffed. 'You give yourself too much credit.'

'Then explain it.'

Silence greeted her on the other end of the line. For a moment Darby thought Vivian had hung up. Then the woman said, 'It's who you are.'

'Oh. And who is that?'

'Death,' Vivian said, without malice. 'You invite it. That's not hyperbole; it's well documented in your file. Everywhere you go, you leave bodies in your wake. You're as relentless as a cancer cell, programmed to do one thing and one thing only: hurt, destroy and kill in the pursuit of your personal agenda.'

'You don't even know me.'

'Doctor,' Vivian said, 'I see you every time I look in the mirror.'

Darby propped a foot up on the railing.

'As far as I'm concerned, Noel is in danger as long as he's near you,' Vivian said. 'I'm not willing to have him become collateral damage on your mission to find Cooper – not that you're going to find him. He's dead, and you know it. Goodbye, Doctor.'

54

When Noel opened his eyes, he was surprised to find it well past 9 a.m. He hadn't slept so long – or so deeply – in what felt like ages.

He wasn't surprised, however, to find Darby no longer in his bed.

She had texted him, though, saying she was downstairs in the main dining room, and asked him to join her for breakfast. She had sent the message fifteen minutes ago, so he figured he had time to grab a quick shower.

He texted her back on the way to the bathroom, his muscles sore, and when he put the phone down he saw himself in the mirror, the red claw marks across his chest and shoulders, the back of his waist and buttocks.

His phone buzzed. A text had come through. The sender was listed as 'Unknown'. He read the two lines sent to him.

YOU WOULDN'T STOP CRYING INSIDE THE CAR THAT NIGHT, SO I GAVE YOU SOMETHING SPECIAL TO CALM YOU DOWN. YOU LOVED IT SO MUCH YOU FELL ASLEEP SUCKING IT.

The main dining room was as tall and wide as a school gymnasium, with high ceiling fans blowing the heat from the two enormous fireplaces back down to the guests, the air uncomfortably warm and smelling of bacon, sausage, eggs and all the other food placed in steaming buffet trays set up along long tables. The restaurant was packed, filled with bright morning sunlight coming from the floor-to-ceiling windows facing the ski lifts. The diners and people milling about the buffet tables or waiting at the build-your-own-omelette station were dressed in various states of ski gear, some even wearing their ski boots, which forced them to walk slightly hunched forward and to lumber awkwardly, *clump-clump-clump*, like better-dressed versions of Frankenstein's monster.

A few minutes of searching and he eventually found Darby sitting at a table in the rear, away from the windows, so the sunlight wouldn't reflect off the screen of her MacBook Air. She was talking on the phone and scribbling on a yellow legal pad. He caught several men eyeing her, even the ones who were sitting with their wives or girlfriends. She hadn't eaten yet; all he saw on the table was a glass of water.

Noel went to the coffee bar. He was aware he was sweating, and it took him a moment to stop his hands from shaking. All he could think about was that text. He had a solid idea who had sent it – but of course couldn't prove it. And he had a solid idea of what the text implied, of course, and even if he had no memory of it the thought made his stomach bottom out. He wanted to reach inside his head and pull that thought away, as though it were a visible, living thing.

Most of the people around him were talking about what had happened yesterday, the body in the cistern, and he learned the lodge had lost over half its guests. The ones who decided to stay behind had been given a reduced rate – provided they signed a waiver acknowledging that they had been informed of the health risks of the water inside the cisterns and were being provided with bottled water.

As he slowly carried two mugs of coffee to Darby's table, something else began to haunt him: his dead sister. Last night he had fallen asleep seeing Karen's bloated face, how her eyes seemed to stare up at him, accusingly, from the surface of the water. *You abandoned me when I needed you the most and now look at what's happened. Look at what you did.*

The sadness and guilt (there was plenty of that) that swept through him weren't just for Karen but also for him – for them. When he was surrounded by families and couples in large groups, as now, everyone here bright-eyed and happy and eager to hit the slopes, he wondered what his life and Karen's would have been like if that night had never happened, his mind pushing him into a parallel universe. Maybe they would be here right now, dressed in their own ski gear, his parents here too, maybe looking after Karen's kids, maybe all of them about to hit the slopes. More than anything, he wondered what it would have been like to wake up each morning feeling . . . not necessarily whole but not haunted.

Darby hung up and placed the phone down on her pad. She had taken lots of notes. She didn't see him until he was practically next to the table, and when she did he felt that familiar awkwardness that always came the morning after sleeping with someone for the first time. He wondered how she was feeling. If she would bring up what had happened last night or choose not to talk about it at all.

'Good morning,' he said, placing the mugs on the table.

She studied his face carefully. 'Are you all right?' she asked.

He had no intention of telling her about the text. Even if he wanted to, there wasn't any proof: whoever had sent the text had used one of those programs that deleted it within seconds after being read. The text was gone.

'Just tired,' he said. 'Didn't sleep well. You?'

'Me neither.'

Noel pulled out the chair beside her and sat down. 'Well, you look positively beautiful. As always.' He sensed her discomfort – saw it in her eyes. 'Did I say something wrong?'

'No. Not at all.' She placed a hand on his forearm and squeezed, and smiled, meaning it.

'You should do that more,' he said, picking up his mug.

'Do what more?'

'Smile.' He took a sip of his coffee. 'You have a killer smile.'

Darby stared at him for a moment – not defiantly, not wishing he wasn't here, but trying to read him.

'This is the part where you say, "Thank you, Noel."'

'Thank you, Noel.'

'And then you say, "And by the way, Noel, you look impossibly handsome this morning."'

'You do,' Darby said, turning back to her legal pad. 'I'm sure women tell you that all the time.'

'But it would mean so much more coming from you.' When her eyes jumped up to meet his, he held her gaze for a moment, to let her know he was serious, then nodded to her pad. 'What'cha got there?'

'What I wanted to talk to you about.' Darby crossed her legs as she reached for her mug.

'Before you do,' he said, 'may I tell you about an interesting development in the case?'

Darby grinned around her mug. 'I'll allow that.'

'Thank you. Caitlyn called me.'

'The girl from the real-estate office?'

Noel nodded. She had called him while he was in the shower. 'She asked if she could speak to us privately,' he said.

'About what?'

'The house. More specifically, the prayer room.'

'The what?'

'That's what she called it, "the prayer room". She said a lot of the houses in that neighbourhood have these secret prayer rooms, where parents would put their kids to punish them, so they could be alone and, you know, pray, get closer to God.'

'Did you tell her we know she called someone?'

'I did. She got real nervous when I asked too. Said she'd tell us everything when *we* met.' He saw the question Darby was about to ask and said, 'Caitlyn asked if you were coming. I asked her why and she said this – and I'm quoting her here – creepy old guy came into the office yesterday asking questions about you. Something about finding your car keys and wanting to know how he could get in contact with you.'

'Name?'

'He didn't tell her. Or so she says. Personally, I think she's frightened.'

'Where is she now?'

'At home with her mother. Wants us to meet her there as soon as we can.'

'Let's go,' Darby said, and began packing her stuff up.

Noel tried to engage her in polite chitchat as they waited for the valet to bring the car around, but she didn't feel like talking, didn't want to talk. She wanted to use the time standing here in the fresh air to organize her thoughts – more specifically, a theory she had been nursing these past four hours.

Then she realized Noel had stopped talking to her. He was toying around with his phone, checking emails. She needed to address this now, before they got under way.

'I'm sorry,' she said.

Noel looked up, his eyes hidden behind a pair of Oakley mirrored sunglasses. 'For what?' he asked.

'I'm not ignoring you. I'm just thinking.'

'It's fine. No worries.'

'I have a tendency to get lost inside my head. I forgot to ask: how are you doing this morning?'

'You mean with my sister?'

Darby nodded. 'I should have asked you earlier.'

'I'm . . . fine, thank you.'

'I've been thinking,' Darby said, shifting the strap of her briefcase to the other shoulder, 'maybe you should go home.'

Noel didn't answer.

'This might take a long time,' Darby said. She could see him staring at her through his sunglasses, his eyes darting across her face. 'Even if it doesn't, you're putting your career on the line if we're found to be working together.'

'My career,' he said flatly.

'Yeah. We're heading back to Fort Jefferson. If Bradley or those other two guys with him find me, my guess is that they'll arrest me.'

'I'm working on that.'

'Vivian? I don't think she's eager to help.' *Especially after the phone call I had with her this morning*, Darby thought.

'Listen to me,' he said quietly and took off his sunglasses. She left hers on, a pair of Ray-Ban aviators. 'I'm a man of my word. When I tell someone I'll do something, I do it. No excuses. This job? It doesn't define my character; it's the other way around. I'll see this to the end because I owe Karen at least that. Cooper too. It's not up for discussion.'

Darby kissed him, wanting to believe everything he'd said, wanting to believe there were people in the world like her who placed value in words and delivered on promises. People like her and Coop.

55

'Karen,' Darby said once they were on the road. 'How long had she been hunting the Red Ryder?'

Noel's brow creased in thought. 'How long?' he asked.

'When did she get serious about it?'

'Since . . .' He adjusted the rear-view mirror, thinking. 'Well, for as long as I can remember. Why?'

'She ever share any notes with you?'

'She scribbled down stuff, would call me with ideas and theories — that sort of thing. But if she had some sort of, you know, file system, or folders on her computer, she never shared them with me. Or Vivian. And I doubt she had such a system in place because in those days she was drunk or high or both.'

'You ever share case files with her?'

Noel shook his head vigorously. 'Absolutely not.'

'What about Vivian?'

'I can say with absolutely one hundred per cent certainty that Vivian did not share anything with Karen. Vivian almost always refused to discuss the Red Ryder with Karen — that job fell to me — because Vivian wanted her to move on with her life. We both did.'

'So it's fair to say what she knows about the case she got from all those books written on the Red Ryder, Internet searches and websites, chat rooms.'

'I'd agree with that.'

'What about discussing potential suspects? There are names floating around on the Internet.'

'I've seen them too, and, while some of them look good on the surface, they were all thoroughly investigated and cleared. But, to answer your question, no, we never shared any information about any suspect – not that there were ever that many. What Karen did was . . . She moved around a lot in the beginning. When she wasn't staying with a family, she was either in private rehab or, after a suicide attempt, a private medical facility – always private, any chance we got, because those places didn't have to worry about bending state or Federal regulations; we could slip her in under a false name, no questions asked or red flags raised.'

Darby nodded, looking out the front and side windows, the flat world excruciatingly bright even with her sunglasses, the sun glinting off the snow.

'Nine times out of ten,' Noel said, 'she landed there because she had convinced herself she had found the guy who was the Red Ryder and attacked him, or was caught stalking him.'

'What kind of proof did she have?'

'Zero. All she had to go on was that she had seen his face that night. And for as long as I'd known her she was convinced he was trying to hunt her down and kill her. Most of the time she was either drunk or high, and with the mental disorder – well, you get the picture. During the periods when she was trying to get clean and sober – even then she believed he was still stalking her. Said he'd call her wherever she was and breathe into the phone. Sometimes she'd follow a guy and get caught by the police and we'd have to get involved, or she would contact Vivian or myself through the mail – mainly me, because she didn't like dealing with Vivian – and she'd give us some guy's name and address, sometimes providing us with evidence, like a piece of paper the guy had handled, maybe a glass or a soda can.'

'And you investigated each person?'

'We ran the guy through the computers, sure, but not one of them added up to being the Red Ryder – not even remotely in the ballpark. We'd show everything to Karen. Meet with her and show her she was wrong.'

'How'd she take it?'

'Not well. She said he was stalking her and she was pissed and angry and hurt we didn't believe her.'

'Was she on her meds those times?'

'No. She refused to accept that she suffered from manic depression. And she was probably still using, or drinking. But if the letter she sent me is true – *if* – she not only got clean and sober seven years ago, she went back on her meds.'

'After she suddenly decided to leave WITSEC.'

Noel nodded. 'She made the call, not us. Just ran off. Never contacted either of us. Then seven years later I get a letter from her with evidence.'

'And during that time, you never tried to track Karen down?'

'Now and then. If I'm being honest, I didn't put much effort into it.'

Probably because he'd felt overwhelming relief from having had that burden lifted from him, Darby thought. 'No one knows who the Red Ryder is,' she said. 'Suspects popped up during the decades, but not a single one of them ever amounted to anything – unless there's something I don't know about.'

'No, you're right.'

'When I did my dissertation on the Red Ryder, I don't remember any suspects who lived in or came from Montana.'

'That was the first thing I checked, when the handwriting came back as solid,' he said. 'Those early suspects that turned up on the police's radar, even the ones Karen thought might be the Red Ryder – Vivian and I went through each and every one to see if there was some tie to Fort Jefferson or to any other place in Montana. We found three, but two of them are dead, and the other is serving thirty for the sale and distribution of methamphetamine.'

They were on the highway now, and, as she reached inside her briefcase, she was gripped with that irrational yet overwhelming feeling she'd had when she first arrived here, how the already massive sky seemed to get larger and larger, about to reach down and swallow the earth. It made her feel small. Insignificant.

'For the moment,' she said, 'let's assume what Karen said in the letter is true: that she was clean and sober, and taking her meds. She'd stabilized. There's no way she believed she could have done, all by herself, what every other law enforcement agency, with all of their combined manpower, computer databases and forensics experts, had failed to do: find the Red Ryder. So what's the next best thing?'

'What do you mean?'

'There's no way *she* can find him, so revenge is off the table, wouldn't you say? Revenge and justice?'

'I buy that.'

'So the next best thing – the only thing she's got left – is closure.'

His brow furrowed again, only this time he rubbed his forehead with his hand, as though the word 'closure' had given him a sudden headache.

'Victims of violent crime need closure,' Darby said. 'Usually it comes in the form of the perpetrator being arrested and then sentenced. I'm not suggesting this works for everyone, because it doesn't. But knowing the perpetrator was caught and, hopefully, imprisoned, does allow the victim to have an ending – an opportunity to heal.'

'Only Karen didn't have a chance at any of that because the Red Ryder was never caught and tried for his crimes.'

Darby nodded. 'As the years piled up, deep down I think your sister knew the chance of uncovering the Red Ryder's true identity in her lifetime was slim to none. And yet she wanted – *needed* – some sort of closure. She needed to know who did this to her, and why, and she was never going to. The only way she could achieve some measure of closure was through the use of a surrogate – someone who would understand not only the horrors she'd endured that night but also the pain and torture she went through after –'

'She had me. I was a victim too.'

'You were, but you were too young – had no memories of what had happened to you, to her, to your family. She needed to talk to someone who'd gone through the exact same horror *she'd* experienced that night – as well as the horror of what had happened *afterwards*, when she survived. I think your sister devoted her time, energy and resources to tracking down the only person who could truly understand her and, maybe, provide her with some measure of closure in her lifetime: the Red Ryder's last known victim.'

Darby was reaching into the briefcase sitting between her legs when Noel straightened a bit in his seat. He swung his head to her.

'You're telling me Jennifer Byram is *here*? In Fort Jefferson?'

'She would be easier to find than the Red Ryder,' Darby said, removing the leather folio containing her legal pad. 'What if your sister *did* find Jennifer Byram? What if Karen found her and moved in right next door?'

56

'I checked all the properties available for rent when Karen moved here last year,' Darby said, 'and there were much cheaper properties – and ones closer to downtown. We're talking a difference of two, three hundred bucks a month in rent. Karen comes here, a single woman with no kids or a job, and she ends up renting a house that's more expensive and we don't know why – and we need to know why because I'm telling you she chose *that* house for a specific reason.'

'And you think it was to live next to Jennifer Byram?'

'It's a theory.'

'Small problem,' Noel began.

'The realtor showed Karen four properties. I have the copies you gave me.'

'So why look at four?'

'Smokescreen,' Darby said. 'Karen didn't want to let anyone know that she was trying to move next door to Jennifer. And think about how odd it would seem if Karen had walked into a realtor's office and said, "I want to rent *this* property." The realtor would have asked why. Karen would have needed to come up with a lie – a solid one. But if she saw, say, four properties, she could simply choose the one she really wanted without tipping her hand.'

'Okay. Let's find out who lives there now and see what –'

'Already did that. Title and the name on the mortgage are the same: Stanley Joseph Avery. He's fifty-eight, works in construction for a place based off Fort Jefferson called Ezekiel Building. Wife's name is Zuriel.'

'Zuriel? What kind of name is that?'

'Means "God is my rock". Had to look it up on Google. It's a boy's name, but whatever. They have two children – girls. Tricia is thirteen, Miriam is eight.'

'How old is she? Zuriel?'

'Don't know yet. I have someone working on it.'

'Who?'

'PI who works for my lawyer, guy named Booker. Here's where it gets interesting,' Darby said. She had the folio open and was flipping past pages. 'Zuriel's maiden name is Matthew. The PI ran both her married and maiden names through all the databases. The woman has no credit cards or any bank accounts – has never had a credit card or opened a bank account.'

'You got a picture of her?'

'No. There's nothing.'

'What do you mean, nothing?'

'My guy swears neither Zuriel Matthew nor Zuriel Avery has an online presence on any of the social platforms – Facebook, Instagram, Twitter, Vine –'

'Vine? Never heard of that one.'

'Allows you to post thirty-second videos. Same deal with the husband, no online presence.'

'What about the kids?'

'If they're on any of these platforms, they're using a screen name because my guy can't find a single thing.'

'How deep did he dig?'

'Deep enough for him to say there's no way anyone in this family has an online presence.'

'What are they, Amish?'

Darby removed a folded piece of paper from a side folder. 'The Byram girl was born and lived in a time when we didn't have all this technology. There are only two pictures of her that I could find online.'

'One good picture is all we need.'

Darby unfolded the piece of paper. On it was a laser-printed colour copy of the last photograph taken of Jennifer, when she was twelve. It had been taken at someone's pool: Jennifer, wearing a red one-piece and her skin the colour of caramel, her brown hair wet and slicked back, leaning forward with her hands on her bony knees, mugging for the camera.

'This is the picture that ran in all the books about the Red Ryder,' Darby said.

'I recognize it. You have a colour printer stashed inside that briefcase?'

Darby shook her head. 'The lodge has one,' she said. 'The girls working the reception desk let me use it. I've also got a hi-res copy loaded on my MacBook. The Byram girl would be in her, what, early fifties now?'

'Around that.' Noel was tapping his thumb against the steering wheel, thinking.

'Caitlyn's home is close to Karen's neighbourhood,' Darby said. 'How about we make a quick detour first?'

'I think I better call Caitlyn, let her know we're running late.'

Karen's neighbourhood looked different in the late-morning sunlight. Not nearly as remote and lonely as Darby had originally thought but an actual neighbourhood, where all you had to do was walk a little way to see one of your neighbours. Most of the houses were set back from the road and hidden behind trees, a mailbox mounted on a post at the end of the driveway.

'What's wrong?' Noel asked her.

'Nothing. Just my first time seeing this place in broad daylight.'

Noel pulled up against the kerb. Darby took out her MacBook and showed Noel the high-res picture of Jennifer Byram. He studied it for a moment and then finally nodded and opened the car door. There was no need to talk; they had already discussed how they were going to approach this, if Zuriel Avery was home.

Darby's pulse raced, her skin tingling in anticipation as Noel rang the doorbell. She glanced over her shoulder, looking past the pristine white blanket of snow in the front yard and past the trees to the main road, the sun warm against her scalp. She could see some of the houses there and wondered where the Red Ryder lived, if he had been tracking them and was now somewhere close by in these woods, watching, when the front door opened.

57

The woman who answered the door looked as though she had recently been released from a hospital. She leaned on an orthopaedic cane and wore white sneakers with Velcro straps instead of laces. The oval face beneath the brittle and lifeless blonde-grey hair was puffy from lack of sleep, her fair skin carved with wrinkles. Her blue eyes, though, were bright, and she was smiling.

Jennifer Byram had blue eyes.

'Good morning,' Noel said, Darby studying the woman's face from behind her sunglasses. 'Are you Zuriel Avery?'

'I am. How may I help you?'

'I'm Agent Covington with the Federal Bureau of Investigation. This is Dr Darby McCormick. She's a consultant with the Bureau.'

The smile faltered as a nervous tremor moved through her. Which didn't mean anything. It was a completely normal reaction when you found an FBI agent suddenly on your doorstep. 'Okay,' Zuriel said, her voice and posture guarded. Nervous. She stared at Darby's motorcycle jacket, wondering why a woman, let alone a doctor, would be wearing such a thing.

'I'm sorry to bother you,' Noel said, 'but we're hoping we could get some information from you regarding your next-door neighbour, Melissa French.'

Noel's tone was relaxed. Informal. The woman, Darby noticed, clenched her cane at the mention of Melissa – Karen.

'You mean my *former* next-door neighbour,' Zuriel said, straightening, like she had suddenly caught a whiff of a bad odour.

The woman had higher cheekbones than Jennifer Byram, but they could be acquired by having dermatological fillers or surgery.

Darby wished it were the dead of summer instead of winter. Instead of wearing baggy jeans and a white turtleneck underneath a dull pink sweatshirt, a small gold cross hanging on a thin gold chain against it, Zuriel might have answered the door in shorts and a T-shirt, the scars from the bullets and the life-saving surgery on display, a roadmap back to that traumatic moment in her childhood.

'May we come in, Mrs Avery?'

Zuriel Avery considered it for a moment or two, Darby sure the woman was going to say no. If she did, there was nothing they could do. They weren't working an investigation, and Zuriel wasn't a suspect or a witness. They were here simply to gather information.

'Of course,' Zuriel said. 'Of course, please come in. Forgive my manners.'

The inside was warm and fragrant with the smell of freshly cooked bread. The white lace curtains had been drawn, filling the living area and part of the kitchen with a drowsy light. A few logs snapped inside the wood stove in the corner.

The young girl with the blonde hair Darby had met last night sat at the rectangular kitchen table along with another girl, this one taller and older and thinner. The thirteen-year-old sister, Tricia. A pair of thick textbooks were open in front of them; another was in front of the chair their mother had vacated. On the other side of the table and facing the girls was a stand-up whiteboard displaying what looked like algebra.

Zuriel shut the door. Darby stared at the whiteboard. 'I homeschool my children. These are my daughters, Tricia and Miriam.'

Both girls got to their feet at the same time and stood with their arms folded. They wore white turtlenecks underneath brown smocks with multiple pockets – a sewing experiment gone horribly wrong. The older one smiled brightly. The younger one, Miriam, stared down at her textbook – but not before glaring at Darby, to let her know her presence wasn't welcomed.

'Good morning,' Tricia said.

Miriam didn't speak or lift her head.

'Miriam,' her mother said sternly. 'Don't be rude.'

'Hello.'

Darby said, 'We met last night, actually.'

'Yes, I heard. Miriam opened the door when Sissy told her not to, and now she's being punished.' Zuriel looked from Darby to Noel and said, 'My husband had chest pains in the middle of supper, and we took him straight to the hospital. He's okay – not his heart but a torn pectoral muscle. Sissy was left in charge and she told Miriam not to answer the door but she did. Isn't that right, Miriam?'

A solemn nod from Miriam.

'Girls,' the mother said, 'take our guests' coats and hang them up, please.'

After they handed over their coats, Zuriel stared at Darby's shoulder holster.

'What kind of doctor are you?' Zuriel asked.

'The kind that carries a gun,' Darby answered.

Zuriel made a face, like this was something a lady would never do.

Noel said, 'Mrs Avery, may we speak to you privately? Some of our questions are . . .' He let his words drift off, leaving Zuriel to fill in the blanks.

Zuriel nodded in understanding.

When her daughters returned, she said, 'Girls, go on upstairs.'

'Momma,' the older daughter said. 'Can Miriam and I bake bread?'

'Fine. Go on, then. Wait.' Zuriel turned to Noel, Darby openly studying the woman's lips without her sunglasses. 'May I get you water or a glass of milk? I don't have coffee, tea or soda. We don't allow caffeine in our house.'

'We're fine, Mrs Avery. Thank you.'

The girls, excited at getting a break from their school-work, gleefully left for the kitchen, which fortunately was walled off from the living-room area. Even better, a radio had been turned on, playing a song that Darby guessed was soft Christian rock: a young woman singing a ballad about a highway to heaven.

Zuriel resumed her seat at the head of the table. Noel sat to her right, Darby to her left. She shut the textbook and pushed it aside. Darby noted the name of the publishing company printed on the side and recognized it. Not that long ago, it had been all over the news for agreeing to print textbooks for public schools that removed evolution and Darwin and substituted Creationism and a belief that dinosaurs roamed the planet 4,000 years ago and coexisted with man. The textbook had had huge sales among ultra-conservative Christians.

Darby also noticed that the woman seemed to want to speak only to Noel because he was a man. Darby suspected Zuriel Avery was a devout Christian woman. In her world, with its strict value system and hierarchy, men were second to God.

Had Jennifer Byram's parents been religious? Or had she, like Karen, discovered Jesus somewhere along the way?

'Melissa French,' Noel said.

Her features collapsed, as though Noel had mentioned the name of someone who had caused her a great deal of pain. Her shoulders slumped and her head bowed slightly as she studied her hands. Sitting this close to her now, Darby saw that Zuriel's upper lip had the same double curvature as Jennifer Byram's – the characteristic known as a Cupid's Bow. A lot of women had it. It didn't mean the woman sitting here was Jennifer Byram.

Noel looked at Darby from across the table. Darby shrugged and shook her head.

Noel said, 'I take it you knew her, Mrs Avery.'

A slow nod from Zuriel, her lips pursed. 'I thought I did,' she said, her voice pinched tight.

'What happened?'

The woman took in a deep breath and quickly collected herself. The sound of kitchen cabinets and drawers being opened and closed, and bowls and other things being placed on counters filled the momentary silence.

'She just up and left without saying goodbye,' Zuriel said.

Noel flicked his attention to Darby and then he said, 'I take it you two were friends.'

'That's what I thought too. Melissa moved in next door, oh, must've been nine, ten months ago. I went over there with the girls about a week or so after Melissa moved in so we could introduce ourselves. Brought over a banana bread too. You would have thought I handed her a filet mignon, the way Melissa thanked me.'

Noel had his hands folded on the table and leaned forward, listening deeply.

'I took her everywhere,' Zuriel said after a moment. 'Introduced her to my friends and brought her to my church. Had her over for dinner and barbecues, even birthday parties. And I was glad to do it, because Melissa was a good, kind woman who became a good friend. Or so I had thought, until she just up and left.' Zuriel shook her head, clearly hurt and mystified at what she had done to deserve such treatment.

Noel nodded in understanding. 'I'm sorry,' he said, meaning it. 'How well did you know her?'

'Well enough to let her babysit my girls, have 'em sleep over there sometimes with Baby James. He's my nephew. Melissa loved babysitting kids, was great with 'em. I paid her in the beginning and then later on after we became . . .' Zuriel didn't finish her thought.

'What?' Noel prompted.

'I didn't have no brothers or sisters. I was an only child.'

Like Jennifer Byram, Darby thought.

'Meeting Melissa,' Zuriel said. 'It was as though I had

found my own Sissy. Sister. We shared everything, practically did everything together.' She smiled bitterly. 'I know now it was too good to be true.'

'Why's that?'

The woman's thoughts turned inward. Her eyes filmed and then, as if realizing what was happening, she blinked back her tears. 'Melissa isn't who she pretended to be,' Zuriel said, slumping back against her chair. 'I saw the police cars over there the other day. Whole bunch of 'em. What did she do now?'

'Now?'

'She was in trouble with the law. Wasn't she?' She shook her head sadly, the gesture of someone who deep down had suspected a certain truth about a person and, after choosing to ignore it, came to realize that her instincts had been correct from the very beginning. 'I knew she was hiding something,' she said, glancing toward the doorway to the kitchen, where her girls were banging around, talking. 'I sensed it.'

'She ever say anything to you?'

'Not in so many words. Melissa was one of the saddest people I've ever met.'

Noel, Darby noticed, had retreated to some private, walled-off area within himself so he could speak about his now-dead sister. 'Sad about what?' he asked.

'I wish I knew. There were times when she'd burst into tears for no reason. Sometimes I'd stop by her house and when she answered the door I could tell she'd been crying. Miriam, when she stayed over there, she'd tell me Melissa cried a lot at night in her sleep. Melissa ain't never said why, and it wasn't my business to push. One time, though, she told me . . .'

Zuriel swallowed. Licked her lips. 'One time she confessed that she just felt so lost,' she said. 'So lost and so lonely and so very depressed about life. I brought her to the church. The pastor spoke to her, but it seemed to make Melissa only more upset.'

'Do you know why?'

'Melissa had accepted our Lord and Saviour Jesus but she . . . I didn't think she could accept who and what she was. Whatever sins she was carrying, they were dragging her down, keeping her lost and alone.' She stared at Noel imploringly. 'What did Melissa do? I know it ain't none of my business, but it's been eating me up. I've been worried sick over her.'

Noel looked at Darby and scratched his eyebrow with his thumbnail – the signal that he had nothing left to ask and for her to show Zuriel the photograph of Jennifer Byram.

'Mrs Avery,' Darby said, reaching into her briefcase. 'May I show you a picture?'

58

Darby opened her MacBook. 'This is why Melissa French was here,' she said, and placed the laptop in front of the woman.

'There's nothing on the screen,' Zuriel Avery said.

'Hit a key.'

'Which one?'

'It doesn't matter.'

Zuriel pressed a key and the screen came to life, showing the picture of Jennifer Byram.

It was as if Zuriel had awoken from a deep sleep only to discover a long-bladed hunting knife had been shoved into her stomach; her eyes widened in surprise and then fear, her mouth forming a silent 'O'. The blood didn't drain from her face; instead, her cheeks flushed with colour. She straightened her shoulders and gripped the arms of her chair to push herself up, on to her feet. But she didn't move, just glared at the computer in shock and hatred, as if it had unearthed a secret she was sure had been successfully buried, never to return.

In that moment, behind the puffy face and the folds of fat, the brittle grey hair that had been dyed bleach-blonde, Darby saw the tanned twelve-year-old girl in the red one-piece who had mugged to the camera, her whole life in front of her, any road she chose lined with gold and possibility and the unlimited joy of youth.

Darby said, 'Hello, Jennifer.'

Zuriel Avery – Jennifer Byram, the Red Ryder's only other surviving victim – looked up from the MacBook and glared at Darby, wanting to reach across the table and murder her.

'You knew,' Darby said. 'All this time, you knew Melissa French was Karen Decker, didn't you?'

Jennifer Byram didn't answer the question.

'Karen's dead,' Darby said. 'She killed herself.'

Jennifer's eyes slammed shut. She looked on the verge of crying.

Darby leaned in closer. 'Karen believed she had found the Red Ryder,' she said.

Jennifer, her eyes shut, was shaking her head.

'Jennifer, look at me.' She wouldn't. Darby said, 'The Red Ryder is alive, and he's living in Fort Jefferson or somewhere close by. You have to help us –'

The daughters walked into the living area, the younger carrying a wooden tray holding thick slices of homemade bread with a stack of white plates and three glasses of water, sprigs of mint stuck to the ice cubes. The tray seemed too heavy for the girl's hands; Miriam struggled to carry it, and Darby thought the girl would drop it. But her older sister reached over Miriam's shoulder and grabbed the tray, steadying it, easing it to the part of the table next to Noel.

Then Miriam focused on her mother. 'Momma, what's wrong?'

Jennifer wiped at her face, forced a smile. 'Nothing's wrong, baby girl. I'm just feeling sad, is all.'

Miriam glared at Darby as Tricia said, 'Please have some of our homemade bread.'

Noel smiled politely.

Tricia said, 'I brought you some grass-fed butter from the farm.'

Darby wasn't looking at the girls; her attention was locked on the mother, Zuriel Avery/Jennifer Byram, the woman staring down at the table. 'If you don't want butter,' Tricia said, 'I can bring you some preserves we canned ourselves. We have raspberry, blueberry and boysenberry.'

Noel, his eyes on the mother, said, 'I'm fine, thank you. Would you girls please excuse us for a moment? We need to talk to your mother.'

'Mr Covington,' Miriam said, 'I need to know if you accept the Lord Jesus Christ as your personal saviour.'

Noel turned to the young girl. Darby did too and saw Miriam's face staring imploringly at Noel, waiting for an answer, as her sister's hand came up from one of the side pockets of her smock, holding a box-cutter.

59

One time, after Karen had been arrested for stalking a 69-year-old retired schoolteacher she was utterly convinced was the Red Ryder, Noel had gathered his courage and asked his sister what it felt like to be shot. This was a week before he was due to be shipped overseas for his first tour in Iraq, before his daily life would consist of visiting sun-blasted shithole towns and villages in the daylight, then raiding them at night, under the cover of darkness. It didn't matter if the sun was up or down, dozens of people – a lot of women and children, far more than he had ever imagined – wanted either to blow his head off his shoulders or to blow him up with an IED planted in the road, or inside stacks of rotting garbage, or, on one memorable occasion, inside the dead body of an Iraqi policeman.

'It's not like on TV or the movies,' Karen said, picking up a French fry from a grease-stained container and dipping it into a plastic cup of ketchup. They had been sitting in an interrogation room somewhere in the Midwest, although Noel couldn't remember where. What he did remember was the two of them sharing burgers and French fries and drinking chocolate milkshakes while Vivian dealt with the people in charge, again using all of her muscle and connections to sort this out, make it disappear.

'Dad loved spaghetti Westerns with Clint Eastwood,'

Karen said, picking up the sweating paper cup holding her milkshake. '*High Plains Drifter* and *The Outlaw Josey Wales* and *The Good, the Bad and the Ugly*. The bad guys, when they got shot, they'd grip their chests or backs and, you know, stumble about theatrically, pretending to be in great pain before they collapsed against the ground and died. That's not real life.'

Karen wiped her mouth with a napkin. 'The moment that bullet hits,' she said, 'your body is flooded with adrenalin, so you don't feel much of anything. But at some point you realize what's happened to you, and then you realize you're going to die, and all the things you ever wanted or wished for in your life – the good stuff, like wanting to be married and have kids, and even the stupid, meaningless stuff like I never got to own a Ford Mustang – it's all coming at you, flooding your head. You realize you'll never come close to touching them let alone achieving them. You're alone – only this loneliness is something you can never recover from, but the scary part is everything you are, what you wanted and wished for, what you fought for and won – none of it matters, because in that moment you no longer matter, you're leaving. Forever.'

Noel was looking across the table at Darby and catching the alarm exploding on her face when he felt something sharp pierce the left side of his throat, near his collarbone. Pain ripped its way up his neck and across his jaw and to his ear before he jumped to his feet, grabbing at his neck and knowing what had happened but not understanding how or why. Blood – his blood – sprayed against the faces of the two girls, across the loaves of white bread, and, as he stumbled against the wall, clawing at his throat and unable to talk, he looked out the window, the bright-blue sky hovering over the tall pines reminding him of a late-summer afternoon he'd spent on the beach with Karen, Vivian having moved her there to dry out while Vivian made arrangements to give her another identity and another chance at a new life. Karen, wearing jeans and a baggy sweatshirt, sat in a beach chair, hugging her knees to her chest. It was her second day without booze or coke, and Noel remembered how his sister had looked at him once, like all she wanted was for him to hold her hand and lie to her, to tell her everything was going to be okay, her life still full of potential and possibilities. Morsels of happiness.

60

Darby jumped to her feet so fast she knocked back her chair and almost turned the table over when her thighs hit the underside of it. The table crashed down to the floor, scaring the older girl, the one holding the box-cutter.

Noel was up on his feet too, spinning wildly, madly, bouncing off the wall and window behind his chair and spraying blood, one hand pressed against his neck and the flap of white-belly skin dangling from it, the other clawing at the air as though it contained the antidote he needed not only to save his life but to turn back time.

Darby already had her hand on the safety of her handgun, her eyes on the two girls, both of their faces red and wet. The older girl looked as if she had just finished her first ride on a rollercoaster: blinking with excitement and nearly breathless, the fear already dwindling, soon to be forgotten.

Miriam was furious. She looked up into the face of her sister and screamed, '*It was my turn! You promised!*'

Darby had her nine out as the eldest handed the box-cutter to her baby sister, like she was passing a baton. Noel had collapsed on the floor near Darby, the blood pumping and spurting between his fingers so dark it looked black.

'*Drop it,*' Darby shouted. She felt Noel's hand clawing at the cuff of her jeans and she saw the eight-year-old beaming at having finally been given the box-cutter.

'*Drop it*,' she shouted again, only this time she backed up to give herself distance between the target – targets, she reminded herself, there were three targets here.

But only Miriam was moving. Her sister looked solemnly down at the table and the mother remained seated, hands folded on her lap and slowly shaking her head. 'You have no authority here, missy,' she said. 'Only God.'

'*Grab her, Sissy!*' Miriam shouted as she darted from around the table, making her way toward the living room – the fastest route to the front door. '*Grab her and hold her down so I can cut her throat!*'

The older one didn't move and the mother remained seated, their heads bowed, as if what was happening wasn't worthy of their attention. Darby told herself the girl was evil and needed to be put down – the sister and the mother as well. Put them all down like rabid dogs because whatever this was, it was a part of them.

But she couldn't kill a child. She beat the girl to the door and threw it open, the sunlight and cold, fresh air that greeted her feeling as though it belonged to another world.

Darby ran down the steps.

No, an inner voice countered. *Turn around and blow the kid out of her shoes and then go back inside the house and put the rest of them down.* Then *make the call.*

She didn't stop running. She glanced over her shoulder and, incredibly, saw the girl following, the box-cutter gripped in her tiny, bloody fist.

Darby ran past the end of the driveway, into the street, and turned right.

Stopped running.

Straight ahead, people were standing on opposite sides of the street, as if waiting for a parade. Had to be several dozen people, and when they saw her, they filed wordlessly into the street together and started coming her way – fathers and mothers holding the hands of their youngest children. A boy no older than three was holding a rock, being led forward by his mother. A few men were armed with shotguns, but almost every male she saw was holding some other weapon – rocks and baseball bats, even a tree limb, its end having been whittled to form a spear.

Darby turned, and was unsurprised to see another crowd heading her way – with Sheriff Powers at its head, the only one who wasn't holding a weapon.

A small army surrounded her.

The town of Fort Jefferson.

Behind Powers she saw faces she recognized: the man who had picked her up at the accident site and driven her to the Moonlight Mile Lodge; the two young women who had checked her in. Darby saw the chubby one with the braces and remembered how she was inconsolable that evening when Karen Decker had been found inside the water cistern. *You helped arrange that – helped make it look like Karen killed herself*, Darby thought.

Thought, *That's why Karen's face couldn't be seen in the video.*

You, everyone in this town and the people at the lodge – you're all working together.

Something hard, like a small rock, hit her back. Darby whipped around and saw a doughy-faced mother grab the arm of a young boy who couldn't have been older than four.

'You do *not* throw a single rock until you are told,' she hissed.

Miriam stood at the edge of the driveway smiling, as though she had just entered a room and discovered a surprise birthday party had been arranged for her.

Fifteen rounds in her magazine and she had another fifteen in the spare clip tucked in her shoulder holster. Thirty rounds total and she knew she would never survive, but she could take people with her – starting with the sheriff.

Darby brought up her weapon.

Powers smiled.

Go on, his smile said. *I dare you.*

She pulled the trigger.

Click.

The sheriff's smile grew wider, his eyes hungry. She pulled the trigger again.

Click-click-click-click.

'Don't bother,' Powers told her, less than fifteen feet away from her. 'We disabled the firing pin.'

But when? The only time she hadn't had her gun on her was last night, when she went to see Noel. She had locked her gun in the room safe.

But hotel employees could bypass any room safe, because they had the master code. They had the codes and keys to every room, every space inside the lodge. She remembered the young kid who was cleaning her room on the evening Karen's body was discovered and wondered if he had accessed her safe.

Miriam had joined Powers. The sheriff waved her away and Miriam stood defiantly, seething, the wind ruffling her hair and her brown smock. The people simply moved around her, not taking any notice of the box-cutter gripped in her small hand or the blood on her face and clothes, and then the crowd swallowed her.

They had formed a circle around Darby, clearly itching to use their weapons on her, to beat her and throw rocks, bleed her right here on the street in the middle of the day.

Is this what happened to Coop?

Powers was clearly the one in charge; he stood apart from the others. He sized her up and down. Behind him, she saw the young woman from the realtor's office, Caitlyn.

She's a part of this too.

Powers saw where she was looking and said, 'I had her call Noel. We were waiting for you at her house, but then I saw you took this detour, courtesy of the GPS tracker we installed on your car.' He reached into his pocket. 'Way I see it, you got yourself two choices: submit or fight.'

A boy not much older than Miriam edged his way past the throng to the front. He moved behind Powers, carrying a red plastic beach bucket full of stones.

'*Stone her now!*' a voice cried out. It sounded like a young girl's.

'*No!*' This from Miriam, who had suddenly pushed her way through the crowd. Her cheeks were mottled red, not from the cold winter air but from anger. 'No, it's *my* turn.'

The boy holding the bucket said, 'The Lord God teaches us women should be seen and not heard.'

'Hush, the both of you,' Powers said, 'or you'll be spending some time in the prayer room.' The Ziploc baggie pinched between his fingers held a folded handkerchief. Then, to Darby, 'The stone or the rag? Which do you prefer?'

'Jackson Cooper,' Darby said. 'Where is he?'

Powers sighed, like he was dealing with a child. Everywhere Darby looked she saw savage faces and more than a few knowing smiles and grins. No one answered.

'The stone or the rag?' Powers asked again.

Miriam struggled to keep quiet, no doubt wishing she had the strength to knock the sheriff aside and tackle Darby, take the razor to her throat.

'Last time,' Powers said.

'What did you do to Jackson Cooper?'

'You don't get to die knowing all the answers,' Powers said. 'That comes later, if the Lord God decides you're worthy.'

Darby said nothing, a part of her brain thinking she could push her way past the crowd and start running, outrun them all, a marathon to nowhere.

'It won't work,' Powers said, as if sensing her thoughts. 'We'll catch you.'

The sun felt warm on the back of her head and shoulders, with Darby not knowing what to do, feeling powerless.

'Decision time,' Powers said.

'The rag.'

Disappointed faces everywhere and a few groans.

Powers pulled the handkerchief from the bag.

Balled it in his fist and stepped forward.

The sheriff placed one hand on the back of her head and Darby tensed, ready to fight. She could break his nose and one of his arms before she hit the pavement.

Powers smiled. 'Go ahead and try,' he said. 'Either way, I'm gonna leave here satisfied.'

When he pressed the wet rag against her face, Darby sucked in chloroform and another chemical she couldn't identify, and she thought of Coop, hoping that whatever was going to happen she would be delivered to him, in this life or the next.

Then, as she began to drift away, as her body began to slump, she heard Powers say, 'That's it, just give into it. Go ahead and sleep. All the answers you ever needed are coming, everything's gonna be just fine.'

February
Day Unknown

61

Darby slowly came awake to the softness of a pillow against her cheek. She was lying on her side, on a mattress. A blanket covered her – what felt like a down comforter. She felt warm. Safe.

Then she remembered what had happened inside the house and on the street, the mob of people wanting to stone her to death.

Whatever chemicals Sheriff Powers had soaked into his handkerchief were still inside her; it seemed to take a great effort to open her eyes. When she did, she saw a beige wall lit by a soft light coming from somewhere behind her.

Her brain reacted to the dim light by sending a spike that shot across her forehead.

Darby moved her limbs and discovered she wasn't bound or gagged – at least as far as she could tell. The only sound she heard was her own breathing.

She shut her eyes and took in deep breaths, reminding herself that she was alive. That whatever was happening would not only pass but that she would deal with it.

You've been here before, a voice said.

Stay here, the voice said.

Go back to sleep.

And she did.

*

When Darby next woke, she was still lying on her side. Her eyes fluttered open and she saw the same soft, warm light. She was no longer facing the wall but a pair of bunk beds. They sat directly across from her, a matching set with dark-blue comforters and pillows.

Miriam was sitting on the bottom bunk.

Darby flinched – or at least had the sensation of it. She found she couldn't move. Didn't have the will for it.

Miriam's cheeks were wet and red with anger, her eyes puffy and bloodshot from crying. She seemed to be doing everything in her power not to jump to her feet and lunge.

'I *hate* you,' the young girl said.

Said, 'I want you to be dead.'

Darby tried to answer. The words had formed inside her head and were on her tongue but she found she didn't feel the need to share them. She heard a man's voice, soft and warm, coming from somewhere inside the room:

'Miriam, remember what the Bible teaches us about understanding and compassion.'

The girl bunched the fabric of her dress in her fists, her eyes burning with rage, and something else – loss. Darby was sure she'd seen that too.

The man said, 'Now come on, baby girl, you've got work to do.'

Miriam didn't move. 'You ruined *everything*,' she told Darby. 'You're going to rot in hell. Every last one of you.'

Miriam burst into tears. She grabbed at her face and started stomping her feet, as though she were raging against the world's coming to an end, Darby closing her eyes and drifting away, back into the darkness.

The next time Darby came awake, she moved her limbs.

Found that she hadn't been restrained.

Her boots had been removed but she was still wearing her jeans.

Her shirt.

She didn't hurt anywhere, hadn't been hurt, as far as she could tell. The pain from earlier was gone, replaced by a dull headache, her mouth and throat as rough and dry as sandpaper.

Her limbs felt heavy as she pushed away the comforter and then sat up, swinging her legs off the bed.

It was a queen, big enough for two adults.

Nice sheets.

A dark-brown, low-pile carpet separated the bed from the bunks. That, and a hard plastic storage compartment built into the wall, the top holding a pair of lamps, both of which were turned off, and an alarm clock, which was unplugged, no time on it. Someone had left her a clear plastic glass full of water and a plate with bread, cheese and an apple.

'Drink some water,' a voice said. 'You'll feel much better.'

It was the same voice she'd heard speaking to Miriam earlier.

Darby turned to her left, looked down the length of the bed and saw a slightly built man sitting in a hard plastic chair. He was hunched forward, elbows resting on his knees and his legs spread wide to give his hands room to work on removing the skin of an apple with what looked like a black KA-BAR military knife. He had brought a small lamp over so he could see what he was doing.

When she finally managed to focus on his face, she saw the old man from the diner, the one who'd worn the rainbow suspenders and a black T-shirt and cleared away the plates. Now he wore a pair of pressed khakis with a white shirt.

Darby took in a deep breath, felt her brain-fog start to clear a bit. Sitting on either side of him were a pair of long bureaus. Behind him was a sliding door, which was closed. She saw another sliding door to her right, just off the foot of the bunk beds. That door was also closed.

She noticed something else: no windows.

Not a room inside a house, because the space was narrow and confined, like the cramped quarters on a submarine. Where was she?

'Would you like this?' he asked, and held up the apple, the curled skin dangling off it reminding her of a snake. She shook her head, and he went back to peeling his apple.

'Can't stand the skin,' he said, concentrating on his work. He was well into his sixties, maybe even early seventies, and had soft white hair that was neatly combed. 'Was that way ever since I was a little boy. Good thing too, because the skin is where all the pesticides reside, you know. Can't get the poison out no matter how hard you scrub.'

Darby stared at the glass of water.

'Go ahead,' he said. 'There's nothing in there that will hurt you.'

Darby grabbed the glass, not caring what might be in it, and began to drink. When her glass was almost empty, he said, 'If you want more, there's a full bottle on the floor next to your bed. You should eat too. You've been pretty much out of it for a good amount of time. You're going to have one God-awful headache when the withdrawal kicks in.'

Withdrawal? From what?

'I'm sorry,' he said, like he actually meant it, his eyes as clear and blue as a Caribbean ocean. 'I had to keep you under so I could get some work done.'

Darby drank some more water. He stared at her for a moment, then smiled. 'Not what you expected, am I?'

Actually, you're exactly what I expected, Darby thought. He was average in so many ways, in height and looks, in size. And he had the most open, kind face. His voice was so soft, his eyes so caring, like those of a priest she'd known from her childhood, a man who saw her sitting in the church pew and, after one look at him, she wanted to bypass the confessional and tell him her sins right then and there, the words *monster* or *predator* never once entering her mind.

Which was the point.

He said, 'Cooper told me you wrote your dissertation on me.'

Hearing his name was like a knife, the blade piercing her stomach and then slicing its way up her torso.

He said, 'Do I disappoint?'

'Do you have a name?'

'Lucius.'

'And your name before that?'

'Does it matter?'

'I suppose not. Where am I?'

'I know you have a lot of questions. I do too. May I make a suggestion? That door right there' – he pointed with his knife to the door next to the bunk beds – 'is for the bathroom. Take a nice long, hot shower. You'll feel better, and the steam will help clear your head.'

Darby didn't move.

Eyed him as she drank some more water.

The man named Lucius chuckled softly. '*Please* don't tell me you think I'm going to try to rape you,' he said. 'That's so not my style. And there's a lock on the door, by the way.'

'Maybe you'll shoot or stab me instead, like your other victims.'

'You're not a victim.'

'Then what am I?'

'My guest.' Lucius smiled. 'You can sit there if you want, and we can talk after I'm finished eating – got to keep my blood sugar up – but, if I were you, I'd take advantage of the shower now. Life feels so much better after you're clean, and you make better decisions. That's my opinion, anyway.'

Darby knew he wanted her to submit to his will – to have her take the first step on whatever sadistic journey he had planned. But she did want to take a shower, scrub away the dread crawling across her skin, clear her head and use the time to think. Because whatever was about to unfold, she needed all her senses working.

'Zuriel Avery,' Darby said.

'Yes?'

'She's Jennifer Byram.'

'She is.'

'And all this time she's been alive and living in Fort Jefferson. With you.'

'I'm afraid I'm not following.'

'She's alive and Karen Decker is dead. Why?'

'Oh, I see. Jenny's my daughter. We changed her name – our names – when we came back to Montana. I had to protect my baby from that monster, in case he came looking for her.' A bright, humorous light came into his eyes as he bit into his apple.

'You killed her mother – tried to kill her. Why?'

He held up a finger, telling her to wait until he'd finished chewing.

'Jenny wasn't supposed to be there with her mother that night, but there she was. Frankly, I was surprised she survived. But I'm glad she did. Seeing the pain she went through from the multiple surgeries, the months and months of rehabilitation – and the psychological trauma, there was a tremendous amount of that – seeing suffering like that up close day after day can really satiate a certain man's appetite.'

'So she knows you're the Red Ryder. That you killed her mother and tried to kill her.'

'She has no idea about that ugly business. Poor thing.'

'And the rest of your acolytes?'

'Some things are best kept private.'

'Why did you?'

'Why did I what?'

'Kill your wife.'

'Because my wife, may she rot in peace, refused to accept the special kind of love a father has for his daughter, if you catch my meaning.'

Darby felt the water in her stomach wanting to come back up.

'That reminds me,' he said, reaching into his pocket, 'I want to show you something.'

62

The man named Lucius came back with an iPhone.

'I saved this for you,' he said. 'Thought you might like to see it.'

He placed the phone on the floor and slid it across the carpet.

The screen held a paused video of a CNN anchor-woman. The red banner scroll along the bottom read: MANHUNT FOR TOP FORENSIC PSYCHOLOGIST.

Darby pressed play.

Dr Darby McCormick, the anchorwoman said, had not only attacked and killed Agent Noel Covington, she had also killed Agent Phillip Bradley. And then came a press conference given by Sheriff Powers: 'I accompanied Agent Covington to a property where Dr McCormick was harassing the family and refusing to leave. She was upset about the recent death of a friend and was having problems coming to terms with it. When she refused to leave, she attacked and killed Agent Covington. With a box-cutter.'

Powers had more lies to share: 'After escaping, she shot and killed Agent Bradley, who had also accompanied us to the premises. She is considered armed and dangerous, and we've put out all the proper alerts.'

They staged the crime scene just like they did with Coop, she thought.

Next came a brief but chaotic interview with Vivian Whitney, the Deputy Chief of the US Marshals. The prim and tiny woman with short, grey hair was bundled into a winter coat, fighting her way, with the help of a pair of big men, through a sea of TV cameras and microphones. She had no comment, the anchorwoman said, but there was much speculation that she had flown out to Montana to assist in the manhunt, which was being spearheaded by the FBI.

The video ended and Lucius said, 'That's about the gist of it.'

'Covered all the bases.'

'We try.'

'Let me guess: you were listening in on all our conversations, too.'

'Most of 'em. We planted listening and tracking devices in the cars.' He gave her a proud smile, but it quickly collapsed. 'Let's get something clear,' he said, his voice grave. 'What happened to those men? Why you're here with me? It's your fault. You have no one but yourself to blame. If you didn't go poking your nose into matters that don't concern you . . .' He shrugged and took another bite of his apple. 'Excuse me for talking with my mouth full, but you should've gone home.'

Darby looked at the ceiling. 'How far underground are we?'

'Far enough.'

'Fallout shelter.'

He nodded. 'This one's on the older side. The others are much more high end. Think underground condos, all of 'em connected together. This place right here's my own private space, where I do most of my entertaining.' His gaze lingered on her for a moment. 'My grandfather built this shelter and pretty much every home and building in this town. Very religious man, he was. When he wasn't working, he was preaching. Had his own following – people thought he was real special 'cause he believed in the old-fashioned values – man works, woman stays home and raises the kiddies, instils morals and the teachings of our Lord Jesus.' He chuckled and added, 'You, my dear, would *not* fit in here, not with that mouth of yours.'

'Sorry to hear that.'

'Women like you . . .' He checked his watch, didn't finish the thought. 'My daddy took over the construction business, and then I did right after I moved back here with my daughter. I thought the fresh air would help her, you know, recuperate.' He smiled. 'I branched into high-end shelters right after 9/11 – they sold like hotcakes. Still do.'

She had read about bunkers being sold as condo units and built in secret locations in places like Colorado, Montana and Wyoming – places where people feared the government was not only going to take their guns but their homes and land. It was a booming business for the Glenn Beck crowd, who were eager to stock up on rations for the end of days, or for the time when the government would take away their religious freedoms, whichever came first.

'What are you?' Darby asked. 'White supremacists? Gun nuts? What?'

'I'd like to consider us a bunch of like-minded people who share the same value system. To preserve a certain way of life.'

'Which is?'

329

'Living under the banner of God and not allowing government people or interlopers like yourself to take away our God-given right to carry firearms and say the Pledge of Allegiance, keep the queers from marrying each other. Truth be told, I don't care about all that stuff. The things I want out of life are much simpler.'

Darby slowly got to her feet, Lucius watching her with mild interest.

Don't ask about Coop, she thought. *That's what he wants you to do.*

'Something on your mind, Doctor?'

'I've decided to take a shower.'

He picked up on her word choice. Smiled.

'I think that's an excellent idea,' he said. 'Take all the time you want. There's no reason to hurry.'

The bathroom was large enough to accommodate a shower with a glass door and, across from it, a toilet and a vanity unit with three decorative bulbs mounted above a medicine cabinet. Lucius or someone else had placed a folded white towel on top of the vanity, along with travel-sized bottles of shampoo and conditioner, a paper-wrapper sliver of soap, a toothbrush and toothpaste. As promised, it locked from the inside, just a quick slide of a small deadbolt.

She checked the medicine cabinet and the small drawers for something she could use as a weapon, but the shelves were bare. When she undressed, she found two cheap bandages on the crook of each arm, her forearms freshly bruised and covered with red welts from injections. She had been injected at least nine times — more than enough to make her physically addicted to whatever he'd given her.

Has to be heroin, she thought. If it was, she'd start experiencing the first wave of withdrawal symptoms in six to twelve hours: general nausea followed by the chills, vomiting and –

You can't think about that now, a voice said. *Deal with what's right in front of you.*

The water was hot and strong. She stood under it, inhaling the steam and scrubbing her skin, gathering her courage for what was coming next.

She knew too much about the inner landscape of sexual sadists. Lucius – who once upon a time had called himself the Red Ryder and murdered thirty-two people, taunting the police before deciding to come here with his maimed daughter – was not only extremely intelligent but had had plenty of time to dwell on and prepare for whatever he had in store for her – and, whatever it was, she was sure it involved Coop.

Was he down here with her?

Was he still alive?

Was he close to death?

Was he going to torture Coop in front of her?

Let him be alive, Darby thought. *No matter what happens next, I'll deal with it as long as I can see him one last time. Tell him how much he means to me.*

How much I love him.

Darby was towelling herself off inside the confined space when she heard a soft knock at the door.

'Sorry to bother you,' Lucius said, 'but I forgot to ask: if you have a headache, I can get you some Excedrin or Advil. Or aspirin.'

'I'm all set.'

'There's a robe underneath the sink, if you'd like to wear it.'

Darby put her clothes back on, relaxing slightly in their familiar comfort. The shower had, in fact, helped. Her head felt clearer. She felt more like herself.

Think.

She placed her hands against the walls and looked at herself in the mirror, to mentally prepare herself for whatever was about to happen next. It would be awful, ungodly; it would be designed to psychologically tear her down. Make her beg for it to stop.

She had one scrap she could cling to, a characteristic that all sexual sadists shared, and it was this: show no fear and do not beg. Your pain, fear and degradation feed the monster.

If I'm going to die, she thought, *I'm going to do it on my terms. At least I'll have that.*

Darby slid open the door, ready to greet whatever was waiting for her on the other side.

63

Darby stood in the doorway. While she'd been in the bathroom, Lucius had moved his chair closer to the foot of the bed. He sat facing her, a leg crossed over his ankle, hands laced behind his head. The knife he'd used to peel his apple rested against his groin.

'Feel better?'

Don't answer. Behind him, on the bureau, she saw his iPhone, only it had been set up on a portable tripod, the camera pointed at the bed. He smiled at her, all white teeth.

'Come on in and join us,' he said.

Us. Darby wanted to run into the room but didn't, just took a couple of steps and then stopped and propped her forearm against the bunk beds, her gaze locked on Lucius the entire time. From the corner of her eye she could see Coop's head resting against the pillows Lucius had propped up near the footboard. His eyes were shut, the skin around them the colour of eggplant, the bruises fading, the cuts starting to scab over. She knew he was sleeping and not dead because he moaned, like a kid who didn't want to wake up and go to school. His arms had been pulled over his head, his wrists handcuffed to the bar along the footboard, and she could see that each ankle had been handcuffed to the bars of the headboard, that he was barefoot and bare-chested, his midsection and thighs covered by a white sheet.

But she kept her gaze on Lucius, on the dreamy, far-away look in his eyes, that of a man who had reached a destination that until now he'd only seen in his dreams.

'Come in and say hello,' he said.

Darby said nothing, didn't move, too busy experiencing that same surreal, dream-like state she'd felt when she ran up the driveway and looked back to see an eight-year-old girl covered in blood and holding a box-cutter, chasing her: that what she was seeing couldn't possibly be real.

But it was real, as was what was happening here in this place buried deep in the ground. She watched as Lucius uncrossed his legs and leaned forward, one hand holding a 9-millimetre equipped with a silencer. He rested it on his hip, on top of the knife, and said, 'Don't be rude. He's been asking for you. Come in and say hello.'

Darby fought the urge to look at Coop, even when his eyes popped open for a moment, when he called for her. She looked only at Lucius as she moved into the room, taking small steps, as if to prove she wasn't in a hurry.

'Cooper here's been a real good boy,' Lucius said. 'A little stubborn in the beginning, but once we got to know each other better he brought me up to speed on Karen Decker, the note and piece of paper she'd mailed to her brother, everything. Ain't that right, Cooper?'

She sat down on the edge of the mattress. Coop struggled to open his eyes, couldn't keep them open. Her gaze finally broke from Lucius's when she saw the needle marks and sores on Coop's bruised forearms, in the crooks of his elbows. His skin was marred with different cuts and gashes, as though he had been in a fight, some of them deep and crudely stitched.

'Heroin,' Lucius said. 'Same stuff I gave you, only I had to give the poor boy something for the pain. He put up quite a fight.'

Coop's handcuffs rattled against the metal bars.

'Coop,' she said. 'I'm here.'

He didn't answer, moaned.

'He's got some pretty bad cuts,' Lucius said. 'Some of 'em are infected.'

She ignored him, looked only at Coop. *What did they do to you?*

'I didn't do that. The cutting,' Lucius said. 'That's my granddaughter's doing.'

Darby lifted her head.

'I had to give her someone to practise on,' Lucius said. 'And I owed her.'

'Owed her?'

'For the night I visited Karen at her home. I told Miriam she could help me with the next one, but I wanted to spend some special time alone with Karen, right here where we're sitting. Miriam found out – her older sister's got a big mouth – and she came running over that night screaming so loud I thought she was going to wake up the entire neighbourhood. I made it up to her by giving her some alone time with Cooper. Man, I wish he'd wake the hell up. Cooper! Come on, boy. Wake up.'

Coop's eyes fluttered open, then shut.

Lucius sighed. 'Guess we'll just have to wait,' he said. 'You got any other questions? It'll help pass the time.'

'The video.'

Lucius frowned. 'What video?'

'The footage of Karen at the lodge, taking the elevator to the roof.'

'Oh. *That*.' Lucius chuckled. 'What about it?'

'That wasn't Karen.'

'No, no. Had a gal who was the same height and roughly the same weight as Karen. Put her in a wig and Karen's clothes, told her where to look each and every step of the way, so the cameras wouldn't capture her face. Did a few dry-runs to make sure we got it right. We wanted the video footage to show that Karen went up there all by herself.'

'How did you manage to get Karen up there?'

'Maintenance elevator,' he replied. 'No cameras, and Karen was real cooperative, thanks to the pills I gave her before we arrived. She was pretty much unconscious by the time we got her to the lodge. I carried her up that little ladder to the cistern, and *ka-plunk*.' He shook his head sadly. 'Hardest thing I'd ever done in my life – not carrying her, I'm talking about not being able to enjoy her while she was here in my playroom. Had to make sure it looked like another junkie suicide, but business is business.'

'Why not just dump her on the road?'

'Where's the fun in that?'

Coop's eyes fluttered open again.

Stayed open.

'Darby,' Coop croaked. 'It's you.'

'It's me.'

'Am I . . . Is this a dream?'

She forced a smile, placed her hand on his cheek. 'I'm here,' she said, her fingers stroking his beard.

'You came.'

'Of course I did.'

'You found me.'

Darby felt the sting of tears. Felt so grateful and relieved – and scared. So scared.

She said, 'Go back to sleep.'

'Don't leave me.'

'I won't, I promise.'

Coop's eyes were closed, his voice slurred when he said, 'He's here. The Red Ryder.'

'It's okay.'

'I screwed up. Shouldn't have gone back to the house by myself. I should've –'

'Shh. It doesn't matter now. We'll have time for all that later.'

His eyes fluttered open. This time they looked bright. Clear.

'I love you,' he said.

The elastic band that had been wrapped around her heart snapped, and she could breathe again. She felt she could do anything. Endure anything.

'I love you so, so much,' he said.

'Close your eyes and rest. I'll –'

'Don't leave me. Please.'

Darby leaned forward and kissed him gently on the lips, feeling their dryness.

'I love you too,' she said.

Said, 'Always have, always will.'

And he relaxed. She heard him let out a sigh that reminded her of her father's final breath after being disconnected from the machines keeping him alive, a relaxing sound that said everything was okay. He had found what he was looking for.

Lucius said, 'I'm glad he's still alive – and that you're here with us. Otherwise, I wouldn't be able to bear witness to the special love you two so clearly share.' His voice was so calm, oddly nurturing. 'Take off your clothes please.'

Darby didn't move.

Said nothing.

'No reason to be shy,' Lucius said quietly, a hungry brightness visible in his eyes. 'I know you like sex.' He bowed his head slightly, as if embarrassed by his choice of words. 'I saw how you and Agent Covington went at it.'

She felt cold all over as the knowledge hit her: Noel's room had been fitted with hidden video-surveillance cameras that most likely had audio too.

Lucius said, 'Don't worry about Cooper being able to get an erection in his current state. I gave him a Viagra.'

Darby wasn't listening to him – wasn't seeing Lucius or Coop or her surroundings, because she had retreated inside herself, thinking about how she'd privately dreamed of this moment for years. How each and every time she had buried it – not because she didn't love Coop or desire him physically, but because he was too important to her as a friend to risk it. How whenever she allowed herself to daydream of the actual moment, she had never imagined it happening under the circumstances in which she found herself right now.

And Lucius knew that, his eyes damp and glowing with heat as he grabbed the edge of the sheet and pulled it free.

Darby looked only at Lucius.

He said, 'Show me love, Doctor. Share it with me, prove that I'm not a hopeless case.'

And when she didn't move: 'Pleasure or pain. What do you want?'

Darby looked only at Lucius, her face free of emotion as she placed her hand on Coop's chest.

'Not your hand,' he said. 'Use your mouth.'

64

Darby pulled away her hand.

Lucius's eyebrows jumped in surprise.

She folded her hands on her lap.

'Go on and do what I said.'

Darby didn't move.

Lucius sighed. Bowed his head and shook it side to side, his lips pursed.

'See,' he said, looking up, his eyes dead, 'where we are right now? This place doesn't exist in what you'd call normal time.' His voice had changed, as though someone else in the room were speaking – a creature imitating a human voice. 'Here? In *my* playroom? I'm God. Your job is to cater to my every single whim and desire, and right now I want –'

'No.'

He brought the nine up and Darby felt her heart leap inside her chest.

'You're gonna learn that I'm not in the habit of repeating myself,' Lucius said. 'Now do what I said.'

She didn't move. When he cocked back the hammer she didn't move and she wasn't afraid because she had found Coop; she was sitting right next to him and he'd said he loved her.

Lucius screwed the silencer against Coop's temple and pushed Coop's head to the side, against the pillow. Darby didn't look or say anything, even when Coop moaned, even when it looked like Lucius was going to pull the trigger.

'Use your mouth,' he said.

Coop moaned, 'Darby? You still here?'

Darby heard the words and they meant nothing to her – they were as meaningless as motes of dust scattering through the air, insignificant. She had already receded into a place deep within herself where no one was allowed, a space that held the truth of everything she knew and believed, and she knew and believed this with heart, mind and soul: the moment she gave into any one of Lucius's demands, he would own her. Shed a single tear or show him in any way she was suffering and he would own her. She was as sure of that as she was of her love for Coop – and there was no way she would allow the monster to see her love.

Better to die with it as her last thought.

Better to die with *him* begging.

Darby got to her feet.

65

Lucius stared at her, incredulous. Darby knew Lucius wouldn't shoot Coop in the head because the monster needed Coop alive, to get her in line and keep her in line, make her bend to his will. He had to hurt Coop, not kill him, and he could do more damage with a knife than with a gun.

But Lucius had chosen the gun, which meant his options were limited. When he pulled the nine away from Coop's head and pointed it at the headboard, at Coop's foot, Darby lunged.

Lucius squeezed off a round, the sound no louder than a muffler backfiring. The shot landed somewhere behind her and she didn't look or care because she had jumped over the footboard and thrown herself at Lucius. His chair toppled backwards and he landed against the floor, startled, but also seemingly oddly delighted; he smiled like a man who had opened the door on Christmas Day to a friend he hadn't seen in ages, standing there on his doorstep holding bags stuffed with gifts.

Lucius was an old man, somewhere in the neighbourhood of seventy. Darby wasn't expecting to encounter strength equal to or greater than her own, so she was surprised by the power in his hands and body when he grabbed her by the neck and slammed her against the bureau. He was fast and wiry, and before she had a chance to defend herself he had pushed her sideways, in the oppo-site direction, and slammed her against the floor, the sudden impact knocking the wind out of her.

She was nearly straddling him when he tried to turn the nine on her, to shoot her in the leg. She grabbed the wrist of his gun-hand; with his free hand he grabbed the side of her head and threw her against the bureau, the sudden impact bringing the iPhone and its attached camera stand toppling down on them. She hadn't let go of his wrist, had both hands on it now, and her nails dug into the thin skin there as she shoved the gun away from her face. Lucius squeezed off another round, the shot hitting the ceiling.

With his free hand he landed a solid blow against the side of her chest, right near her stomach; she felt her strength waver and then disappear when he hit her again, and again. Darby still held his wrist and, forcing her body to turn sideways, she threw her back against his stomach. She was still holding his wrist when he reached over her and hit her in the stomach, and she threw back her head and heard and felt something crack. She did it again and again, like someone experiencing a seizure, the back of her skull connecting with different parts of his face, the delicate bones there, until she had freed the gun from his hand.

She scrambled off him now with the gun, and Lucius lay there, his face no longer resembling anything human – nose broken, the orbital bone surrounding his left eye caved in, giving his face a sunken look. She had dislocated his jaw; his mouth hung sideways as he coughed and gagged and spat like some creature from a horror movie, tongue thrashing like a fish caught on a hook.

Lucius was trying to scramble to his feet when she swung and hit him in the Adam's apple. The fight completely left him and he collapsed, quickly flopping on to his side and curling into a foetal position so he could breathe, his face turning crimson, almost purple, as he wheezed, struggling to suck in air through the blood flooding his broken windpipe.

Darby straightened and saw a couple of his bloody teeth lying on the carpet. The KA-BAR knife lay a few feet away. She went for it.

(*Turn off the camera and do it*, said a voice that was not her own. *Cut him. Slowly. Make it last.*)

Darby powered down the phone. When she gripped the knife's handle, her thoughts turned to Karen Decker, dead and floating inside the cistern, all alone in the dark; the depression and despair that had consumed Karen's every waking moment and how she had tried to kill those feelings with booze and drugs; and how, when the pain wouldn't die – when it came back stronger and meaner – she had tried to kill herself not once but four times. Darby thought of Jennifer Byram, who had been sexually abused, tortured over the course of her life by her father, a man who had killed so many others, had ruined so many lives – Darby wanted to stay down here for days and slowly torture him in this place where even God Himself couldn't hear.

Darby was holding the knife the Red Ryder had possibly used on his victims. What a fitting end to use it on the monster. Then she thought about the families of all his victims, how they needed to see the monster in court so they could put a name to their suffering. Have peace.

Maybe.

And *maybe* that was more important than her anger and her need to satisfy her own urges, however dark and justified. Darby placed the nine and the knife on the bed and turned her attention to Lucius's trouser pockets, where she found a handcuff key mixed in with a couple of Werther's Original hard candies; in his back pocket was a magnetic keycard and a prayer card with a line from Psalm 61: 'Hear my cry, God. Listen to my prayer. From the ends of the earth, I will call to you, when my heart is overwhelmed.'

The handcuff key worked on all of Coop's handcuffs. She used them to hog-tie Lucius.

Darby grabbed the sheet and draped it over Coop, who was shivering, his skin pimpled with sweat.

She said, 'Can you hear me?'

Coop didn't answer. She examined the 9-millimetre handgun. A Glock 22. She checked the magazine, saw that it contained the standard fifteen rounds.

Coop moaned.

Darby leaned in close and spoke into his ear. 'I'm here,' she said. 'You're safe.'

His eyes didn't open; they darted from side to side beneath his eyelids, as if searching for her inside a dream. Darby was looking down at his bruised face and wishing she could reach him when she heard a door open somewhere outside the room.

66

Darby got to her feet. She had the knife gripped in one hand and, in the other, Lucius's nine, with its attached silencer and sixteen rounds.

The moans of two men – one a man she loved, the other a man who wasn't a man at all but a monster in great pain – filled the small room where she stood. The smell of blood flooded her nostrils as she raised her nine, pointing it at the doorway, the room beyond cast in gloom. All she could see was part of a bare wall, and the same low-pile brown carpet.

Someone was humming, the sound moving closer, closer. She didn't hear any footsteps but she heard a heavy door click shut and *thump* against its frame, and before she could even consider whether or not to leave Coop, to move into the adjoining room, a figure marched through the doorway and then came to a sudden stop when he saw Lucius lying on the carpet in all that blood, his pleasant, almost delighted expression collapsing, replaced by fear.

It was the young guy from the lodge – the one who had picked her up in the Ford Expedition and driven her to Karen Decker's home. She recognized the long scraggly beard and the Stetson. He wasn't wearing his boots, only white socks, and he had on dark jeans and a light-green T-shirt with a Bible verse printed in white on the front: 'ALL things are POSSIBLE for those who BELIEVE.

Mark 9:23'. He was holding a bottle of Rolling Rock beer by the neck.

'What's wrong?' Darby asked. 'Not the party you expected?'

He didn't answer, swallowing repeatedly as he stared at the handgun pointed at him, Darby thinking about how nice and cool he'd played it inside the SUV, trying to get information from her.

'Michael,' she said. 'That's your name, right?'

He nodded, then swallowed, frightened. 'Look,' he said, slowly bringing up his hands, 'I'm just doing what I was told. I was told to come here.'

'Following orders.'

'Yeah. Exactly. These people . . .'

'What?'

'My parents are old. Sick. They depend on me. I'm just looking out for them.'

'Where are they right now?'

'In their house.'

'And you're down here in your socks, hanging out, drinking a beer.'

'It's not what you think. I –'

'How many are down here?'

His gaze cut to Lucius.

'Don't look at him,' Darby said. 'He's not in charge any more. I am. How many?'

'How many what?'

'How many are down here?'

He thought about it for a moment. 'Five,' he said. A pause, and then he added, 'Yeah, five.'

'Including you?'

'Including me.'

'All men, I take it.'

He nodded, kept nodding.

'Sheriff Powers?' she asked.

'He's not here.'

'Where is he?'

'Still upstairs, I think.'

'Upstairs where?'

'In the house.'

Darby cocked back the hammer.

'I'll help you, I swear,' he said. 'Just let me go so I can go back home to my parents.'

Darby rubbed the ball of her thumb across the tip of the hammer.

'I'm telling you the truth,' he said, his eyes bright with alcohol. 'I swear to God.'

'Turn around and put your hands behind your back.'

Darby walked up to him, digging the muzzle of her nine against the small of his back, above his spine, as she patted him down for weapons. He was clean. She checked his pockets and found a keycard, a pack of gum and two lubricated condoms that were ribbed for 'her pleasure'.

'You're going to take me to them,' she said. 'Then you're going to show me the way out of this place. You do that and you're free to go. You try anything funny, make me nervous or upset, I'll turn you into a quadriplegic. You know what a quadriplegic is, Mike?'

'A cripple in a wheelchair.'

'A cripple who can't use his arms or his legs. That means someone will have to feed you, bathe you and change your diapers. You won't have any control over your bladder, and

all that sitting in your wheelchair is going to make you con-
stipated, which means some poor nurse is going to have to
bend you over, stick her hand up your balloon knot and
removed the waste herself. And since you don't have anyone to take care of you, Mike, you'll be put in some state-run
facility. You want that kind of life, Mike?'

'No. No, please, I'll do anything, just –'

'Then do what I say.'

'I will, I promise.'

'Lead the way.'

'You mind if I finish the rest of my beer? It'll help calm
my nerves.'

'Sure,' Darby said. 'Drink up.'

67

Darby followed Mike into the adjoining room and saw a light switch on the wall. She flicked it.

The two bare bulbs installed on the ceiling revealed an area with roughly the same square footage as her combined living room/kitchen at her former Beacon Hill condo – a space just large enough to hold a couple of couches, an armoire for the TV, a fireplace and a kitchen table. No furniture here, only shelves that stretched from the floor to the ceiling, each one stocked with canned and nonperishable foods and gallon jugs of water and just about anything else one might need to survive the end of days, a zombie apocalypse or the fallout from a nuclear explosion.

Mike the Driver stopped in front of a grey metal door with a keycard reader. He didn't turn around or look over his shoulder, didn't see what had stolen her attention and made her blood run cold. Lucius had made a shrine on one of the shelves: standing frames holding photographs of his daughter, all taken while she was asleep during various points in her life, her skin exposed so he could capture her scars, the fresh incisions left by recent surgery.

It was the first photograph on the top row that broke Darby's heart, the one of Jennifer in her late teens sitting in a wheelchair outside a hospital, the young girl forcing herself to smile through the pain and giving a half-hearted thumbs-up to tell the person behind the camera, maybe her father, maybe to the world, that the pain she was in would pass because she was a survivor. Like Karen Decker.

Mike cocked his head to the side and said, 'I can't open the door. You have the keycard.'

She gave it to him. He waved it across the keycard reader and she saw the light turn green and heard the lock click open.

The hallway was long and boxy, the ceiling vents blowing warm air against her head. She could see a door at the other end. It didn't have a window, but as she drew closer she heard country music intercut with men's laughter.

'What's going on in there, Mike?'

'Just a few guys hanging out, is all.'

'How many?'

'Five. Including me.'

'I hope you're not lying to me.'

'I swear to God I'm –'

She balled the hair on the back of his head into a fist as she dug the muzzle into his back. 'If I find out you're lying to me?' she hissed against his ear. 'If I feel like I might be in danger? I'll pump a couple of rounds into your spine and take my chances with the boys in the room. We clear, Mike?'

'Absolutely.'

'So glad to hear that.' She handed him the keycard. 'Now open the door.'

With a trembling hand, he waved the card over the reader. The light turned green, and when the lock clicked back he opened the door to a country ballad coming from wall-mounted speakers, the room strewn with colourful Christmas lights installed near the ceiling, the men sitting in comfortable chairs and on couches and dressed the same way as Mike the Driver, in T-shirts and jeans; the air was oppressively hot and smelled of testosterone, sweat and beer.

And in the centre of the room was a bare mattress set up on a table. Iron O-rings with metal chains were fixed to each table corner, and she saw shackles lying on top of the mattress, along with leather restraints, leg-spreaders and other sadomasochistic devices she'd seen at a number of crime scenes – and right then she knew why the men had gathered here, that Lucius had intended to bring her to them after he was done with her, because all the men were smiling as they got to their feet, drinks in hand, ready to party.

She pumped two rounds into Mike's back, and when she felt him drop she brought up the nine and squeezed off a tight double-tap into the chest of the nearest man, then moved the weapon to the bald man standing in the far corner, near a metal ladder that led up to a trapdoor installed in the ceiling. One shot to the head and he collapsed.

When she was done, they were all on the floor.

Mike and a couple of others were still alive, writhing in pain. She wanted to plant a round in their heads, to make sure they were dead before going back down the hallway to Coop; but that would be a waste of ammo.

Darby stood there, watching them bleed out as the ballad switched to an upbeat country song. When she was certain they were dead, she climbed the ladder that led only one way: up.

The ceiling hatch didn't have a lock. Darby had expected to find one, but when she turned the handle it moved freely. She pushed up, relieved when she encountered no resistance.

Paper, light as feathers, rained down on her.

Candy wrappers.

The hatch was inside the prayer room. She poked her head over the top, the colourful Christmas lights from below illuminating the gloom in the chamber, allowing her to make out the mummified remains of the two girls, their dark sockets pinned on her, their lips parted in a scream that no one would ever hear. They were still here and the candy wrappers were still here, because the sheriff hadn't removed anything – and had no plans to do so because he was a part of everything. This cult.

Darby turned and retraced her steps back to the bedroom. Lucius was still alive; she could hear him breathing. She went to Coop, lifted him up into a sitting position. His eyes remained shut. She hung his heavy, muscular arm over her shoulder and then she stood and, with his feet dragging, carried him out of the bedroom and through the hall to the other room, the party room.

Coop couldn't walk, let alone climb a ladder. She'd have to leave him here. After she eased him to a sitting position beside the ladder, she went to retrieve the bed sheet and quilt to keep him warm. She wrapped the sheet around him and then gently shook him awake.

His eyes fluttered open. 'Darby,' he croaked. 'You're here.'

'Everything's fine,' she said. 'But I need to go get help. I'll be right back, okay?'

His head lolled around on his shoulders as he looked about the room, trying to take in his surroundings.

'Where . . . are we?'

Darby kissed his forehead.

Smiled, her eyes bright with tears.

'We're going home,' she said.

68

Darby didn't have a flashlight – couldn't find one on the shelves stocked with food. But she found the phone Lucius had given her to watch the news coverage.

Up the ladder again, the nine tucked in the back waistband of her jeans, the phone in her pocket. When she entered the hidden chamber, she grabbed both items, using the phone to light her way through the dark.

She went down on her knees and put her ear to the chamber door, straining to hear over the blood pounding in her head. Satisfied that no one was standing on the other side, she gently pushed against the small door, her body shuddering with gratitude when she discovered it was unlocked. She climbed out, into the house's hidden heart.

Darby reached the spiral staircase and checked the phone for a signal.

No bars.

She wasn't wearing her boots, only socks, so she didn't have to worry about her footfalls announcing her presence, in case someone was inside the bedroom, waiting.

What had Mike the Driver told her about the sheriff?

He's in the house.

But was he alone?

Up the stairs, taking one at a time and pausing to listen.

She was coming up to the landing when she checked the phone for a signal. Still nothing. She decided to put the phone away, not wanting the light from the screen to wink underneath the bookcase, in case the sheriff and whoever might be with him saw it.

A razor-thin beam of light burned against the bottom of the bookcase.

If he, or anyone else, is inside the bedroom, a voice said, *they won't be expecting you.*

How many people could be waiting inside the bedroom? Two? Four?

How many people in town knew about this place?

She had five shots left.

Make them count.

Darby found the latch and pulled, *click.*

She pushed open the bookcase to bright sunlight.

And there, lying on the bed, was Sheriff Powers, reading a big paperback book that rested on his stomach: *Chicken Soup for the Soul.* He was the only one there.

His eyes widened, then turned hard.

Scared.

Right then Darby knew he was here alone. She moved to the foot of the bed, the nine trained on him. The bedroom door was open all the way and she didn't see anyone standing in the hallway, and she didn't hear anyone moving around downstairs. If someone else was here, the smart gamble might have been for Powers to yell. She would have taken him as a hostage, and when his men ran upstairs she would have seen she was outnumbered and outgunned . . .

But none of that happened. He held the book, studying her, his gaze turning inward as he tried to figure a way out of this.

'The remains downstairs,' Darby said. 'Who are they?'

'Don't know their names.'

'Where are they from?'

'Before my time.'

Darby could see the beads of sweat along his hairline.

'I know what you're going to do,' he said. 'Mind if I say a prayer first?'

Darby didn't answer.

Powers closed his eyes. He sounded relieved, as if a great weight had been lifted off his shoulders, when he spoke. 'Our Father, who art in Heaven, hallowed be thy name. Thy kingdom come, thy will be done, on earth as it is in –'

Darby shot him in the thigh, the round tearing through his femoral artery.

After the screaming stopped, and after he staggered out of the bedroom and collapsed on the landing near the stairs, his body growing still and his lips moving sound-lessly in prayer, she removed his sidearm, holding it with a tissue, and placed it on the bed. She would tell them he had pulled the gun on her before she fired. With no wit-nesses, it would be easy to sell the idea she had killed him in self-defence.

She took out the phone. All the signal bars were full. She dialled the operator and asked to be connected to Montana's US Marshals' office.

29th of February
Monday, Leap Day

69

Working in any capacity in law enforcement, whether on the street or behind the desk, you heard all sorts of stories about drug addiction and the withdrawal process. Heroin withdrawal, Darby had been told, occupied a certain level of hell because opiates stole not only your mind and body but also your soul.

The stories she'd heard were right.

For four days inside the Montana Army Hospital, where she and Coop had been secreted, Darby existed in a fevered, dream-like state in which she went from hot to cold, her body soaked with sweat, as if she had just emerged from a pool. She couldn't stop scratching her skin or vomiting. They had to feed her intravenously, and the nurse, whose name was Suzanne, injected drugs into the IV line to help Darby manage the withdrawal symptoms. They didn't do any good because her body treated the cure as though it were poison, and throughout the entire process, anytime she was awake, she had a headache that felt like someone had buried an axe in the centre of her forehead. She found she could manage it if she kept her eyes shut and if the room was as dark as a grave, without sound.

Locked inside the dark, she reviewed what she knew, which wasn't much.

Marshals from the Montana office came to Karen

Decker's house and immediately arrested her. While she was lying on the foyer floor, her hands yanked behind her back and cuffed, she told them everything. She didn't need to tell them about Cooper or ask for medical help; she had done all of that in the phone call.

Afterwards, she had endured a gruelling interrogation inside a room similar to the one where she had first met Noel and answered their questions until the withdrawal hit. The last thing she remembered was vomiting into a trashcan, a female marshal holding back her hair for her. Everything that happened after that was locked in fevered dreams that made little to no sense.

But Coop was always waiting for her in her dreams. Only it wasn't a dream because he was alive and safe, and he loved her. That allowed her to sleep.

On the fifth day in the hospital, Darby summoned up enough energy to drink a glass of room-temperature water without throwing it back up.

'That's great,' Nurse Suzanne said. 'You're making such great progress.'

Coop, the nurse said, was much worse. He had told Nurse Suzanne that he believed he had been given heroin on a daily basis since his capture. *That's almost a week*, Darby was thinking when the nurse said, 'It's amazing, really, that he didn't OD, given the amount in his system. He's got a long road of recovery in front of him because, well, technically, through no fault of his own, he's an addict.'

'When can I see him?'

Suzanne's smile was pained, her voice as quiet as a librarian's when she said, 'Soon.'

'I need to see him. Need to –'

'He's still unconscious. In addition to treating his withdrawal symptoms, we're treating his infection. It's called *Staphylococcus aureus*.'

'MRSA.'

Suzanne nodded. 'It's resistant to a lot of the antibiotics we use to treat ordinary staph infections. But don't worry too much, Ms McCormick. I think he'll be just fine. And so will you.' She had a warm smile and kind eyes. 'You two have plenty of time.'

Time, Darby thought, and felt herself relax. She had Coop and he had spoken words she had secretly longed to hear.

I love you, Darby.

I love you so much.

And she had said, *I love you too.*

Until the stars fall from the sky.

And Coop had relaxed because she had found him, and he had found her. Finally. And now they had time. Darby closed her eyes and drifted off into a peaceful, dreamless sleep.

They came late the next morning, as Darby was eating breakfast, her first solid meal.

The FBI agents wanted to get her statement. Stan Davies, the cop from Bozeman, was with them.

Darby told them everything that had happened. By the time she'd finished answering their questions, the sun was gone, the windows dark.

'The remains inside the house,' she said as they were packing up their briefcases and gathering their coats. 'You haven't told me who they are.'

Davies answered the question. 'We don't know,' he said. 'We may never know.'

Vivian Whitney was there the next time Darby woke up.

She was a small and compact woman, Vivian. Neat. She stared down at Darby, disappointed, as if her waking had interrupted Vivian's plan to smother her to death with a pillow.

The woman's eyes burned with anger. And grief.

'I was hoping to speak to you before I left.'

Darby licked her lips. 'Noel,' she began.

'I loved him as if he were my own son.'

'I'm sorry.'

Vivian searched Darby's eyes to see if it was true.

'Tell me what happened to him,' Vivian said. 'Word for word.'

Darby told her.

Vivian excused herself to use the bathroom. When she returned, she seemed pale underneath her makeup, her eyes bloodshot.

'We found the bunkers or whatever you want to call them. And guns,' Vivian said. She stood by the chair where her briefcase rested. 'Enough to arm a Third World militia. From what I've been told, almost everyone in this town was planning for the fall of the government, or an apocalypse – whatever you want to call it. The government calls it an act of terrorism, which falls under the FBI's umbrella. The Bureau is trying to round up all the people involved in this cult, although a handful took the coward's way out.'

Suicide, Darby thought. 'How?'

'Poison. I won't know more until the toxicology reports come back. That will take weeks.'

'How many?'

'The FBI didn't tell you?'

'No.'

Vivian turned in her chair, retrieved her worn leather briefcase from the floor and rooted through a file. 'I don't have an exact number, and I don't know any names,' she said.

Then she began flipping through a stack of 8 × 10 crime-scene photographs.

'This is the only one that will mean anything to you,' Vivian said, and handed Darby a photograph. It showed Jennifer Byram lying on her back, on a bed, her arms draped around the shoulders of her two daughters, who were snuggled up against their mother, seemingly in a peaceful sleep. Dead.

'The house is a crime scene, so the sheriff moved Byram and her girls to a small hotel in Bozeman,' Vivian said. 'When word got out that you were alive, she poisoned herself and her children. He killed himself, by the way.'

'Who?'

'The old man hog-tied in the fallout shelter. I take it you did that.'

Darby nodded. 'His name was Lucius,' she said. 'He was Jennifer's father. The Red Ryder.'

'He rubbed his neck up against a metal burr in the bed post until he managed to sever his artery and bleed out. As for whether or not he is, in fact, the Red Ryder –'

'He is.'

'There are forensics tests we need to run, evidence that needs to be examined. It's going to take some time. With any luck, we may be able to put that awful business to bed.'

Darby placed the photograph on her lap and turned her attention to the window. All she could see was the sky. It was a cold, hard blue, free of clouds. It was enough.

'The good news – the *wonderful* news,' Vivian said, her voice thick with irony, 'is that you and Cooper are alive to fight another day. What a miracle.' Her eyes were bright and burning with purpose, like a general who realized she had lost a major battle but was still determined to find a way to win the war.

70

The following morning, while Darby was watching CNN, Nurse Suzanne came in holding a breakfast tray. The woman was smiling.

'Mr Cooper's awake,' she said. 'He's asking for you.'

Darby was pulling back the flimsy hospital sheets when the nurse said, 'No. Eat first. That's the deal.'

After she finished, Darby allowed Suzanne to help her sit up but she refused to sit in the wheelchair.

'I'm not paralysed,' Darby said.

'But in your condition, you might still fall. Why chance it?'

'I'm walking in there by myself.'

The woman sighed. 'I won't stop you.'

'Good. You know what you could do for me? Help me to the bathroom. I want to shower first.'

It was difficult to stand. As she washed herself, she had moments when she felt dizzy, her legs acting like they were about to buckle. But the excitement she felt – the gratitude – of being able to see Coop gave her all the strength she needed.

Darby studied her reflection in the mirror. She thought she looked good. Healthy and strong. She wished she had some makeup, though, some lip gloss and just a touch of eyeliner, some concealer to hide the bags under her eyes. She didn't have her clothes – they had been taken as evidence – and there was no way she was going into Coop's room wearing a hospital gown.

When she came back into the room, she told the nurse what she needed. It took Suzanne about twenty minutes to gather everything, and when she returned she was holding a purse and a pair of yoga pants and a T-shirt that was a little on the small side. 'It's the best I could do,' she said about the clothes. 'The makeup is in my purse. Help yourself to whatever you need.'

The hall and reception area were noisy, full of soldiers and various government types – Feds, she assumed, given their sharp suits. Everyone was staring at her.

'First room there on your right,' Suzanne said. 'Let me help you.'

'No. I can do it on my own.'

Suzanne watched Darby shuffle across the hall, using the wall for support.

Coop's bed was elevated, his face turned to the window, which glowed with the last afternoon light. His bare chest was covered in bandages. He looked pale and, even underneath all the muscle, seemed so incredibly fragile.

He didn't notice she was there until she sat beside him, on the edge of his mattress. He rolled his head slowly to her. His eyes widened, then closed into slits. He smiled weakly.

His voice was hoarse, barely above a whisper when he spoke. 'I thought I dreamed you . . . I thought I'd die without seeing you again.'

She wanted to cry in gratitude and relief, but didn't. She needed to be strong. For him.

'Did they tell you the good news?' he asked.

'About the staph infection? They said –'

'No, the other good news. That I'm officially a heroin addict. A junkie.'

His eyes grew wet and he turned his head to the window.

Darby grabbed his hand. He tried to pull it away, but he didn't have the strength, and she wouldn't let him go. 'We'll get through this together,' she said, rubbing her fingers against his callused palm. 'We always do.'

He said nothing, just stared out the window, Darby wanting to pull him close to her, find a way to put him inside her and keep him there because he was medicine and food and breath. He was everyone and everything she needed and wanted.

'I shouldn't have gone in there alone,' he said.

'Gone where? Karen Decker's house?'

A slow nod and he licked his lips. 'The first time I was in there, it kept bothering me, how neat and tidy everything was,' he said, his eyes searching the sky beyond the windows. 'It was too clean – too perfect.'

She rubbed his hand, only half listening because she no longer cared about Karen Decker or the Red Ryder or anyone else; she was overwhelmed by the fact they were both alive and sitting here together, a new road in front of them because of the words they'd shared in a shelter buried deep in the earth, a place where Karen Decker and others had begged for their lives.

'So I went back there,' Coop said. 'I went back there late at night because something was nagging at me and I didn't know what, so I went through the house and examined every inch of it. Every nook and cranny, because I was certain something was there and all I had to do was find it. And when I was in the bedroom, examining the bookcases, I stumbled – and that's the right word – I *stumbled* upon the lever for the secret door.'

'I found it. The passageway inside the house.'

'The bodies?'

'Yes.'

Coop nodded, kept nodding. 'Who are they? Do we know?'

'No. Not yet.'

'I saw them. I saw the remains, and there I was, alone in this secret chamber buried inside this ordinary-looking house, and part of me – just closed. I don't know how else to describe it. But right then I knew I was done. That I didn't – couldn't – do this any more. And when I was –'

'It doesn't matter,' Darby said. 'What matters is –'

'They were waiting for me in the bedroom. Lucius and the sheriff and some of his people, and they all had police batons. I don't remember what happened, but when I woke up I was locked inside this room, and there was this girl there who had a knife. Couldn't have been more than eight, maybe ten years old.' Coop blinked several times and then closed his eyes, kept them closed. 'She was there to practise how to cut, and Lucius, her grandfather, was there, teaching her. His granddaughter. An eight-year-old girl.'

Darby was about to speak when Coop suddenly turned his head and faced her.

'I'm so sorry,' he said.

'I found you. That's all that matters.'

'What you told me . . .' He was too weak to finish.

Darby said the words for him. For them. 'I love you

too.' She brought his hand up to her mouth and kissed it. She smiled down at him. 'Until the stars fall from the sky.'

Coop had drifted off to sleep when a woman who looked like she had been sculpted from God's hand stepped into the room. She stood nearly six feet tall in high-heeled boots that went up past her knees, and she looked ridiculously beautiful, her features flawless, all perfect angles, not a single blemish.

Not a Fed, Darby thought. Too stylish. The woman wore black leggings – everything she wore was black, the skirt, blouse and chunky cardigan sweater. A female Fed wouldn't dress that way, and she wasn't carrying a sidearm or a badge – and her black hair, thick and coarse, was long and spilled artfully over her shoulders. *A TV reporter*, Darby thought, *maybe a lawyer*.

Only the woman had a wadded-up tissue in her fist, and her eyes were bloodshot from crying.

'Darby?' she asked. She had a British accent.

Darby got to her feet, wobbling slightly. The woman took her into her long and slightly perfumed arms, and hugged her fiercely against her cashmere-covered chest.

The woman wept, shuddering.

'Thank you,' she cried. 'Thank you for saving him.'

Darby gently removed the woman from her arms. 'I'm sorry, but have we met?'

'I'm sorry. Yes. I mean, no. No, we haven't, but I've heard so much about you. I'm Amanda. Jackson's fiancée.'

Darby felt the room begin to spin.

Felt the sting of tears and blinked them back – *willed* them back, as Amanda said, 'I'm sorry we had to meet under these circumstances.'

Don't cry, an inner voice screamed. *Don't you* dare *break down in front of her.*

'They called me late last night,' Amanda said, dabbing her eyes with the tissue. 'Told me what happened and then some government men came over and put me on a private plane.'

'Good,' Darby said. Her voice was not her own, and her face felt hot and damp. 'That's good.'

And it all made sense now, why Coop had been acting so oddly that night at Logan Airport, why he had been paying her so many compliments – why he had gotten so drunk. He was trying to find a way to deliver the news that he was engaged.

Amanda cupped Darby's face in her elegant and smooth hands. 'Thank you,' she said, and kissed Darby firmly on the forehead, as if wanting to brand her.

Amanda was crying again. 'Thank you for bringing him back home to me.'

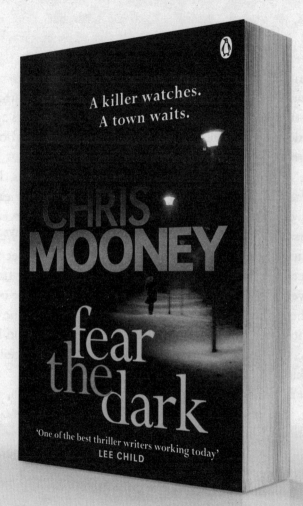

'I didn't mean to kill her, Sarah. It just –'

'Happened. I know,' she says in that quiet, soothing voice that made me fall in love with her all those years ago. She swallows and forces a smile. 'I understand. You don't have to explain yourself.'

We've done this dance before – too many times, I'm ashamed to admit. And, while I'm genuinely sorry each and every time, I also genuinely believe Sarah does, in fact, understand. This isn't wishful thinking on my part. We've been together a long time, Sarah and I; there are no secrets between us. Besides, Sarah couldn't keep something from me even if she wanted to. She's not a good actor, for one, but the reality is that she's not capable of deceit. Doesn't have it in her. She's too meek, still wears her heart on her sleeve. One look at her face and I know what she's feeling. Thinking.

We're sitting together on the living-room couch, the place, it seems, where we always end up having this conversation. I knock back the rest of my bourbon – my third – and stare into the fire, wondering, again, if there is such a place as hell.

'It just got away from me. Again.'

'I know,' she says quietly. 'Still, maybe you should have –'

My glare stops her cold. The firewood snaps and hisses.

'Should've what?' I prompt, aware of the heat climbing into my voice. Sarah knows better than to beat a dead horse. I've already apologized. The subject is closed. Done.

She takes another delicate sip of her white wine and stares down into her glass, like there's an escape hatch hiding somewhere at the bottom. I see how I've hurt her, and I take our glasses and place them on the coffee-table. Then I snuggle up next to her and take her hands in mine. Her smile is tight – not out of fear but because even now, after all this time together, she's still embarrassed about her crooked teeth.

'You're beautiful,' I say.

She reddens and stares down at my hands. The skin is still pink and sore from the hot water and the vigorous scrubbing with the brush. It took a good twenty minutes to remove the blood – especially the blood caked underneath my fingernails. I was so angry, so consumed by rage, that I forgot to put on the gloves. I need to be more careful next time.

And there will be a next time. We both know it.

Sarah clears her throat. 'A walk,' she says timidly.

'What?'

'We should take a walk. The fresh air will do us both some good.'

'Honey, it's the middle of the night. And it's freezing out.'

'I don't care.' The tentative smile on her face is as fragile as an eggshell.

My heart sinks when I break it. 'I'm exhausted,' I say gently. 'Maybe tomorrow night.'

She puts on a brave face. 'Whatever you want.'

'Thanks for understanding.'

She nods, keeps nodding.

I cup her face in my hands, fighting back tears. She swallows, nervous.

'You mean the world to me. I love you. You know that, right?'

'I do,' she says.

And I believe her.

I kiss her forehead. 'Everything's going to be okay.'

I smile. Kiss her gently on the lips. She crinkles her nose, like she's caught a whiff of a bad odour.

'What is it now?' I ask sharply.

'It's nothing.'

'No, go on. Say what's on your mind.' I feel the anger, how it's already moved past the point of no return. I can't help it – can't *stop* it. 'Say it.'

'Shower.' Her voice is barely above a whisper. 'You should take a long, hot shower.'

'Because I stink? That what you're trying to tell me?'

'No. It'll relax you.'

'I'm too tired.'

'I know, baby,' she says, and my anger retreats like dirty water swirling down a drain. She knows I love it when she calls me *baby*. 'It's just that you've got blood in your hair again.'

He just wanted a decent book to read ...

Not too much to ask, is it? It was in 1935 when Allen Lane, Managing Director of Bodley Head Publishers, stood on a platform at Exeter railway station looking for something good to read on his journey back to London. His choice was limited to popular magazines and poor-quality paperbacks – the same choice faced every day by the vast majority of readers, few of whom could afford hardbacks. Lane's disappointment and subsequent anger at the range of books generally available led him to found a company – and change the world.

'We believed in the existence in this country of a vast reading public for intelligent books at a low price, and staked everything on it'
Sir Allen Lane, 1902–1970, founder of Penguin Books

The quality paperback had arrived – and not just in bookshops. Lane was adamant that his Penguins should appear in chain stores and tobacconists, and should cost no more than a packet of cigarettes.

Reading habits (and cigarette prices) have changed since 1935, but Penguin still believes in publishing the best books for everybody to enjoy. We still believe that good design costs no more than bad design, and we still believe that quality books published passionately and responsibly make the world a better place.

So wherever you see the little bird – whether it's on a piece of prize-winning literary fiction or a celebrity autobiography, political tour de force or historical masterpiece, a serial-killer thriller, reference book, world classic or a piece of pure escapism – you can bet that it represents the very best that the genre has to offer.

Whatever you like to read – trust Penguin.